"Jonathan Leaf's entertaining murder mystery-insider's guide-*roman à clef* gives you a marvelous tour of the so-called City of Angles—because everyone's got one—as his protagonists strive to scale the slippery and treacherous walls of Fortress Hollywood. If Carl Hiaasen is Florida Man, then Jonathan Leaf certainly has Los Angeles covered."

—**ALEXANDER ROSE,** Author of *Washington's Spies* and Producer of *Turn: Washington's Spies.*

"Jonathan Leaf's scintillating debut, *City of Angles,* is even sharper than its whip-smart title. Part noir, part exposé of Hollywood's dirty little secrets, and all fun and games, the tale teases and satisfies in equal parts. Flashing a shrewd sense of humor that feels like a knowing wink at a Tinseltown bar, Leaf's prose treads nimbly between the crisp and the lyrical."

—**CHRISTOPHER YATES**, author of *Black Chalk* and *Grist Mill Road*

CITY OF ANGLES

CITY OF ANGLES

ANGLES

JONATHAN LEAF

BOMBARDIER
BOOKS

PUBLISHED BY BOMBARDIER BOOKS
An Imprint of Post Hill Press

City of Angles
© 2023 by Jonathan Leaf
All Rights Reserved

ISBN: 978-1-63758-788-1
ISBN (eBook): 978-1-63758-789-8

Cover Design by Tiffani Shea
Interior design and composition by Greg Johnson, Textbook Perfect

Post Hill Press
New York • Nashville
posthillpress.com

Published in the United States of America
1 2 3 4 5 6 7 8 9 10

To my beloved wife, Christina

"Our loss is their loss."

—**OSCAR LEVANT** on hearing that
Milton Berle had converted
from Judaism to Christian Science

CHAPTER 1

There is a kind of apartment building that everyone in Hollywood has been in. The design of the rooms is identical, or nearly so. Plate glass covers the closet doors, and cheap ceiling fans are above your head. A pool sits in the middle of the structure, and, though constructed in a prime earthquake zone, it stands on stilts. Beneath are the coveted parking spaces.

Because the insulation in these buildings is virtually nonexistent and the heating is poor, they can be chilly on summer nights and frigid in the winter. The tenants are warmer, though. Consistently friendly and affable, they await that one big break that's surely around the corner: the guest-starring spot that will be a recurring role, the pilot script that's about to be picked up, the financing for the picture that only requires one well-heeled benefactor.

Were they all delusional? Billy Rosenberg saw them in passing every day as he lived in such a building, and one morning in the year before the pandemic he asked himself that question.

As he was possessed of a large DVD collection, several movie posters, and a great many books, these reflected back to him from the plate glass, making his apartment seem cramped. It struck him that he had spent too much time in the room, alone, often when the sun was shining. Too many hours had passed, surfing the web or typing unread scripts. So, grabbing his laptop, he strode over to a local coffee shop. His reaction upon entering it was the one he had each time he walked in: astonishment at how many attractive folk were inside.

Sitting down, he flipped on his computer and began working. Stopping, he watched the people. The prettiest individuals from towns all over the country, they had been uniformly drawn to Los Angeles by the firm conviction that they were singular and fated to a special destiny. Awareness of that prompted him towards other ruminations. Gradually, then, he realized that he had fallen into a fugue state, and thunderously loud as it was, it took him a moment to recognize that a woman at his side was addressing him. As such, he could only be sure of her second sentence. She was asking if they had met in an Alexander Technique class.

The voice was low and soft, but there was nothing in the expression of her eyes that corresponded to the smile she offered. It was as though the bottom half of her face was hysterically intent on seduction, and the upper half appraising him like an expensive tennis racket. Yet he knew the accent. Even with the decibel level, it was unmistakable. It was what they called RP: Received Pronunciation, the precise, crisp, non-regional mode of speech taught in acting classes.

He examined her more closely. Her eyes were intensely blue, and her nose was fine and straight. What you could not miss was her chest. Her breasts were large, unnaturally taut and fake. Trying not to stare, he admitted the truth to himself: While he might insist that he did not find silicone implants attractive, and though he really was, in a measure, repulsed by them, his penis was twitching as he tried to keep his eyes at the level of her gaze. Reflecting on this, he hesitated before saying that it couldn't have been there that they'd met, but he was sure they had been introduced, they must know each other through mutual friends.

"Do you smoke?" she asked.

Since she was inviting him outside, they left their coffee mugs and put their laptops in their cases in a safe spot behind the counter, near the barista. Then they ambled out to the sidewalk.

Taking one of her cigarettes and her match, he yielded to a habit he did not possess. Since she was obviously a natural flirt, he asked himself how much she believed that they knew each other and how much she was interested in him. His face was not preternaturally lovely, and his shoes said every bit as much about his level of success as his car—and the way he held himself—did. Was this an exercise for an acting class? A response to a momentary fit of tedium? Spitefulness towards a boyfriend for some soon-to-be-forgotten slight?

The sky was gray, and the February air chill. Not wearing tights and garbed in a top calculated to show off her cleavage, she was getting goose flesh, and, as she observed him noticing this, they exchanged warmer expressions. Then there was that strange sense of intimacy that you can have with another person when you've wandered off together from a party in the early hours. This feeling was so strong and sudden that he asked himself if he could invite her back to his apartment, just two blocks away.

Then, as though this thought—and the doubt prompted by it—registered in his eyes, this demonstrating his uncertain place, he felt her again cooling, appraising him clinically once more, shaking her black bangs with a mixture of possibly assumed sexual assurance and vague mocking.

So, an hour later, as he reentered his apartment, he asked himself why everything in the city was so alluring yet so inconstant. Picking up his phone, Billy stared at the number she had punched into it. Her name was Vincenza Morgan.

CHAPTER 2

Vincenza loved film noir. She adored Veronica Lake and Lana Turner, Lauren Bacall and Jane Greer. Her hairstyle imitated Bettie Page, and she liked to wear the sort of stockings that so consistently flattered Barbara Stanwyck. She had coffee table books on these old-time stars, and she sometimes wondered how she would look in a black and white picture with dramatic lighting and moody shadows.

That was a fantasy. What she was confronted by the following afternoon was real. It was as tangible as a bridge or an airplane, and, while it had the same quality of mystery as an old movie, those tales were a retreat from the struggles of her life. But she was faced by a terrifying problem: A corpse lay in her trunk, and she had no idea where it came from.

Set to audition for a role in a Reese Witherspoon movie, she was in an underground garage across the street from the studio in Culver City where her tryout was to take place. There is an elaborate social structure attached to movie parking spots, and her first reaction to being told to park outside the studio lot was irritation. Now it was gratitude. It was fortunate that her car was where no one paid attention. She had gone to the trunk because its warning light had come on, and, after getting out of the car, she had walked around, put her key in the lock and started to lift the lid. She stopped when she realized that what was peeking out was a pair of legs folded crosswise over a man's torso.

As no one was around her, she reached in with her left hand, feeling his calf. It was room temperature and stiff. Accidentally biting her lip, she resisted the impulse to scream and closed the lid of the trunk shut.

Yes, she needed to phone the police. Yet she had no time. Mad though it was, this had to wait. If the existence of a cadaver in the trunk of her car inspired shock and dread, she could not drop the audition. She remembered it too well: She had called off another tryout three months earlier when she was in the grip of a high fever, and, afterwards, her agent had scolded her in a way meant to leave no doubt that he was open to dumping her as a client. There was no subtext. She was not to miss an audition again, not if she were receiving chemo and confronted by the amputation of a limb. So there she was, trying to tell herself that it would be all right and that she should just go ahead and perform.

She wished that she was Lizabeth Scott or Claire Trevor and about to be romanced by Robert Mitchum or Sterling Hayden. The man would be wearing a wide-brimmed hat with a gat in his hand, and together they would tackle the whodunit, puzzling out the nature of the crime and the malefactor responsible. But while she knew from experience that there would be handsome, square-jawed men on the studio lot, none was waiting for her.

Exiting the underground lot, she came out into the afternoon sun. Facing her was the gate in front of the studio complex, and crossing the street, she approached a security guard. Showing him her pass, she was waved in. She put on her oversized sunglasses and marched towards the soundstages and offices. Mercedes, BMWs, and Bentleys were all around: glistening autos with thick coats of paint. She tried not to think about how the California sun had faded the leather of her shoes and bag. She told herself that she was in control. She tried to remind herself of all those necessary clichés, starting with "it's always darkest before the dawn." If what was happening made no sense, somehow or other it was all going to be all right.

Pulling her phone out of the bag, she checked the time. She needed to compose herself. This was not merely to regain her poise. She had to redo her makeup and hair. Perspiration was accumulating around her wrists, forehead, and armpits. She had ten minutes before she was due for the audition. Experience told her that she might have another hour waiting outside the producer's office. The sides—the pages of script that she was to perform—were in the bag draped around her shoulder. The part was small but significant, and she had rehearsed it for three and a half hours.

In the last few years, several friends had gotten these sorts of roles, built up their resumes, then won leads on TV shows or in studio features. It had happened for them. Why couldn't it for her? This, not the body, was what she needed to focus on. Breathing deeply, she asked herself what the movie was about and what her chances of being cast were. Witherspoon was the star. The part was that of a bitchy stewardess who didn't want to let the heroine, arriving late, onto a flight. Marked on the sides were directions telling her that she was to go to a room in building number twelve, and she examined a map of the lot. Streaming past her were those employed at the studio: D-girls, secretaries, flunkies, gophers. There were also directors, producers, and actors. On other days, these were people she would have liked to meet.

Reaching the building, she opened the door, turned left, and headed along a wide, carpeted hallway. Other actresses were already present. Among this number were familiar faces, women she had been up against before. Taking off her sunglasses, she gestured her hellos. A

D-girl noted her arrival and instructed her to park herself on one of the chairs.

The greetings she received from the other actresses told her that they had heard about the indie picture she had just finished shooting. There was envy and resentment in their supposedly joyful congratulations. They knew who else was in the film. The "how amazings!" were laced with strychnine. How was it that this—the dead man in her trunk—had come to be there? It had happened right when she was on the cusp. She had not run away. But it seemed that was what this city and life itself were: You went on with things, playing your role, pretending that everything was fine when a catastrophe was happening. Now this was occurring on a scale a thousand times greater. None knew. No one sensed it. Just the opposite: Perhaps it was the hint that she was about to be someone which prompted the D-girl to slide over to her, mentioning that they wouldn't be seeing her for at least forty minutes. Did it say something that she didn't need to *ask* where she was in the queue?

So notably solicitous, the assistant next directed her to the bathroom, which was down a flight of stairs. Reaching it, Vincenza checked herself in the mirror, brushing her hair, fixing her lipstick, straightening her dress. Then she advanced into a stall. Not sitting down but closing the door firmly shut, she pressed her cell phone tightly to her ear. There were two messages from friends, asking what was she doing that night. That everything went on as it always did: This was simultaneously comforting and petrifying. How could it be that the other actresses didn't suspect the trouble she was in, that what they saw was just a woman on the verge?

Checking herself in the mirror a second time, she brushed her hair once more, swallowed a mint to cover the smell of cigarettes, and exited the bathroom, walking up the steps and reentering the room. Sitting down on one of the metal folding chairs they had put out, she felt something she had not in some time: heart palpitations.

She knew that all they saw was her legs and her enhanced chest and her lips and mascara.

Staggering into the audition room, she was faced by four people placed behind The Table. This is one of the established institutions of the entertainment industry, one whose sole purpose is to humble actors. For The Table is an otherwise superfluous piece of furniture whose sole value lies in its creation of an artificial barrier establishing a division between those who are casting and those anxious for their favor. Most often it is faced by a single chair. Placing yourself in this seat can feel a bit like undergoing interrogation, if with the difference that you must first spend hours learning lines, teasing up your hair, painting yourself with blush and lipstick, and working on the correct presentation of your cleavage, after which you linger for long stretches, waiting to be called. Within the room, there is usually a casting aide who serves as the "reader." This person performs the scene with you. To make matters still more stressful and difficult, frequently he is not of the same age, race, or gender as his character.

And that was indeed the case. Thus, in trying to present her rendition of a snotty stewardess who refuses to let Reese Witherspoon onto her flight, Vincenza was acting with a "Reese" with the height and build of a middle linebacker. Where she had practiced the role by staring down at what was supposed to be a somewhat older five-foot-two-inch woman, she gazed up at a heavyset young man with a soul patch.

The producer, Vincenza gradually deduced, was the one providing the guidance, though it was hard to believe that the producer could be an attractive woman younger than she was.

Vincenza tried to tell herself that she was not distracted. Yet she knew that this was not the case. One thought preying on her was this question of how soon it would be until the carcass began to smell, and, in the run-up to her audition, she had pulled her phone close, taken off her sunglasses, and searched the internet to find out.

Then she had asked herself if this might be potential evidence against her and if there was any way to bury the query with the body. As it happened, the minimum amount of time was said to be a day. She tried not to ponder it. She needed to be present. So she looked to the petite bottle blonde in the fancy suit: the producer. A Brit, she spoke in a deep, staccato voice, one punctuated by a snorting sound that suggested that she had a deviated septum. Gazing down and away from Vincenza, the woman stared at her resume, set on the back of her eight-inch-by-ten glossy.

"Vincenza," she began with an unexpected gentleness, "you're doing one thing I really like, one thing which we really haven't seen from anyone: not focusing on Reese's character. Showing the audience that she's the least of your concerns. And that's exactly right. I guess what I'm saying is that you're the first who actually understands the scene. But what I'm not getting is the full meanness. Can you do a bit more of that? Show us what a cunt you are?"

Even after twelve years in Hollywood, Vincenza was unnerved by the producer's use of the word. But she knew to nod, taking her note. Inhaling once more, she looked to the windows left of her, just above eye level. Outside, the sun was dipping below the horizon, the sky taking on a striking medley of tones: lavender and scarlet, bronze and magenta. Could it be that her preoccupation with the body's possible odor was assisting her in the audition? Instinct told her to stand up and to instruct her scene partner to take his place in the chair. She was in command. She had to play that.

She tried not to let them see her anxiousness. Had they liked this reading? It was always impossible to tell if you were going to receive a callback. What she knew now, though—and had not grasped before—was that she had done the right thing in scrupulously following the script: that it was better to be examining it than to be staring at the casting agent and the producer but changing the words. She had learned, too, how important it was to depart the room with a professional but bland politeness, a manner verging on indifference.

Back in the waiting area, she took off her pumps, slipping them into her handbag. In their place she put on her faded, open-toed, low heels. Departing, she switched her phone back on and gazed up. Light came from many directions: illumination from the studio buildings and from the overhead lamps in the lot. A sliver still emanated from the descending sun, falling below the western edge of Culver City.

Trudging forward, she went through with her customary review. (She did not want to call this one a post-mortem. That was a little too *apropos*.) The movie's director had not been present. Nor had the casting director. But she had managed to impress one of the producers, it seemed.

Putting on her large sunglasses and employing them as a shield, she refused to make eye contact with the passing faces. Then, reaching her car, she removed them and gazed about once more, making sure no one was nearby. No, there were just a great many automobiles fitted in between painted lines. So, inhaling deeply, she stepped to her car's trunk and pulled out her key chain. Yet her hands were shaking, and she knew that she was not going to be able to press the button, opening the lock. Nor was she prepared to dial the police.

Pulling out her phone, she searched for the nearest police station. It was almost around the corner—on Duquesne Avenue—barely two blocks from the studio gates. Starting the ignition, she drove down Culver Boulevard, by an old-fashioned post office building. That was on her left. Swinging right onto Duquesne, she passed the Culver City Hall. Next to it stood the police station. Designed in Depression-era Works Progress Administration style, it was a long, white-stucco building flanked by flagpoles and palm trees. A half dozen black-and-white police cruisers were planted in front. Vincenza felt her heart beating. The palpitations were almost audible, and she drove by, circling around and driving up to Irving. Then she threaded her way down Washington back to Duquesne.

She went past the police station three times. The immediate question was where to park. The real concern was how to enter and tell the police that there was a dead body in her trunk, and she had no idea how it had gotten there. It was as though she was choking.

Whom might she call? Her first thought was her frequent scene partner, Sara Kertesz. But what could she do? The men she worked for in her day job might know how to dispose of a corpse. She did not want to be indebted to them. She did not wish to think about her mother who was 2000 miles away. The only person she could summon to mind potentially of use whom she could trust was an acquaintance in the religious sect she was attached to, the International Church of Life. A new faith, it attracted its members for a multitude of reasons. One bore relevance: The Church *did things*. She had assumed that this faculty would be employed to save the species. Perhaps it might be put to use saving her.

Pulling over and parking in a strip mall, she opened her driver's side door and lit a cigarette. Who was the man in the car's rear? How had he gotten there? On at least two instances she had provided her car to other members of the Church. It struck her that in making her independent film she had also loaned the vehicle to her producing partner and the crew members. Who might have copied the keys?

CHAPTER 3

The following afternoon Billy was waiting for a meeting, one confirmed an hour earlier. It had been rescheduled seven times. He had been in Los Angeles long enough not to take offense. It was how the business was. The apex predators—producers, executives, actors, directors, and agents—told their assistants to follow the practice. Those not at the summit were phoned each day to say that their scheduled conference had been put off. This would happen up until the moment when a hole suddenly appeared in the predator's schedule and the lesser light might be slotted in. The reason for this practice was that if Meryl Streep were to decide at the last minute that she wanted to see you, you rearranged your afternoon. So it often took weeks for someone like Billy to have a meeting that had been previously scheduled—if it took place at all.

As he was led into the offices of the production company, which were on the studio's lot in Culver City, he reminded himself to be warm but not intimate, friendly but not effusive. The woman receiving him was the company's principal assistant (as the head of their operation was in London, where they were about to begin shooting a picture based on the Arthurian legends). Her name, she had explained with a beaming look that he had learned meant nothing in the way

12

of genuine interest, was Gwendolyn Weiner. The name puzzled Billy as she certainly did not look Jewish. Her butch haircut and manner suggested that she was gay. Was this, then, the last name of her female companion, and, if so, why had it not been hyphenated, as was customary? He knew better than to ask. Rather, he took his cue and seated himself opposite her in a handsome, burnt sienna leather chair that matched to expensive beige carpeting.

Her eyes were of a contrasting color, a watery blue-green that glinted as she fixed them upon him. Behind her, light slanted in from a large third-floor window.

"Susan told me how amazing your idea was," she said, referring to the absent executive. "But we wanted to hear about it from you. In person. We're glad you could finally come."

Billy tried to keep the necessary straight face when he heard this as they both knew that he had waited weeks for the meeting.

"Of course."

"The idea is to shoot this as a backdoor pilot, yes?" she went on. This was a term for a TV movie that could be used to set up a subsequent series with the same characters and setting.

"That was one idea I'd had."

She paused, and then leaned forward, clasping her hands together and smiling officiously. "Tell me more."

"Well, at some level, it's just a variant on a detective show. Because that's part of what a bounty hunter is: a licensed detective. And the first thing she has to do is figure out where the person she's supposed to capture is. Then she has to bring that person back, which could involve shooting, car chases. The runny-and-jumpy stuff. Each episode involves some kind of mystery. Why has this person fled? What happened? Is the fugitive guilty? And then this is also a feminist story, because it's about a woman with a kid trying to make it in this male-dominated business of bounty hunting, or, as it's called among the professionals in the trade, skip tracing. It's a whole vibrant subculture we'd have to explore. With its own laws, jargon, customs…"

Billy had practiced this pitch in front of his apartment's plate-glass mirrors, and he was surprised by how cleanly it had come off, even somehow sounding fresh in his own ears. He could see, though, that Gwendolyn was not persuaded by it, and he knew from experience that it was unlikely that she had done anything more than read the initial scene or two from the script, the part called the teaser—this along with the notes on it that had been given to her by her own assistant. The trick at this point was to project a relaxed mood when you sensed resistance. If you tried to push back, you were bound to lose them for good.

Yet he was one month behind on the rent, four months in arrears on student loans. What was more, he was in that unfortunate spot which every writer in Hollywood is bound to be at some point: His agent wasn't taking his calls, and he wasn't sure if this meant he no longer had an agent or if it simply indicated that he didn't have an agent who cared in the slightest degree about him as a client. (There is a not insignificant difference). So, he tried to come across as blithe and relaxed as he was able, awaiting her reply.

Short as Gwendolyn Weiner's hair was, it bounced nonetheless as she nodded. It was the sort of response that was most common in Hollywood: a grinning, bright-eyed, shake of rejection.

"It sounds like every plot—every episode—would have to be shot in a different state. Sounds awful expensive."

Billy hesitated. How could he properly agree with the criticism while also dispensing with it? Although the executive had been compelled to smile as she rebuffed him, he was now obliged to thoughtfully and graciously absorb this blow without seeming too desperate in his acceptance of it.

"Yes," he began, "that's right. *Quite* right. My agent thinks with all the neighborhoods and styles of architecture and terrain we have around here that we could film most of it locally. But there are obviously scenes—every so often—that would have to be shot out of state."

"Interesting," she said, pausing to reflect and to consider whether she might be risking some of her accumulated capital as an executive to express interest in a pitch from a writer who appeared to stand on the totem pole below the line at which the timber meets the soil. "Maybe I should think about this more."

The translation into ordinary English of this last part was easy enough for Billy. She was asking if she should read the script. What Billy was unsure of was how to prod her to do this without saying this directly, thereby breaking the unstated protocol that a writer was never to challenge an executive for her dereliction in not reading what she had professed to.

"I have a thought," she said, sitting back in her chair. She was serious and not smiling. The blue-green eyes seemed to be looking partly inward. This, he knew, was a welcome sign. After all, executives had no need to be glad-handing when they were contemplating doing you a favor, and if they wished to do business with you they would not want to show weakness.

"We have a script that needs a polish. On a few scenes," she said. "Would you be interested in doing that? Then, when you've finished and we've looked at it, we could talk more about *The Bounty-Hunter with a Curling Iron*."

"I'm actually pretty available right now," he allowed. "Go ahead."

"It's with *Arthur Rex*. The studio thinks that the relationship between Arthur and Lancelot doesn't have enough subtextual elements."

"Well, I'm good at subtextual. I mean, I think I'm known for that." He waited for this statement to sink in. "I take it you're looking for ideas from several writers."

She nodded once more, this time without smiling. "Yes. And you're all right with that—though it means we might not use anything you give us?"

"How fast do you need it?"

The number she quoted to him as pay was enough to live on for at least six months, and, as he had nearly depleted a small inheritance that he had received in an IRA account, he was not about to argue over the amount. There was even the added benefit that the money would have to be sent through his agent, and that might—ever so possibly—resurrect that relationship. With this in mind, Billy focused himself and made a determined effort not to show that he was all that pleased or surprised by the outcome of the meeting, retreating with a polite clasp of palms and the most matter-of-fact smile he could summon.

Leaving the office, he almost felt like skipping, and he glided back to the studio parking lot in a cheery mood, one only broken by an unexpected sight. Suddenly, as he gazed to his right, he saw that Vincenza Morgan was traipsing along, parallel to him. But, as she was wearing sunglasses and seemingly preoccupied, he was invisible to her.

CHAPTER 4

Vincenza hadn't re-opened the trunk. It was six in the evening. There were offices in the strip mall—a dentist and an acupuncturist, among others—and people were starting to leave for the day. That meant there was a chance as she opened it that folk slipping past her on the way to their vehicles might see. And, as she still wasn't sure who was inside, there was no reason to phone her friend at the Church of Life, not yet. There was something else, too. Her phone had just rung, and faster than she could ever remember, she was being instructed that she was to return to the studio the following morning for a callback. New sides to prepare for her next audition would arrive by email.

She wanted to go to the police. But how could she explain it? Forcing herself to breathe, she put out the cigarette and hopped back into the car. Setting out on a string of roads, she decided to return to her apartment in Hollywood. She had to think. That would be easier once she got home. At noontime, the journey could be made in twenty minutes. It was, after all, little more than a passage of a couple of miles traveling east on Venice Boulevard, then a few more heading north on Highland. Now it might take hour.

The rush hour traffic wasn't all that was slowing her down, though. She couldn't safely open the trunk in the garage of her building either. So, while she flipped on the radio and partly occupied herself with changing channels, her focus was upon finding a spot along the way where she could pull over to check the cargo space. The great number of cars about made this difficult. Whenever it seemed that she had identified a possible spot, she noticed an angle from which a resident or a passerby might look in. On Venice, there were too many people drifting in and out from the supermarket and drug store parking lots, even with the sun descending, and South La Brea was no better. Scrutinizing both sides of the road, she passed a series of half-empty motels and auto parts stores. All were well-lit. Nor was Highland an alternative. It was jammed with cars and crisply illuminated on every block. The sole option, it seemed, was to go onto a side street past the area of her apartment building, and that presented a different obstacle. The most remote spots were at underpasses and beneath clumps of trees where the homeless congregated. Finally, though, after a good quarter-hour of additional driving, she discovered a spot with sufficient light where she was not fearful of an attack from a street person. Up in the hills, it lay near Bronson Canyon.

She reminded herself of the explanation she would fall back upon if stopped: She was checking for a spare tire. This in mind, she parked the car on a shoulder and popped the latch for the trunk. Once again, walking around the car, she felt the heart palpitations. Gazing about, she turned her head, making sure no one could see.

Then she lifted the lid. With this, the trunk light came on, exposing the body. It had been deposited with the face pointed up but with the legs pressed against the head and torso. Nonetheless, Vincenza promptly recognized him. It was her sometime lover, Tom Selva. Once strikingly beautiful, his skin was a gray-green, and she felt an impulse to retch. Yet she could not turn away.

More startling was the amount of blood, dried a deep shade of brown. Swiveling her eyes in a half-circle, she gazed left, then right, making sure that there was still no one lurking nearby. Then she placed her head inside the compartment. Below the skinny legs, she discerned the cause of death: gaping bullet holes. Even more disturbing was the sight of a revolver plopped onto his chest. Vincenza recognized it as a prop gun used in the movie she had shot, and, without thinking, she grabbed it, lifting it up. With that, she inhaled the scent of gunpowder. It was only as she set the weapon down that it occurred to her that she had just placed a set of fingerprints on what was surely a murder weapon. Indeed, as sweaty as her hands were, she had put a firm imprint upon it.

Should she clean the gun, ridding it of her fingerprints and possibly someone else's? She did not know, though instinct told her that she must get away from an odor—that of the body—which was like sweetly rotting meat. Closing the trunk, she placed herself behind the wheel of the car. Around her was the gathering darkness, and she heard the rumble of distant engines. Hot tears streamed down her cheeks. It took her the better part of an hour to compose herself. Then, unsure of what else she might do, she called her sometime advisor within the Church of Life.

THAT MAN—DAVID CLARKSON—was hunched over, busy studying an overstuffed manila folder. Perched on the seventeenth floor of the Church's worldwide headquarters, he was in an office in an eighteen-story art deco tower. Set just south of Sunset Boulevard, along the edge of Thai Town, its windows offered him a spectacular, unimpeded view of the downtown, and through these he saw its sparkling lights, shining in the darkness. Yet, striding over, he closed the drapes. Then he returned to his desk to once more examine the contents of the file.

The folder was Vincenza's. He was examining it because the head of the Church—the Supreme Pilot—had instructed him to call her and ask her to come *immediately*. The guidance he had received was so clear and unambiguous and yet so devoid of explanation that he wondered what the possible purpose of the request was. For that reason he had hesitated in dialing the number. Although he could not wait much longer, his gut told him that something critically important was at stake and that he needed to know more. He was relieved when he saw that *she* was calling *him*.

The forms in the folder went back twelve years, and most of the information contained within the file had yet to be digitized. The first papers dated to six months after Vincenza—then named Kelli Haines—had arrived in Los Angeles, freshly graduated from Burnsville High in Eagan, Minnesota. These papers constituted her initial psychological profile. The result of her introductory session with a Church counselor, these were from what was referred to as "an exploratory session." In it she had revealed a vast amount. Far more than in a nude scene in a movie, she had been stripped naked.

The first method that the Church used to recruit members was the plainest imaginable: a personality test. The trick lay in the interpretation of the answers. No matter what you said, the tester told you the same thing. Sighing and acting as though it pained him to reveal the truth, the counselor informed you that the exam showed that you were a person of extraordinary potential but badly damaged. Fortunately, he would say, the Church's recognized methods of therapy could heal you.

This approach had worked flawlessly on Vincenza, and the sheets bared the most harrowing aspects of her life: how and why her stepfather used to beat her and when she had decided to stop speaking with her mother. There was more. Scrawled notes revealed that she had been Burnsville High's homecoming queen and that she had an ongoing relationship with a photographer whose claims that he could provide her work as a model were proving false. She had mentioned to her profiler that she drove on side streets because she was scared of highway exits. She admitted that she was fearful of sitting on toilet seats in restrooms. She told her confessor that she was worried about the possibility of blood clots caused by her birth control pills, and she dreaded the onset of her periods when off them. She had panic attacks. The physical description provided matched to what he knew from his own encounters with her: She had radiant eyes and shapely legs, the waist of a waifish adolescent, and delicate skin. Even her ears were well-formed. More, these looks had been improved by plastic surgeons. Not only had they enlarged her chest, but they had thinned her nose and removed the pointiness from her chin. She was an undeniable beauty.

Additional papers in the stack recounted the process by which she had become the Church's servant. This commenced with modest requests. Would she volunteer, helping out by painting the walls of a new house of worship in Glendale? Would she make donations in return for classes and seminars? Within a year she had become a devoted follower.

As the man behind the desk read the documents, he considered the ways in which he was like her. He, too, had come to Los Angeles to act. Breathing in and unconsciously nodding his head, he recalled the time. Ten years had passed in the usual profitless battles: to obtain an agent, to be cast in parts for a reel, to be seen in roles in sketch shows and revivals staged in black box theaters.

Seated in his office reading the folder, he alternated between sipping from a no longer warm cup of coffee and gnawing his cuticles. The Supreme Pilot rarely failed to explain why he wanted something, and it was never a good sign when he left out the background. Yet the file was unremarkable. Hundreds of the files among the thousands in the Church's archives were similar. There were only two distinctive items. The first was that she was so easy on the eyes, though even that was hardly uncommon. The second was that she had managed to persuade several of the Church's best-known young adherents to appear in an independent film that she had co-produced and acted in. It seemed reasonable to think that this must be the reason why the Supreme Pilot wished to see her. But why was he being asked to get her to the Church headquarters that night? Clarkson wondered, and he could not deny that he had a peculiar sense, a foreboding that a pertinent but vital detail had been omitted from what had been said to him.

His own name was indicated by a card on the doorframe outside his office. There had been a time when he had thought that such a marker would be affixed to a strip of oak-paneling on a high floor in a downtown skyscraper: at a top corporate firm with prestige clients. But, when he had graduated from law school, it was the Great Recession, and he had discovered that there was an excess of attorneys in the city and the jobs were going to the graduates from UCLA and USC, not Southwestern Law, the school he had attended while holding down a position as the night manager of a motel. He had been grateful to the Church for his job. Over time his role had become that of its fixer.

Balked in his aim of deciphering the Supreme Pilot's intentions and well aware that it was not his business to press him for an explanation, Clarkson lifted up the phone.

Her tone was hysterical and urgent. "Would you talk to me? I might need some help," she said. "I'm really glad that I was able to reach you. I figured that you often work late."

"Of course, Vincenza. You've been devoted to the Church. As you know, we like to say that we don't have followers. We have lenders. You give us your love and passion and devotion, and we're obligated to pay back the debt."

"I'm grateful to hear you say that. Very."

There was a pause. It was more than anxious.

22

"If you really need help, why don't you come now? To the head-quarters. You know that I consider you a friend."

Clarkson heard her breathing. It was heavy, and she was stammering. He had the sense from the texture of her voice that she must have been crying. Yet she did not respond. There was just the sound on the line of her taking in mouthfuls of air. She was almost panting, and he moved further forward in his chair.

What else could he say to persuade her?

"We could send a car," he added quickly.

He realized that he had made a mistake. That the suggestion unnerved her was audible, and it was underlined by what she said next—that she would phone him back. With that, the phone line went dead.

CHAPTER 5

The affair with Tom Selva had commenced in a fashion only possible in Hollywood.

Eight years before he had been a nobody. While he liked to tell friends that he had "representation," he did not have an agent, and his manager was a hectoring, schlubby woman with no-name clients who worked out of her home-office, set next to the laundry room in her split-level in the Valley. His training consisted of what he had learned from the drama teacher who had cast him in a play in Tarzana. It was his high school's production of Neil Simon's *Lost in Yonkers*, and by most standards he was terrible. He did not sound like a New Yorker, did not look Jewish, spoke in a recognizable Valley accent, and plainly had more experience and confidence with girls than most men in their forties. He rarely seemed to be acting with his scene partners, and his comedic timing was rudimentary.

But the manager—Millie Kleinbaum—had attended it because her daughter had a part. What she saw in Selva was what everyone did: the matching of magnificent good looks with sex appeal. It is a fact that most entertainment industry professionals know all too well: Box office stars typically possess two opposing traits. These attributes are abiding egomania and consuming insecurity. Millie did not fully understand that this was what she was viewing on the stage, but she smelled it. With it came the conviction that she had grasped a winning lottery ticket, that she had found her fortune, if only she could hang onto it.

Once he was signed, she began focusing on him, expending more time and effort upon Selva than she did on the few actors she represented who were the source of the little money she possessed not provided in child support from her orthodontist ex-husband. She had advanced Selva the money to fix his teeth, sending him to her ex. She had prodded him to get his headshots and then gone over them to select the best. She had worked with him on voice and posture. Then she had badgered every casting director she could get on the phone to find him auditions for starting out jobs: commercials, print modeling gigs, industrials.

A full year went by before she could obtain a meeting with an agent for him, and the part that made him famous arrived by happenstance. Unconvinced of his prospects as an actor, his mother had goaded him into assuming the status of a part-time student at Cal State, Northridge. Interested in little besides cars and girls, he had selected an automotive technology class. This placed him in the school's auto body shop when a casting agent for a new movie about the underground racing scene popped in. She was seeking a grease monkey to fix her damaged transmission, not an actor. Still, just like Millie Kleinbaum, she couldn't keep her eyes off him. And she knew that he knew it. Was he someone to bring in for an audition? He was plausible as a working-class car enthusiast. The notion was bolstered when she learned that he had an agent and manager along with a modicum of experience before the camera. Nonetheless, the studio had refused to cast him, and it was only when the actor signed to play the role broke his arm two days prior to the start of shooting that Selva was awarded it.

Once the movie opened, he was a star. Boys across the country knew him as Stevie P., the guy with the amped-up Mustang and the knowing smile. Attempts to make him a darling to pubescent females had proved less efficacious; his barely concealed wolfishness was not what the average teenaged girl newly confronted by periods and acne esteemed. Still, the series of movies in which he starred were among the most popular in the world, and when his "people" failed to get him the range of roles he sought, he had no compunction or sluggishness in dispensing with them. That included Millie Kleinbaum. While their contract had been for two years, she possessed an option by which she could extend it for another two. This led to litigation, which she won. On the day the fourth year ended, her termination notice arrived by courier.

In the midst of this, Selva had been introduced to the Church. What they said made sense. Undergoing their induction tests and speaking to them about his fears and secrets, he had felt for the first time that he had been spoken to honestly. He was comfortable, could talk frankly about things, might say what he had not been able to. The method they employed to test his responses and to remedy them was scientific. There were polygraph machines and detailed procedures by which you could begin to understand the way in which you were held back by repression and anxiety. There was a scheme for better health and nutrition with vitamins and cleansing, and you could discuss things without reserve with their confessors. They understood what he was saying when he brought up the feeling that his friendships in school had been fake, and they had the cause for why this was, explanations. The people within the Church grasped its larger mission and cause. It was exciting to be a part of it.

The Church had doctrines, too. In order for followers to reach the elevated states of consciousness and maturity at which Church leaders felt confident that they might entrust them with its esoteric truths, they had to pass a series of tests, presented over a period of years. Each was a step up. At the hour of his death, Selva had attained the status of FUP. This meant a *fully unrepressed person*.

Those who opposed the Church were EMEs, or *enemies of man's emergence*. Leaders of the Church—men like Clarkson—were referred to as pilots. This is because the Church teaches its members that growing ecological degradation will eventually require our species to transport itself to another planet five parsecs—roughly sixteen light years—away. The pilots, it is presumed, will captain the flights to this new planet where humanity will begin its process of evolution again in a new Eden. Once Church members reach the highest state of understanding, they are allowed to participate in a ceremony at which they are prepared for the tasks they will under-take at the hour of interplanetary journey. Yet, because the Church's thinking so radically conflicted with the beliefs of the mainstream, and as preparation for the day of leave-taking from Earth required enormous passion and commitment, it advises adherents to limit their contact with family members opposed to it, those who are despoiling the planet's air, land, and water. Those who have left the Church and gone back to shameless lives, ones in which indifference to ecological destruction is blithely tolerated, are shunned.

All this seemed so obvious and reasonable to Selva that he found it hard to understand how it could be that there were those outside the Church, people still hostile to its mission and its goals. So he did as the Church leaders instructed him. It had been explained to him that the future society on the new Eden required artists and poets, creative figures like himself. It had also been pointed out that he served the Church and its purposes through his celebrity. He was a shining example of what the Church represented and the values it embodied. His talent and beauty were avatars of what mankind would be after the interplanetary journey.

They had even cautioned him against a modest lifestyle, observing that it might turn those attached to wastefulness and consumption away from involvement in the Church, the necessary first step to man's enlightenment and the species' preparation for the trek from earth.

Devotion inspired him, and it had prompted him to insist that his wife join the Church of Life. He could not marry a woman who was not committed to the cause. It was not just a means by which to judge her character. He did not want his children or their mother left on earth when the day of passage arrived.

Attachment to the Church had affected him in another way, too. Through the Church he had met Vincenza.

Day by day his fame grew. In poorly heated factories in China, people made toy figurines of him. Booths at comic conventions were devoted to his Stevie P. character. A public relations firm took in $23,000 each month to keep sordid tales about him out of the press. He had a half-time hairdresser and stylist and a full-time cook and trainer. He had a production office. He employed agents, lawyers, managers, gardeners, accountants, tax advisors, and a pool cleaner. There was a night nurse and a nanny to assist his wife with their newborn son, and he had leased a BMW for a girlfriend. As his own taste ran to classic motorcycles, he had a collection of them at his compound on a high street in West Hollywood. More recently, he had purchased a bungalow in New Orleans's Garden District.

He had only been twenty-eight years old.

WHEN STILL A BOY, SELVA WAS MOLESTED. The sights and smells lodged themselves inside: the hand holding the engorged member that pitched forward from his father's pelvis, the odors of sweat and gin. Then there was another picture that stayed, left from the morning when the sound of a pistol going off drew him down a flight of steps from his upstairs bedroom in his family's two-story home. At the head of their butcher-block dining table was the chair in which his father sat. The gun he had taken his life with was in his right hand. His ashen face with its bulging eyes was nearly parallel to his shoulders, and blood was draining from the exit wound in his scalp, matting his thinning blond hair.

Only with the Church counselors had Selva felt comfortable talking about this. But the Church was a community, the one place where he did not sense that he needed to war and to take. They valued him, not, as others did, merely for his starring roles in *The Dangerous Race* films.

Within days of the first movie's release, he had found that he was a different person. When he went to a party, he did not need to sweet-talk. Girls just offered themselves, asking him to head into the bushes or the backseat of their cars—even a bathroom—anywhere they might satisfy him. He did not know how most of the agents and gossip writers and photographers garnered his phone number. The calls and requests were incessant, though. It was an inundation.

What he did not receive were offers to play weighty or interesting parts. Fearful that he might not report to work promptly for the sequel, the studio had boosted his pay for the second film to $2 million, and he had made multiples of that with each of the succeeding car crash epics. Yet even when his agents managed to finagle a script for him for a project helmed by one of the name directors—Tarantino, Scorsese—he could not get an audition, and too often he had the sense when he attended more serious industry functions that he was being furtively mocked. It was almost as though they, too, knew about his father. Other actors regarded as no more than charming pretty boys had somehow moved ahead. In a few short years Ashton Kutcher had graduated from *Dude, Where's My Car?* to a featured role in an ensemble drama about the assassination of Bobby Kennedy. Robert Pattinson had gone from vampirism to starring in a period film based on a novel by a nineteenth-century Frenchman. Where was his ascension? Why were late-night comics joking about his acting skills, even as their booking agents pled for him to appear on their shows?

Selva did not know Vincenza well. But not long after they were introduced she had earned his respect. How many other unknown actresses had told him that they were not going to sleep with him because his fiancée was pregnant?

Then, right after his wife gave birth, Vincenza had come to him with a suggestion. Her idea intrigued him. It was to shoot a film about a group of friends, twenty-something actors in Hollywood, who, over the course of a long night, discover that they have betrayed one another, professionally and personally. Other parts would be played by fellow members in the Church of Life, up-and-comers. But his was the leading role. The dialogue would be improvised. The actors would work with Vincenza and her collaborators on developing their characters, and when the film was released they would be given credit for their contributions. The plot—laid out in an eight-page story treatment—was cleverly constructed, and they would enhance it with their own inventions, details from their own lives which would give it layers of authenticity.

To accentuate the drama, it would be in black and white. The inspiration was the great films made by John Cassavetes in the 1970s, movies like *Faces* and *A Woman Under the Influence*, pictures with consummate performers like Ben Gazzara and Gena Rowlands, practitioners of the Method. The stars would trust one another and work just like those had. Three cameras would be arranged around them, and it would be directed to give the audience the sense that what it was seeing was real. There would be lots of overlapping dialogue, and the actors would play off one another, knowing where the interchanges had to go but taking their time getting there. In Selva's crucial scene, he was to tease a dweeby pal rather cruelly, inching his buddy towards a breaking point. At that moment, a woman would reveal that Selva had been having an affair with the friend's wife, and they would start to brawl. At the end, his character died.

The film would be cheap to make as there would be no sets to construct, and it would be performed over a few nights in a twenty-four-hour diner in West Hollywood, one loaned to them in return for its very visible use with its actual name. An ex of Vincenza's who wished to be a producer had managed to pull in $75,000 from a rich uncle. That was the money to shoot the movie, and if all the actors agreed to work for free, they had the funds. Each would have a chance to display not only his creativity but his chops, showing off his skill in scenes of naturalism and high drama. As Vincenza had pointed out, it was exactly the kind of movie that could be programmed at the top indie film festivals, Sundance or South by Southwest, and, once it was out, people in the industry would understand what he was capable of. No one would be mocking him. He wouldn't just be Stevie P., that handsome dope. He would be cast in the parts that got you Oscar nominations. He would attain that next step, the one that had eluded him.

CHAPTER 6

Selling real estate, teaching nursery school, and instructing yoga classes: Those were the most common ways struggling actresses supported themselves. Vincenza had seen how her friends gradually drifted into these occupations, becoming career professionals in other fields without even knowing it.

There were other paths, of course. Some worked the phones, selling subscriptions to the symphony. Then there were low-paid jobs as self-employed taxi drivers. Or you might be hired as a cocktail waitress, bartender, or nightclub hostess. A few of her acting class friends had fallen into porn, and from that point on they were avoided, as everyone had the sense that their condition might be contagious. The brightest worked as SAT instructors.

For seven years Vincenza had manned the register at a marijuana dispensary. It was literally an odd job in as much as the way the store functioned was strange. Because the federal government did not recognize their legality, the dispensaries could not place the funds they received in banks. That compelled them to run on a cash basis. Consequently, the businesses did not attract legitimate operators. Rather, the owners of the shops were small-time hoods. Vincenza's interactions with hers were sometimes pleasant and amusing, but at other times suffused with menace. Pay came at two-week intervals in an envelope filled with bills of varying denominations.

The customers were likewise peculiar. She had quickly learned not to dress in a sexy or immodest way. In a bathroom in the back of the store, she would change outfits when she had to leave for an audition. That provoked comments on the way out from the proprietors, two Israeli brothers, sometime ecstasy dealers. Their come-ons were rarely even on the level of, "You're hot! You know that?" More often it was, "Am I ever going to get a feel?" It had taken her a while, but she had eventually realized that it was banter, however demeaning. It was a business, and they did not want to lose her. What was more, she was perpetually surrounded by other employees. The gay store manager was always hovering about while an extraction technician toiled in the backroom, and, intermittently, there was a cannabis scientist popping in to test the samples delivered by the vendors.

Her unease was more often awakened by thoughts of what might happen to the Israelis' silent partners. On several occasions she had heard the brothers voicing what sounded like threats, as she had seen them with guns tucked into their waistbands.

The job required a large amount of knowledge. Although a computer software system listed all of the items they offered, in order to serve the customers who came in to the shop she had been obliged to memorize detail on their varieties of oils, lozenges, injectables, and edibles, along with their two dozen brands of raw pot. This unrefined product was contained within capacious glass jars, carefully labeled and set in rows. The lot was in display cases. Above these, clipped to racks on the walls, were a huge assortment of vaping instruments, pens for the tongue and hookahs in all shapes and sizes.

In order to learn the differences between these articles, Vincenza had to sample them. Naturally that had led to a mild habit, one that she could easily kick if she wanted to. Still, amidst all the perturbation—knowing that you had once been homecoming queen and now were a store clerk—it was a salve.

The brothers, Eilan and Binyamin, employed her as a cashier and sales assistant alongside a young man who was a determined ganja enthusiast and another actress, a truly breathtaking girl whom Vincenza had met in a class at the Beverly Hills Playhouse. To the brothers' credit, they permitted the women to head off for auditions so long as there was someone present to handle the customers. Although this arrangement sometimes led to conflict, most often it worked tolerably well as neither actress was getting that many auditions, and both were desirous of extra hours. Since the store stayed open until seven at night, and it had to be staffed on weekends, there were ways for the three of them to juggle schedules.

Normally Vincenza's called for her to get Saturdays off. That was when she went to her Meisner Sessions, acting classes that taught you how to listen and respond with intensity and alertness. There she had recognized one of the shop's regulars, a nerdy girl who wore hipster, 1950s-style glasses. Most comfortable at comedy, this woman—Sara was her name—soon became Vincenza's regular scene partner.

Since both women lived within a twenty-minute drive of the class, they would head to one or another of their apartments and get stoned afterwards. Even without the Mary Jane, Sara was someone easy to establish a rapport with. They shared a taste in movies, had similar ideas regarding the men in the class, and neither was put off by her polite refusals when Vincenza suggested that she accompany her to Church sessions. Yet months of these afternoons went by before Sara mentioned the filmscript she was writing and her desire to round up performers to make a movie based upon it. Vincenza was put at ease by the fact that she freely admitted that her interest in collaborating was stimulated by the knowledge that, through the Church of Life, Vincenza knew a number of talked-about actors.

Two more seasons followed during which Sara discussed the screenplay without ever showing it to Vincenza. While she would describe it in considerable detail, somehow she could never be persuaded to provide her with a copy. It had taken Vincenza a while to grasp the truth, that there was no script, just an idea.

Meanwhile, time passed as it does in Los Angeles. Summer turned to winter with little change but for the coming of the rains, and the shift in the hue of the chaparral draping the canyons, which traded gray-green for ochre and brown. Occasionally, Vincenza heard of friends who had gotten meaningful roles she had sought or read about. But there were parts in commercials to prepare for and parties to go to and nightclubs and dates and boyfriends.

When there was a free moment at the shop, she practiced her audition sides with her beautiful but utterly wooden co-worker, the girl she had met at the Beverly Hills Playhouse. Or, following her Meisner Class on Saturdays, she relaxed with Sara. Eventually, Vincenza began showing her the notes she had typed out, outlining their plot. It took most of a year to set down the story treatment. Once that was finished, Vincenza found their aspiring producer and Sara recruited a would-be director, a recent USC film school grad.

This was their team. It was their opportunity. The script gave each a role. If they could just get some of Vincenza's acquaintances from the Church to sign on, they had a solid commercial proposition. They would be seen at last, and not for speaking two lines in a compact car commercial or an ad for chicken wings. And who was the biggest name they could latch on to? Tom Selva.

There were things about men that Vincenza had known almost as if from birth—and certainly from the hour when she had fastened the straps of her first training bra. One nugget of wisdom involved sex: If you afforded it to them too readily, they never took you seriously. She had reproached herself for rejecting Selva when he had propositioned her. He was as desirable as any man she had ever met. But it was not simply a matter of scruples. Had she gone to bed with him when he asked, he would have regarded her as no more than a brief diversion. And she needed to be something more.

An invite to a Church function at which he was being lauded provided the occasion. For most of the evening, phalanxes of people formed around him, and they were in the midst of a high-ceilinged ballroom. It required waiting until he was on the edge of the space in the last hour of the event. That she had put him off before—this and the amount of her chest presented by her blouse—commanded his attention.

She waited for him to ask her what she was working on. That was the cue. The intensity with which he listened to her told others not to interrupt, and she saw in talking with him about it how responsive he was. The appealing aspect was the chance to devise his own lines, to help create the scenes, he said. Too often he had felt that he was a highly remunerated parrot.

The intimacy with which Selva said this touched her, and the way he looked at her made her feel charming, like someone smarter and more poised. However much she knew his reputation, and that he was married, she felt the attraction, so much so that she was forced to break eye contact. Then she felt his hand grasping her wrist. Turning her gaze up, she saw that he was giving her that stare, telling her to meet with him soon to speak about the script.

She had insisted that their get-together be at a restaurant in the middle of the day, and she dressed for it in relatively modest fashion. The top displayed no more than a hint of her nipples. Yet, while she liked Sara, she did not trust her and couldn't be sure that she wouldn't try to cut her out of the project once she met Selva. So it was just the two of them. Handing him the treatment, she focused on proper elocution as she ran through her more thorough explanation of the story and what his part would be.

A week went by. Then there was a text message, requesting that she come to a cottage in Malibu overlooking the beach. This time she attired herself to close the deal.

Was making love to him the price of the ticket? She had waited so long for any real chance, and suddenly she found herself alone with him with the pounding of the surf serving as the soundtrack and the cornflower blue sky and chalk-white sand their backdrop. She couldn't help but think of scenes from cheesy movies and episodes of reality shows set in tropical locales. She wished it were not so cliché. She wished he were not already wed. And yet…

She knew to wait until he had put pen to paper before she relented, and she tried not to admit to herself how much she wanted it to be heartfelt and not transactional. It pained her to notice it, but there it was—he was somewhat perfunctory in the way he saw her out when she left. Probably she was just another girl to him. But she knew: Once he had placed his signature on the sheet there was a possibility of her life becoming something better, and, although sober, she drove away from his cottage in such a state of excitement that she had to stop, pulling over to the side of the road. Tears formed in her eyes, joy mixing with shame and a sense that a long chain of failures and disappointments might be nearing its conclusion.

Things moved rapidly then. Not even a month was needed to attach two more talents from the Church: another talked-about young actor and a charismatic singer named Lorelei who had a song rising up the charts. Lorelei would play the heroine, while Sara would be her troubled friend with a drug problem. Vincenza was the *femme fatale*.

MOVIEMAKING IS MORE A MANAGEMENT SKILL than an art. A hundred things are bound to go wrong. The capable producer and director are masters of adjustment, swift to replace missing actors, substitute locations and equipment, change lines, and make good use of mistakes.

These talents were immediately required on Vincenza and Sara's film, and they were fortunate above all else for one decision made by their novice producer. Conscious of the extent of his ignorance, he had brought on a veteran line producer, giving her the title of co-executive in lieu of her salary. In return, she was organizing every aspect of the production. She had seen to it that the gaffers, lighting technicians, electricians, costumer, prop master, two makeup women, and a half dozen cameramen were present on time, that the craft services people and their buffet were there before them, and that there was an on-set photographer present to take publicity stills. She had begged a favor of a friend who ran a limo company to arrange for the transportation of the stars. She had even checked to see if the tape marks on the restaurant floor were in the right places for where the actors needed to stand in the opening sequence, and she had directed the assistant cameraman on where to re-set them when it became apparent that not all of the principals would fit into the shot.

Equally important was her ability to settle down the cast and provide assurance in a situation that invited panic. The tension was only partly a consequence of the team's lack of experience. Much more, it was the result of the idea that the actors should improvise. That had encouraged self-indulgence, posturing, and camera-hogging. Everyone was trying to upstage Selva. He responded to this in multiple ways. In some scenes he played it super-cool, performing almost exclusively with his eyes, suggesting in this fashion that those acting up a storm around him were void of self-possession and significance. At other moments, he commenced long, digressive monologues, chewing up camera time. He had kicked Lorelei under the table they were sitting at as a way to throw her off when she was speaking.

The plan had been for the movie to be shot in nineteen separate sections, each approximately five minutes long. The treatment called for a revelation or event in each. Yet, although the shoot was only to last four nights, at the end of the first they had completed just three sequences. While their three cameras had been kept on continuously, producing eighteen hours of footage, at most they had a quarter-hour of material that would wind up in the finished version. Moreover, they knew that the final scene, with its gore and violence, required more prep time than any other. Yet the schedule called for shooting that last.

Even so, there was brilliance. In the last scene of the first night, Lorelei's character had exposed Selva's, informing the actor playing his best friend that he had been stopped from getting a big part he hoped for because Selva had told producers that he had been fired from his previous job for disruptive behavior. Then she had told him about Selva's affair with his wife. Everyone in the room was still as it played out, and the expression of shock and rage in the actor's eyes was affecting. Though none could say if the movie was going to be Oscar-worthy, no one who saw that sequence wouldn't know that Selva was more than a mere mannequin.

The first night's shoot ran from midnight to eight in the morning. When it concluded, the limos were there to take the stars home. But, because they knew one another from the Church and they were all young, several of the actors had wanted to stay at the diner where they were shooting to hang out. The line producer had proven her worth again by prodding them to go get rest, lest they be even more exhausted that night. They were binging on coffee and Adderall.

The reliance upon chemical aids became more evident on the second evening. The production's other young star—Tom Hutchins—arrived with a hip flask full of whiskey, which he passed around between scenes. The belief was that it would loosen them up, and it did add to the volatility of the performances. That both cast and crew were bedraggled multiplied the effect. No one had slept much during the daylight hours. This problem was not limited to the cast. The mood of the crew was strained. Yet the pace of shooting accelerated. Where the cast members had been intent at gobbling up screen time, now they wanted to finish their scenes, and the mix of combustible tempers and familiarity enlivened everything they shot. The movie was springing to life.

Much was also happening on the set that the cameramen surreptitiously captured. At one point Lorelei and Selva strolled off. The director hoped that they would settle their fight. Footage showed that they returned with curious smirks, and that he had a hand cupped around her waist.

It occurred to Vincenza that rumors about what had happened on the set could only help sell the picture. Nonetheless, it irked her, the want of respect, that he was displaying his disregard so openly. While she had told herself that she had drained herself of feelings for him, she found herself alternating between ruminations upon methods by which she might revenge herself with specific fantasies of lovemaking. But she needed to keep control of herself—or at least preserve the emotions for the right instant. That was the final sequence of the second night, the eleventh scene.

She was playing Selva's lover. Acting classes had taught her: The trick was to have the audience see you fight back your emotions, to have them hear you try to speak crisply when your words are choked. So she kept a rein on her emotions, battling what was inside to preserve some dignity.

When she had finished her lines, the director called it a wrap, and the cast members straggled out to the limos to go home. As the credited co-author of the story, Vincenza had to stay, and she sat down, drained. It took a decided effort to lift herself up and go to the "video village" they had hastily assembled. This was the alcove in a corner of the room where you viewed the raw footage. What if it were no good? She had invested so much in the project: not only time, but hope.

She watched it once, then a second time with Sara and the director beside her. There was no need to listen to their comments. It was the best she had ever done, understated and moving, and almost in unison she felt their hands on top of her shoulders, congratulating and thanking her.

Once they had departed, she sat down again. The only face left on the set that she recognized was that of the prop master. Spent as she was, she could not help but notice that he was checking the revolver, the one that was to be employed in the movie's last scene.

CHAPTER 7

One month earlier Todd Gelber had been talking with a reporter about an indie film being shot that had somehow managed to attach name talent. In charge of production for the world's largest streaming service, Gelber controlled more money for the making of movies than anyone.

Four weeks later, sitting in his office, he reflected on the conversation. It was when he had first been alerted that Tom Selva, the singer Lorelei, and the character actor Tom Hutchins were in the cast.

Gelber had been a talent agent for twenty years. When the streaming service had offered him the job he held, he had accepted the position gleefully and without reflection. He understood how much money, status, and power it meant. He had been told that being production chief was equal parts fun and stress. But it was proving to be like giving birth. He had not fully grasped the effort and pain entailed in getting a ten-pound baby through the slim aperture of the birth canal.

He was learning how it felt to be the one who gave all the answers. He had to say no almost every minute. It was like being a loan officer for borrowers from the House of Lords. Everyone he spoke with sincerely believed that their rejection was an outrage on the level of the Tuskegee Syphilis Study. You had to know how to articulate a "Hollywood no." All day long you had to say—with what appeared to be perfect sincerity—that you loved almost everything about the project, but you had to pass on it *right now*.

Then there was the matter of information. However much he had needed knowledge as an agent, it was the difference between a single bee who makes honey and the bear who consumes it. As the production chief, he had to be ever with his ears cocked to the ground, listening for noises. After all, the chief who heard about projects too late might never have a chance to bid on them, and it is far easier to encounter projects to which you can say no than to uncover those about which you want to say yes.

As an agent, each day he had made fifty calls and attended four meetings. Now it was necessary to make five hundred calls and attend a score of meetings. Since this was impossible, the position required a full lineup of subordinates with drive and intelligence equal to his own. Yet a team of aides with such capacities and instincts was difficult to find, hold onto, or trust. Would they be plotting against him with the aim of replacing him? Were they planting stories hostile to him in the press? Had they neglected to mention crucial projects, discussions, or meetings? Did they know good from bad? Were they conspiring to assist old friends and allies, placing those relationships above their obligation to their employer?

All this kept Gelber from sleeping. He had averaged about four hours each night since gaining his title. Everyone in Hollywood needed his help and resented his power. That this tech upstart he was working for was gaining a degree of power that threatened the industry's old ways was held against him. Already he had to say no at least once to nearly everyone of influence. In a company town, he was no longer part of the company.

He had tried to get some reckoning of the information flow by demanding that a huge online bulletin board be created, one listing the most important pitches the company was receiving, along with the names of their actors, directors, writers, agents, and managers. The bulletin board could not contain all pitches, though, just those coming from the most established venues, the top agents at the principal agencies. Nor could it tell him about what had not been proposed to them, though this was what was potentially of greatest interest.

For that he relied on his years of contacts and relationships. Of special value was a columnist for one of the trades, the magazines that report on box office numbers, plans for new productions, and the comings and goings of industry executives and their clients. Gelber had known this man from the first day that he had arrived at his old talent agency, as they had been introduced there as trainees in the mail room. For the small price of an occasional bit of salacious gossip, the writer had proved an excellent source of not-yet-public information.

Gelber had a talent for remembering the details of conversations, and in the aftermath of all that had happened since his chat with the writer, he reviewed it in his mind.

The reporter had begun by declaring that the set of the movie was said to be "wild." It was not just "the sucking and fucking," as he had put it with characteristic refinement. The actors were bringing their own lives into the story. "*Very* personal stuff."

Didn't that mean that their reps should be seeing to it that it was killed?

"You're still thinking like an agent," the columnist had replied. This was his way of telling him that the news was useful, and he was owed something in return. As Gelber was uncertain if this were so, he was not going to give in so easily. Hence, sighing theatrically, he had deliberately paused.

In Gelber's office there were posters from the most admired and profitable movies and TV series produced by the company. Unavoidably, he thought of their budgets, some of which had been immense. That reminded him that his position required a measure of caution.

"You don't think I have enough enemies already? I should pick up this little piece of indie shit so I can have that many more?"

"It certainly sounds like you might want to have eyes on the set," his friend had answered him. "My source says that some of the acting has been sweet."

"I know that's what you really care about, Bill: great acting. You'll keep me informed?"

With that and without feeding the reporter anything back, Gelber had apologized, saying that he had to run and they would catch up soon. Then he had hung up. His rapid exit from the conversation genuinely saddened him. Much of the joy in his work lay in this chin-wagging. Yet he had to keep friendly sparring to a minimum.

As an agent, his focus had been on making his revenue targets, lifting up the sum of his clients' annual billings to the number the agency assigned him. That meant battling from week to week and month to month, getting actors to sign onto projects about which they were dubious or finding them work hawking brands of toothpaste and automobiles, life insurance and suppositories. Suddenly he found that he had to figure out how to use his enormous power to produce the movies and series the company sought without losing his job and becoming utterly detested in the process.

Five flights below him on Rodeo Drive tourists idled, stepping forward slowly, stupefied as much by the sights of the shop windows as the attire of the locals. Alongside them were the Hollywood wives at whom they gaped. Out shopping, these women tottered about in five-inch heels. Their plunging necklines crowned leather dresses or leopard print blouses. Their false eyelashes were gargantuan enough to require their own driveways and chauffeurs. Their handbags were either too small to fit purses in or too big for their tiny dogs. He had gotten used to this oddity. What he needed was to be free of this, to be clearheaded and able to come up with answers. Solutions.

Was there a way to make use of what might be a talked-about film? Gelber had been around long enough that he realized that he knew of a way to take advantage of the situation.

CHAPTER 8

Los Angeles is a city of searchers. More than a few religious sects and even entirely new faiths have been created within it. Home to Aimee Semple MacPherson when she alternated between sermonizing and fornicating, it was where Carlos Castaneda authored his spiritual sourcebooks. The greater number of its acting teachers have crafted virtual cults around themselves, and its psychiatrists have fashioned more than a few literal ones. The Pentecostal Church and Scientology were born on its streets. Manson's disciples congregated on an old movie set in the Valley.

Vincenza had been one of these searchers. When her name was Kelli, back in Minnesota, she was the kind of girl of which there is probably one in most towns.

Straight boys gawked at her. Even before she had gotten implants, she had a high bosom that parted in dramatic fashion. By the middle of the tenth grade it was unmistakable, and her skin had that delicate quality which people call peaches and cream—so much so that when people eyed her from a distance, they wrongly assumed that she wore rouge.

She had managed with some degree of grace to stay out of the fights that broke out among the different cliques among Eagan's girls.

Yet there was more to her seeming good fortune. While she was not quite diligent enough to be a member of the school honor society, nearly all her teachers liked her, the women as much as the men, and though it was almost a given that she would be homecoming queen, it was doubtful if more than two girls had resented it. No one seemed to think her uppity because she did not have a boyfriend and only occasionally turned up at school dances and parties.

Caught up in their own adolescent insecurities and worries, few sensed what was happening. They just assumed that matters were placid and cheery. How could they not be for a girl who was so blessed? If she had a brother or sister who knew what was taking place, it would have been easier. But she was an only child.

Sometimes she thought, too, that it would have been better had their home not been on a remote lot. Then perhaps neighbors might have heard. It would have been humiliating, of course, should they have known, suspecting something if not knowing the specifics: that she was beaten and that her mother was taking her stepfather's side, declaring that she *was* dressed in a tawdry manner, that she *had* failed to be an upstanding member of their church congregation.

The cause of the difficulty was the synod they had joined with her mother's remarriage, one that did not permit women to wear pants or to dance. How could she go to school and get along with her class-mates in the present day obeying such restrictions? The beatings made it harder to avoid further ones. For her stepfather especially liked to hit her on her thighs and calves. How then was she to show up in skirts and dresses? She had tried to solve this conundrum by wearing stockings. But what was she to do in summer?

Frequently she felt as though there was something resting upon her chest, what with all these things she could not talk about. Her stepfather was plainly aroused when he punished her, and her mother obviously knew this and hated her for it. How could she speak with others about this when it was difficult enough to try and put her predicament into words, to acknowledge it to herself, to admit what was occurring and not take their side and blame herself? She wondered what boys thought when they stared at her with those expressions of longing. Did they realize that she envied others, that she wanted for one close friend such as most of the ugly girls and least liked boys had?

She had read an excerpt from Freud in her psychology class, and she thought about it often. It was from *The Interpretation of Dreams*, and it had made an impression on her because her most recurrent dream was that her father was alive. Whenever she awoke from it, she would stare at an old photo in which she was in his arms. Just five when he died, she knew even before she learned it in the class that the image of him which she had in her recollections was fabricated.

Her outlet was school theater. Her mother and stepfather would never allow her to be in a play and the notion of auditioning and rejection frightened her. Only because of the persistent prodding of the school drama teacher had she tried out, winning the lead in the fall production. That necessitated further secretiveness, this time towards her parents.

Her hope was that she could keep this from them until the yearbook came out near the end of the school year. Since she never brought friends home and her parents rarely associated with anyone outside their narrow group—the fellow members of their congregation—it struck her that they might not know until she was graduated.

That was the plan.

While her mother regarded her as a rival, this did not mean that she was without ambition for her, and she had worked closely with her on her college applications and tried to stay in touch with her teachers. There, things went awry. One of the teachers in the school said how her performance as Emily in *Our Town* had broken everyone's heart, and that she hoped her mother was as proud as everyone else. That provoked another beating. It was savage.

The next four months was prison. Each day was another scratched off from the calendar. Initially, her mother and stepfather had said that she had showed she was not trustworthy and had suggested that in the aftermath of the incident she would only be permitted to go to college as a commuter. Finally, they relented. Yet all that was irrelevant. She had been waitlisted by Macalester, a competitive school. She had been admitted to the University of Minnesota. So what? If they so hated her acting, then that proved it was her destiny.

She had always been captivated by fame, enchanted by fantasies of herself on the covers of magazines. She imagined herself sensationally garbed on red carpets talking to movie stars. She wasn't going to become a nutritionist or a junior marketing executive. People had loved her performance as Emily, and she felt a joy and a sense of focus during the rehearsals that she had never felt doing anything else. The night of the first performance, though terrifying, was thrilling, and the succeeding nights were equally rousing. It was elation, a kind of delight which told her that there was a life, a better one, out there.

Skipping the graduation exercise, she packed a duffel bag full of her clothes and hitched a ride to the airport. She arrived in Los Angeles with $1,406, not knowing a single soul.

CHAPTER 9

Driving to the biggest date he had ever had, Billy Rosenberg contemplated one question. He had been mulling it over the entire way, and he pondered it again as he handed his car keys to the valet.

"Are we, in fact, on a date?"

All through his days at Dartmouth, he and nearly every other boy in his class had been fixated on a WASP beauty whose parents owned a hotel chain in the Pacific Northwest. Studious and clever, she treated her classmates with a not-so-vague disdain, and nerdy and self-conscious as Billy was, he had never even considered the idea of asking her out. But now she was one of the many struggling actresses in Hollywood, and he was someone with an agent and a few connections.

Not long after his novel about life in Venezuela under Chavez had been purchased in a New York literary auction for $75,000, it had been reported prominently in the class notes of the school's alumni magazine, and he was well aware that word had gotten around about the book's subsequent film sale. That he had been asked to adapt the novel was the reason he had originally come out to Hollywood. It had launched his career as a scriptwriter, and, though things had stalled, others didn't necessarily know that. When they had bumped into each

51

other a few weeks before at a film screening, he had gleaned that Claire was among those who still imagined that he was an up-and-comer. And amidst the would-be starlets and the trays of canapés and drinks at the premiere, she had mentioned to him that she wanted to star in and produce movies herself. Then she had hinted that she had potential backing for that from indie producers.

Was that bravado? An unrealistic hopefulness aided by trays of fruity cocktails? Whatever the case, the pretext for the get-together was a discussion they were supposed to have about the possibility of collaborating, and he had emailed her a pdf of one of his scripts, a contemporary melodrama with a part in it that she might be able to play. Yet if this was supposed to be a business meeting, there was no denying that she had been aggressively flirting with him amidst the chatter about the notion of working together and unexpectedly fond reminiscences of student days in New Hampshire.

Did this coquettishness reflect a need for attention in a city where her good looks counted for far less than these had in the Ivy League? Was it genuine interest? Or might it indicate a sense of how she thought that she ought to be acting with someone who could help her advance her career, which seemed to be going nowhere in the months after she had passed her thirtieth birthday? Or was it some mix of each with the added element of uncertainty that she herself didn't know what her intentions were?

Billy was coming to understand it: Since meet-ups in Los Angeles so often combined business with romance and so much was about self-presentation, it was quite possible that an amount of swagger might persuade Claire to sleep with him even if she hadn't been seriously considering the idea—if she were, in fact, single—and possibly even if she weren't. At the same time, in the #MeToo era, one had to be watchful.

Gazing up, he eyed the bar of a palatial barbecue spot in Koreatown. Most of the restaurant's signage was in Korean, though

English writing in smaller type lay underneath. Taking up the second and third floors of a building occupying the whole of a block on Western Avenue, it was the size of a catering hall and decorated with an equal degree of vulgar abandon. Plush red carpeting covered the floors, and there were giant statues of the Buddha, spray-painted gold, planted alongside the swinging doors to the kitchen. The bar was polished chrome.

To his surprise, Billy saw as he entered that Claire was already there. Large hoop earrings dangled from her ears. Her strawberry blonde hair was freshly combed. Most notable, though, was her matching of blouse and bra. These showed off a surfeit of skin.

Kissing her on both cheeks, he watched as she pulled herself up, advertising the effort that had gone into keeping her calves, which appeared to be even slimmer than in their college days, toned. "It's great to see you," she said.

That was the cue for him to smile and place himself on a round leather bar seat beside her. With conscious effort, he forced himself not to be too warm, not to let her know how moved he was by her presence and her far-from-vanished loveliness. He waited for her to say something, whether polite chatter about old friends or to bring up the script.

He sensed her fear and desperation in the rapidity with which she motioned to the bartender for a drinks menu for him, then launched into a series of queries about college classmates whom neither of them had been especially fond of. He noticed, too, that she was gulping down her drink and holding the large glass it was in with a nervous intensity.

Where, he wondered, was the aloof beauty he had known?

The glass beads of her bracelet reflected off the chrome of the bar, as did the bright red shade of her blouse. He watched these, waiting patiently for the instant when she would mention the script. The drink in front of him provided him with something to do with his hands. This was welcome as he felt the tightness in his throat and the dewiness of his palms.

Her calculation was indicated by the patience she displayed in avoiding the topic at hand. Half an hour passed with a first round of glasses of *soju* almost fully downed before she gave him a firm glance that told him that it was time to converse *seriously*.

"I guess you know," she said, fixing her gray-green eyes on him, "that I've been transitioning from simply being an actress to a hyphenate: a producer and director? I don't know how much I spoke to you about that when I ran into you at the screening."

Billy noticed that as she went into her pitch that she assumed again the manner he had seen in college: cool, haughty and in control. Was this performance of a part she had mastered or did it reflect something more real? He could not be sure. He knew what it meant that she was talking as much as she was of her plans and her alliances in the industry. It said that she wanted the part—even if she had not yet mentioned it. After all, those who had unquestioned power and access presented their responses to your ideas or your writing without telling you about who they were.

But Los Angeles is a city of actors, and everyone is playing a part. His role, he knew, was to be a receptive listener, if not to accept her claims and assurances at face value.

When the bartender halted in front of them to ask if they wanted another round of the Korean rice wine they were drinking, he waited for her to take the lead in signaling assent. As the "producer" in the meeting, she would handle the bill.

Billy leaned forward. The bar was getting more crowded and the increasingly intoxicated patrons were growing louder. While he did not want to draw his line of sight too obviously in the direction of her chest, he needed to draw closer to hear her. Her voice was small, and she was not someone who yelled. At the same time, though that forced him to draw near to make out the words, her manner kept him at a remove. It was as frustrating and alluring as it had been a decade earlier.

Sipping the glass of *soju*, she turned her eyes back to him and presented the philosophical part of her pitch, explaining her convictions: A movie must have something to say. There were too many vanity projects floating about, getting produced and screened, and, while she was undeniably intrigued by the part that Billy had written, she wasn't interested in making any film for *that reason*. What appealed to her above all else was that the story addressed the matter of climate change. She *was* intrigued, and she *absolutely* wanted to talk more about how they might try to make this happen, but—and she needed to emphasize this—she wouldn't be *exploring this question of collaboration* and possibly making use of her patrons and connections if the script weren't *meaningful* and potentially *important*.

The declaration—full as it was of italicized assertions—served as the segue to a further aspect of her pitch: talk about a short film she had written and produced that had been shown at a local festival where it had been awarded a prize. Its subject was the cause of equal pay for women in the construction trades. It was hard not to be amused by the revelation that Claire had cast herself as a forklift operator. It was as easy for Billy to imagine a supermodel playing a grocery store cashier subscribed to Weight Watchers.

Nonetheless, the picture Claire painted was superficially persuasive. She noted that she had been employed by an acclaimed indie producer, and, in her accounting, he had been greatly impressed by her short and was eager to get behind a future project of hers.

What did this really mean? He was able to guess that she had been briefly an intern for this talked-about Jewish producer. If it were true, it might indicate one of two things: Either the producer wanted to sleep with her or he returned her calls because he had her marked out for the role of his second wife, granted her fair-haired Protestant comeliness, her youth, and her intelligence. Billy could surmise as well that the money for the short had come from her rich parents or a trust fund.

The bartender had been making regular pit stops, and, as she went on talking about all the things she responded to in the script, they polished off a third round. Then Claire gestured for a fourth, and with this a thought abruptly entered Billy's mind: Why, he asked himself, had she suggested that they meet for drinks at a Korean barbecue restaurant? The reason she had provided on the phone was that it was roughly equidistant from where he lived in Hollywood and her apartment in Mid-City. It was also public, lively, and theatrical: fun.

Might there be another purpose? She had picked the brand of *soju*, recommending it when he had expressed a lack of familiarity with the beverage and the names of the brands on the drinks list. Transparent and relatively dry, it was seemingly not that different from Chardonnay or Chablis. But he had heard tales from friends that it could be as high proof as vodka or whiskey. Had he just consumed three half-glasses of something twice as strong as a martini? Was that why he was suddenly struggling with his balance?

BILLY'S DREAMS WERE FEROCIOUS. Nightmares alternated with lurid fantasies. He awoke to the early morning light, streaming in through a picture window.

Claire was dressed, and he was in her bed. Her apartment was spotless, modern, and well-appointed. The contemporary furniture screamed out that it had been selected at a design center and manufactured somewhere in Italy. The floors were white and bare. Configured as a single large space, it extended from the bed on one side to an open kitchen, thirty-five feet away, on the other. That was where she was.

The sharpness of the light hurt his eyes, if far less than the memory of what had happened. He wished that he could have blacked it out.

Grossly inebriated as they both were, she had called for an Uber. Before the car appeared, she had mentioned the recent reports of intoxicated women being raped by their drivers, and he had promptly insisted that he would see her back to her place. Fooling around with her in the back of the vehicle, he was all but drooling as along the way they expressed the most thrilling and persuasive clichés. They were going to be partners. They were meant for each other. It was fate.

The problem arrived back at her place when he tried to put his condom on. His erection flickered and went out. It was rather like a birthday candle, if without the compensating virtue of the cake beneath.

Would she be understanding? Or would she treat the prior evening as a great mistake not to be repeated?

Sensing that he was awake, she half-turned her head towards him. Little as her nose was, her profile was not her best look. But the delicate pallor of her skin and the motion of her red-gold hair affected him. There was still a measure of disbelief that he was with her, although this now matched to uncertainty and fear.

Using one hand to jiggle the knob of her espresso machine, she held a cup under the spigot with the other.

"Would you like some?" she asked. "I'm sorry about last night. I can see that it was a terrible mistake. I don't know what we were thinking. *Soju*."

She shook her head and then drew the filled cup away from the machine. Swallowing a mouthful, she turned her face more fully and spat out her next declaration with such efficiency that he did not have time to form a response.

"Please don't misunderstand," she went on, "I mean, I meant everything I said about our working together. I *love* the script. I'm saying that about the idea of putting our lives—our personal lives—together."

What was he to say? He had not been impotent previously on the occasions when he was sober. But would she believe that or care?

Pulling himself forward and lifting up the covers, he rubbed his temples and yawned. He needed to think. He could sense her anxiousness, and he knew it was possible that this was partly driving her rejection of him. How could he put a stop to that without conveying need and fecklessness, emotions that would drive her further away?

Abruptly, a thought came to him.

CHAPTER 10

The more Vincenza contemplated the idea of meeting up with David Clarkson, the less she liked it. She had spent sufficient time in classes and enough hours studying acting to know a false note, and there was something overly welcoming in Clarkson's phone voice. It told her that he was not going to help her, and he might be seeking to harm her. At the same time, the more she thought about calling the cops, the less she liked that option. The police would presume that she had killed Selva. What else could they suppose about the presence of the dead body of her lover in her trunk with the murder weapon set alongside it?

She sat in the front seat of her car, trying to think. Everything told her she needed to drive away. Yet where should she go?

Only as she was starting the engine did it occur to her. Selva's beach cottage was the lone spot she knew of that was apt to be safely empty. Even if he did not have the keys to it in his pocket—itself unlikely—she had seen where he kept a spare garage door opener, and she could park her car in his garage, deposit the body within it and leave. So long as no one was at the cottage, there would be no way to identify her as the one who had abandoned it. Were there a video system outside, she could disable it, and she distinctly remembered Selva's explaining to her that his wife didn't know of the place.

There wasn't an instant for her to ponder this. She had to get to the cottage, and she had to return with enough hours left in the evening that she had time to rehearse her callback sides. If it seemed crazy to be worried about her audition when she was in such danger, this was why was she living in Los Angeles and why had she devoted twelve years of her life to her craft.

What was the best way to get there? The fastest path to Malibu called for the 10 freeway. But since the roads were jammed and this was the direction most of the traffic was flowing, that route would take her a good two hours, perhaps more. And she remained incapacitated, white-knuckled by the sight of the freeway on-ramps. So, packed as it was, she decided to take Sunset Boulevard. Yet nothing was automatic or reflexive. Just as when she had first learned to drive, she had to consciously set her foot on the gas pedal, put the car in reverse, then accelerate into traffic. Even putting her fingers on the radio to switch the channel was a deliberate act. Her hands were trembling.

The landscape around her was a mix of streetlights, phosphorescent lamps, and vague shapes, and, although it was February, in places she saw homes still adorned by Christmas displays. Elsewhere she glimpsed the blank pockets of empty lots and barren hillsides. Then, as she entered West Hollywood, she passed a succession of blocks lined by nightclubs and chic hotels.

She felt her heart beating, and she wanted to light up. It struck her that one advantage of taking Sunset was that it allowed her to open the window and smoke in the car without stinking it up. After all, she wasn't exactly speeding along. In some spots, cars were two feet from her bumpers. Were they close enough to sniff the corpse? Was that why the faces were so unsmiling—or was she imagining this?

Only as she passed Beverly Hills and drove around the UCLA campus did the road cease to be bunched up. But when she neared the

405, the cars increasingly grew huddled again, and her hands clenched as she rode beneath it. Turning south on an extension to Bundy, she sped towards San Vincente. In the midst of this, her phone beeped, indicating a text: additional details on her callback for the Reese Witherspoon movie. The gesture of reaching for it nearly caused her to rear-end the driver in front of her.

Passing through Brentwood, she steered past the golf course and country club. The homes were enormous, and a sea of lights surrounded her. Finally, she eyed the coast highway and the ocean. It was the one freeway she could drive on. The small number of lanes made it bearable, and, swinging onto it, she went faster, racing towards Malibu. On her left was the immensity of the Pacific and the white-caps of the waves breaking against the shore.

She went by the Palisades, the Getty Museum and Point Dume, driving all the way to County Line Beach. That led to a winding mountain road. She had to slow down to make sure that she didn't miss the turnoff. The cottage was on a narrow spot, high up. A number of huge estates flanked one side of the street, overlooking the water. The bougainvillea and the birds of paradise along the driveway were markers to Selva's bungalow. An amber lamp shone above the garage.

It was late, and parking in the driveway, she scrutinized her surroundings, which were eerily void of noise or motion. The sky around her was clearer and brighter, and a crowd of stars circled above her head. Below, she saw the garage opener right where Selva had left it. The windows of the cottage were darkened. Elsewhere, she could make out various driveways farther down the street, though their outlines were indistinct.

Pushing a button, she watched as the garage door ascended. Observing this, she hopped back into her car, angled it in backwards, and closed the door shut. Then she exited the vehicle with the garage light on. She was freezing cold and hungry. Some pot lay in a bag in her glove compartment, and the impulse to step back into the automobile for it was overwhelming.

Finishing the joint, she retreated from the car a second time and paced to its back, which was only a foot and a half from the garage's rear wall. There she pressed the button on her keychain opening the trunk's lock. As it lifted up, she was greeted by a light displaying Selva's once-beautiful visage. His blue eyes stared back, and, without thinking, she placed a hand on his cheek. It was the temperature of a thawing pork chop.

How could she get his body out of the trunk? Slim as he was, he was half a head taller than she, and he outweighed her by a good fifty pounds. Joined to the fact that he was stiff, she could not simply reach in and pull him out. Then a solution came to her. It was to swing his legs and his buttocks up, drawing these over the back edge of the trunk. This was so that she could sit on the ground and pull from his ankles in order to use the force of gravity so that his head and torso followed.

They landed on her then, knocking her over but dropping the body onto the icy cement of the floor. Having done this, she took out the gun, ran a cloth over it to remove her fingerprints, set it upon the cadaver and grasped the garage door controller and opened the door a second time.

Basic common sense told her to leave as quickly as possible. But she was famished in a fashion that only actors can understand. She had eaten just two pieces of fruit at breakfast, nothing since, and through sheer will, she forced herself not to do as she wished, to enter the house, looking for something to chew on. It was hard to think and she was shaking, and, ravenous though she was, she restarted the engine.

She headed back taking a different route, crossing back through Topanga and Laurel Canyon. The clock on her dashboard showed that it was just a few minutes shy of eleven when she reached Franklin Canyon. Parking her car in her underground garage, she hiked up two flights of steps to her apartment. She could not remember one night when she had come home so tired, not even during the year when she had worked as a waitress.

Still, she was fearful in approaching the door, and, famished and exhausted as she was, she was tentative in entering. The relief she felt in seeing that it was just as she had left it that afternoon was counterbalanced by the knowledge that what remained in her fridge was just a plain yogurt and a third of a tub of cottage cheese. Only as she was getting into bed did she realize she had forgotten to see if there was a surveillance camera outside the beach house. What could be done about that? She had to put it out of her mind. Frightening and inscrutable as her situation was, she had to prevent it from taking over her thoughts of the day ahead. It was bad enough that she had failed to rehearse her scene and the callback was early in the morning.

CHAPTER 11

"In Hollywood you have to be a big dick, not have one," David Clarkson observed. He was smiling as he said it, making use of the skills he had honed as an actor.

Those years of unsuccess had taught him. Above all he had learned how to read subtext and how to seem knowing and shrewd. The deluge of actors, producers, and agents in Los Angeles renders it a place—more than any other—where people are attuned to vibrations, to sensing what has not been said, to grasping what is coming into vogue. A decade of trying to make it as a thespian and living among this tribe had etched this into Clarkson. He knew when a clothing style was about to become trendy or when someone wanted a hug, praise, or chastisement. He understood as well that the city was one where people unexpectedly fell or rose, often because of unforeseen reinventions. So you had to be alert with everyone, and you had to remember that nothing you said was an aside, nothing incidental, that every statement was a sales pitch, a presentation, a performance.

He bore this in mind in speaking to the assistant to one of the Church of Life's most important members, a much-admired writer-director and two-time Academy Award winner. He was trying to hit the notes required to be the aide's pal. This was of particular value as he required a favor of him, and, as the assistant had just joked about his self-doubts regarding the dimensions of his middle leg, Clarkson was flattering him, suggesting that he was soon to be a *somebody*, telling him that this was more important than his endowments, while also talking in his language. It was a mode of speech Clarkson despised. But he knew that there was no point in "being himself." In order to serve the Church and to perform his job he had to be a thousand people.

That was especially true then. Two hours of studying Vincenza's file—most especially including that handwritten report of her first Church confession—had persuaded him that he had to go to Culver City to see her. The night before he had left the office in the early evening and driven to her apartment, which lay between Hollywood Boulevard and Franklin Canyon. But she was not there. Yet, after phoning him, she had sent him a text saying that she could talk once she was finished with an audition in Culver City at 9:30 a.m. the next morning.

He was determined to intercept her there.

There were two obstacles. First, he had to get from Thai Town to Culver City during the morning rush hour. That could take upwards of an hour, if not more, depending on how backed up the westbound lanes of the freeway were. Second, he had to arrange for a pass, letting him onto the studio's lot. This was why he was calling the assistant: to cadge a brief meeting with the director providing him with one.

The joshing finished, the assistant paused and then got to the matter at hand. "You're sure you have to see him here, this morning? What's this about?"

"We've been thinking about a birthday party—a surprise party—for Richard, our Church's Priest Counselor for your boss, and I wanted to chat with him, get his involvement."

"You can't do that over the phone?"

"I have to be in Culver City anyway, and, while I don't think it will take long, yes, I'd rather do it face-to-face."

The assistant hesitated before relenting. "What time were you thinking? Guess I could slip you in." The tone of voice told Clarkson that there would be a debt, one which a pilot in the International Church of Life was easily able to pay.

REACHING THE STUDIO GATES AT NINE, he arrived with some confidence, and, waved in and parked, he marched over, planning to just quickly pop in to say hello to the director he was visiting. That, though, was where things went awry. For they had kept him waiting, and the director *wanted* to talk. More, important as he was, Clarkson couldn't just slip in and politely depart. So by the time he returned to the parking lot it was nearly ten-fifteen.

Even so, he remained convinced that he would catch Vincenza on her way back to her car. To that end he circled around the lot three times, pretending that he was being choosy in selecting a spot, rather than delaying in exiting, and it appeared he had seen her at a remove. But then another driver in an SUV blocked his field of vision, and, when he gazed back once more towards the dark-haired woman with the oversized sunglasses, the one resembling her, she was gone.

This prompted Clarkson to message her to say that he was at the studio. Why didn't they catch up nearby? While there was no answer, he headed to the suggested meet point. His text called for getting together at Gregorio's coffee shop five minutes later. Yet because he was passing through the studio gates behind an extended line of cars and the security people were arguing with one of the drivers, it took him ten minutes to escape. Then he hit a pair of red lights. Incredibly, it had taken him almost twenty minutes to reach the shop, which was just four blocks from the studio, and when he arrived Vincenza was nowhere to be seen.

Was it possible that she had gone to the wrong Gregorio's, the one in the opposite direction? Or had she mistakenly placed herself at the Gregorio's located on the studio lot? Clarkson wondered. Getting out of his car, he walked in and ordered an herbal tea. Then he waited. He was afraid of what might come from calling or texting her another time. Listening to her voice the night before, he had sensed her fear. It was out of character that he had misread her reaction, and he was not about to make the mistake a second time. Thinking about what he should do next, he saw on his phone a message from the Supreme Pilot asking him why he had not brought Vincenza to the Church headquarters.

Clarkson sipped the tea and considered the situation. He was not eager to tell the Supreme Pilot what had taken place—that he had failed to find her. He knew his employer's temper, and he had seen him strike women and even men when incited. Still, he tried not to worry. This was probably a minor affair, wasn't it? All he was being asked was to ferry a woman to their headquarters. In any event, he had done so much for the Church that it was hard to believe that it could matter greatly if he failed. He had handled secret abortions, illegal adoptions, and tortious litigation. He had dirtied up those who had left the Church, moved sums into offshore accounts, and led publicity campaigns to make gay actors appear straight. He had intimidated those intent on writing books and articles critical of the Church, and he had pressured or paid off women who had been attacked or molested by higher-ups. He had done what was desired and what was necessary. He was all right, wasn't he?

Driving to her apartment near Franklin Canyon, he arrived with the intention of staking out the building. Perhaps he might stop her as she was entering or leaving. Parking a block away, he returned on foot. Then he entered the underground garage and settled himself on a flight of cement steps. He tried not to look at his watch as another half an hour went by. Neither she nor her car had appeared, and those coming into the building, edging in their vehicles, were staring at him, puzzled as to why he was there. Necessarily, striding to the gate of her building, he pressed the buzzer for her apartment. Yet, again, there was no response.

Events, he realized, were getting ahead of him. That was made clear by a phone call he received as he paced back to his car. On the line, speaking breathlessly, was an aide. He was with a girl, he said, someone he had brought to the Malibu beach house that the Church provided to its most important followers, Tom Selva among them.

"I found something in the garage," he said.

CHAPTER 12

Billy Rosenberg's grasp of the situation was more intuitive than analytical. What he instinctively understood was that if he was going to reawaken Claire Hesper's romantic interest, he had to be in control of something and to show mastery over it. That was why he was making them breakfast with the various items in her fridge.

There weren't many of these, as it was evident that she was a classic trust-fund girl: Although her open-plan kitchen was only slightly smaller than Mongolia, she ate almost all of her meals out and seemed to have as much acquaintance with cooking an omelet as Billy did with the use of nanoparticles.

She had explained that the eggs in the fridge had been purchased on Christmas Eve for an eggnog recipe. That meant they were past their sell-by date. There was also salt and pepper and butter, along with some generic form of artificially colored cheddar cheese. This dairy was a brighter shade than her hair. Although he had had to make do without onions or mushrooms, he was setting the omelets onto their plates. He watched as she bit into one of the eggs, marveling at his powers of creation.

"I wish I knew how to cook."

Her outfit appeared to have been chosen with considerable calculation. In the aftermath of his failure, she had picked out a relatively heavy bra that disguised the nipples she had flaunted the night before. But, perhaps reflecting her determination to persuade him of the necessity of giving her the part she so desired, she was wearing a short skirt that displayed her legs, which she repeatedly crossed and recrossed, seemingly oblivious to the effect that this had upon him.

"I'm so impressed with your ability to write a woman, a strong woman. Have you always known how to do that? It shows a lot of sensitivity."

Billy turned his palms face up to suggest that he couldn't understand the gift any better than she. Outside, the sun was beginning to rise towards the meridian. It drilled into his eyes, and as they were seated on barstools that flanked her immense tabletop, it was an effort not to slouch. This was relevant as he was five-foot-nine: just two inches taller than she. He wanted to give her a winning, confident smile, the kind that won the day in a romantic comedy. Yet he was keenly aware that his teeth weren't straight, and, if he was not ugly, he had neither the looks nor the poise of the leading men that he encountered with startling frequency.

"You have other scripts that you could show me?"

He nodded and watched as she nibbled, placing tiny portions of the omelet onto her tongue, chewing these minute allotments with care. It was obvious that she was starved but uneasy eating in front of him. The exhibition reminded him of something he had noted previously: In no city outside of the Third World was hunger so much the prevailing theme of daily existence. He could not but suspect that it was less frequented in Somalia.

"Do you have a sister? I mean that you have such a sense for women."

Billy admitted that he did. With that, she pushed the half-finished plate of food away, trying to make the act seem nonchalant. "You know I've always considered you a friend, but I really know very little about you."

The way she said this seemed to imply a certain openness, a willingness to admit the possibility that they ought jointly to be *something*, more than mere work partners, whatever this might be. But he hadn't the slightest notion of what the appropriate response to the observation was, and his confidence, which had never been great, had been whittled down by his experiences in Hollywood such that, if provided with a method for doing so, he would have shaved each morning without inspecting himself in the mirror.

"I guess we don't really know each other," he said.

The lifelessness of his response prompted her to pull her head back and offer him a courteous Cheshire-cat grin. Whatever opening he might have possessed had just been sealed off, it seemed. It had happened that quickly.

"Perhaps we should share a cab back to the restaurant. To pick up our cars?"

"Yes, though we'll know not to drink this time," she said.

The sense that he was being forcefully pushed away annoyed him more than it deflated him, and he found, rather suddenly, that he wanted to argue with her. That she was tempting him with the display of her calves and feigning ignorance about what she was doing made him want to punish her. It was cruel and humiliating. Didn't she sense how he was feeling about his impotence?

"Should I put the dishes in the dishwasher?" he asked. "Or is today one of the days that your maid comes in to do all of your cleaning? Your maid keeps it so spotless."

They both knew the meaning of this remark. As they had attended a particularly "woke" college, they had shared in the sense that they were part of a cadre of more enlightened and just people: those dedicated to battling inequity. And he was puncturing that, mocking her standing, pointing out who she was and how she lived.

It took him a moment to realize what he had done by challenging her in this fashion. He was asking her how much she was willing to tolerate in order to obtain the role she wanted. Would she put up with him when he was a jerk? Would she judiciously parse her words when they had disputes, accepting a measure of his authority? They were both conscious of what had happened and that it was a power move, if one only possible in the peculiar circles in which they had lived.

Because her skin was so pale, her anger or embarrassment showed at once in a flushing of her cheeks and brow. What surprised him was what else was observable: Her eyes and the rest of her body hinted at arousal. It occurred to him that it was possible that she liked fighting, and, if that were so, that it might not be wise for him to try and mollify her.

"In college, I kind of always thought you were a closet conservative," she said. "But you're judging me?"

"Please. You're judging me for being impotent, though I was wasted."

"I had no intention of doing—or trying to do—what we...tried to do. It was the *soju*."

He knew that he couldn't point out that she was the one who had ordered the drinks. That was challenging her too directly.

"I'm just saying that *you* are judging *me*."

"Yes?"

"You are."

"I see. So you would be fine—wonderfully impressive, no doubt—now?" He was astonished by the viciousness with which she said this. It made him want to walk out and be done with her.

More intriguing though was what he saw then in her face: She loved his rage. Indeed, watching her, he couldn't help but suspect that she would have preferred if he had wanted to hit her. She was either

72

not the person or no longer the person he had imagined. She was in his arms once again, though, and a moment later they were headed back to her bed.

The theater of it had proved irresistible.

THE TIME AFTER THE LOVEMAKING was almost more awkward than what had preceded it.

Although Claire was acting sweet and romantic, Billy had a strange vibe. This became more pronounced when she put on her shoes, which had three-inch heels. Barefoot, he stood alongside her; they were equally aware that she was now taller than he. The discomfiture this engendered was the prompt for her to pace over to her armoire. From it she pulled out a linen jacket to wear on top of her cotton blouse. They had called for a taxi, and they were putting on their clothes. In moments they would head back to the Korean barbecue restaurant to pick up their cars.

Billy had that feeling he often did in Los Angeles: that everything was a transaction, and, if you were overly aggressive in declaring that a purchase and sale had been made, you invited the opposite party in the deal to cancel it and renegotiate the terms. At the same time, he knew that he would be greatly insulting her and calling her a whore were he to ask her if she was dating someone or if there was anyone else in the picture.

Not sure what to say, he listened as she filled up the noiselessness with a stream of patter. The talk was about the audition she had that afternoon, which she had to prepare for. Billy's suggestion that he could work with her on it, acting as her scene partner, was met with a determined insistence that he must have writing to do and that she didn't want to take advantage of their "friendship." The impersonal way in which she said this last word was jarring, and his face registered his unease.

Was the word choice a misstep on her part or a deliberate act? Billy couldn't be sure. But he saw that she knew it had bothered and affected him.

She kept her body turned away from him as she penciled in her eyeliner and fixed her lipstick. While he was the writer, she, as the talker, went about explaining herself.

"Look," she began, "I just think that we have to be circumspect. You're very smart. I knew that at Dartmouth. Always. And I think that's sexy. But—and you may find this hard to believe, yet it's true— I've never gone to bed with a man like that before. I mean, I wasn't even sure we were on a date, to be honest. And then…"

"Of course."

"We'll see where this is going."

"Naturally."

"It has to work for both of us."

"Of course."

"I mean, I hope you liked it."

All he could do in response was nod.

She sat down on the bed then as he belted his pants and put on his shoes. Watching, she gave him a melting smile, one that not only implied a blossoming of emotion but attraction and intimacy. Then she stood up. This seemed to signal that they were done with the discussion, and, as such, she went to her phone to make certain that their driver was ready outside. That was the cue for hustling him out of her apartment.

Her sendoff at the restaurant was likewise smiling and blithe, if hard to read, and he drove back to his apartment with alternating feelings of euphoria and mistrust. He couldn't believe that she had slept with him. He couldn't believe that she would make a habit of it. Elated as he was, he was conscious that he was skating on a pond with inch-thick ice.

CHAPTER 13

The alarm had woken Vincenza up at five. Standing up and flicking on the switch to a table lamp, she gazed at herself in the mirror. She could see herself finally in other people's eyes. Yes, she had a figure indeed. That was visible even in the semidarkness. She was tempted to turn on the light over her head so she could see it better.

But she needed to rehearse, and she felt more comfortable doing so in the haze. The next two hours were toil, working over and over on the scene with different manners and in contrasting voices, nervously smoking one cigarette after another while trying to assess and interpret the underlying meaning of the scene and the motivation of her character. Then she had showered, coiffed her hair, done her makeup, and headed for the studio.

Brought into a much smaller waiting area in a different building for the callback, she greeted the other actress with a half-smile. It was just the two of them. Half an hour early, Vincenza read the side once more and then followed her usual ritual of going to the bathroom to check herself and consume a mint. The presence of the other woman, someone she knew from the Church, prompted her to think once more about her connection to it.

Many actors had been funneled into the Church through acting teachers who were acolytes. These guides explained to their students that if they really wanted to augment their skills and enhance their opportunities as performers that they should attend a membership meeting. Belatedly Vincenza had come to see that this was the right means by which to enter the faith, for those recruited by a favored acting teacher were placed on a preferable track. Since the instructor saw the student as *their* project, they went out of their way to refer them to industry contacts, also taking the time to give them detailed instruction regarding the ins and outs of the business. That included tutoring in the vital process of reading for parts, something Vincenza had lacked but this other woman had received. Was that why the other girl, her competition, was more established? Vincenza's thoughts were interrupted by a gesture from the D-girl telling her it was her time.

She did not know what to make of the speed with which the audition went or of the director's reaction and presence. He had not given her a single note or suggestion. Was that good or bad?

Because they had provided her with a prime parking spot in the regular studio lot for the callback, the walk back to it was brief, and it did not permit her a moment for a cigarette. It barely offered time to scroll through her emails and messages.

One text especially prompted her notice, though, as it was from Clarkson. He was at the studio, he said. Some reflection as she drove out of the lot made her more nervous and uncomfortable. She believed in the faith. She would be among those transported to a pristine and unspoiled planet, somewhere far away, out in the night sky. What she was not sure now was whether she could trust the Church leaders. The coincidence of Clarkson's presence bothered her even more than his offer to send a driver to pick her up the night before.

Returning to her secluded spot in Bronson Canyon, she parked her car. Then she went to the trunk. Inside it she had placed a pair of rubber gloves, along with bottles of bleach and water and a pile of sponges. Setting to work, she scoured it thoroughly. This took longer than she expected, and by the time she was done she felt that she was ready to perform Lady Macbeth's "Out, out damn spot" monologue with a new truthfulness and authenticity. Hearing it, Judi Dench would have begged her for acting lessons.

Spent and desperate for a nap, Vincenza drove back to her apartment and went to bed. There were too many thoughts in her mind, though, for her to sleep, and reflexively she strode over to her window and gazed out onto the street. What she saw there frightened her. A man in a navy-blue track suit was parked in a bronze minivan, not forty feet away. Unmistakably, it was one of a half dozen which the Church used for its particular jobs. She recognized it from the reserved space kept for them in the lot in front of its headquarters.

In the twilight, it was impossible to see the face of the driver, especially as she was peeking out through a sliver of the drapes. Visible, though, was a plastic coffee cup he was holding in his hands. Slowly drawing it towards his mouth, he was watching and waiting. This was not a matter of unmotivated fears. Something was happening, something involving the Church, something directed at her, and she had to get away. Dressing quickly, she grabbed her keys and her purse. She headed around the interior courtyard of the building, snaking past its swimming pool, moving swiftly to a staircase leading down to the basement garage. Carefully, she paced down its steps. Yet, before she reached the bottom, she took out her car keys and peered ahead. The space was dimly lit by long fluorescent tubes that cast blue shadows on the roofs of the automobiles and on the damp concrete of the floor. The only sound was the persistent humming of a building generator in a far corner.

Pausing, she looked and listened, trying to observe a flickering of light or another noise that might tell her if someone was present. Then, after what seemed like a minute, she glided towards her car. Advancing as quietly as possible, she opened the driver's side door, placing herself within it. Starting the ignition, she put her foot to the gas, set the transmission into drive, and sped out, accelerating towards the exit on the side of the building opposite her apartment. This set her on a path away from the tracksuited man. She was even more alarmed, though, by what she saw as she turned onto the street. Another figure, seemingly sent to keep an eye on the other side of the structure, was in an identical minivan.

These were men from the Church. They weren't police. Detectives could simply knock on her door. And she knew the color and style of the minivans. This was not her imagination. It was not madness. She wanted to do what characters in Hollywood movies do, driving at thrilling speeds in order to escape peril. But the street she was on was too narrow and too short. In fact, almost as soon as she reached the road, she had to slow down for the approach of the intersection with Franklin Avenue. Meeting it, she stared in the rearview mirror.

The man in the second minivan was pulling out, trying to keep up. That spurred her to make a sharp left, jerking forward, heading east. It took her a moment to understand what she had done: She was going directly towards the Church's headquarters in Thai Town.

With that thought in mind, she swung left again as she reached Western Avenue. That turned her towards Griffith Park. She knew from experience that hikers parked their cars there before commencing their march up The Trails to the Greek Theater and the Observatory. The extended canopy of a line of tall trees shaded both sides of the road making it an easy spot in which to disappear amongst the multitude of joggers and walkers, stretching and readying themselves for the climb to the city's heights. This was the place to go.

The second bronze minivan was half a block behind her when she braked. Working her way around a pair of the hikers, she hooked the car into a parking spot on the roadside and cut her engine. That presented the man following her with a choice. He could gamble that she was planning to enter the park, go up to its gates and pay for entrance, trailing her in his car. Or he could try to find a space of his own. That would require him to drive around. Aware that either approach would occupy him, she took advantage of the time to take off the sweater she had wrapped around her shoulders. Then she grabbed her sunglasses from her glove compartment, put them on, darted out of her car and joined the gathering throng.

They were all sorts: young actors and actresses, lawyers and teachers, vacationers and tech geeks, nurses and nature enthusiasts. The number was leavened with a sprinkling of seniors determined to keep themselves trim. There were also yellow buses awaiting children coming down who had just made school trips to the Observatory.

Wearing sneakers and the dark glasses, she was nearly indistinguishable from the dozens of other brunettes moving up the hillside. This disguise was nearly completed by the unearthing of companions. For turning about, she spotted a fit-looking middle-aged couple. Almost beside her, they were prepping for the hike. When they smiled at her, she returned their expression. This led them to ask her if she wished to join them. With that she fell in with the pair. She could not have been more pleased: Anyone spotting the three of them would have presumed that she was their daughter. And it was not long, in fact, before they were chatting away, talking of small things like whether or not she hiked the canyon regularly. They lived in the neighborhood, the woman allowed, and they did it every day. That wakened a discussion of the relative merits of different blocks in the area and favorite stretches of Griffith Park. Vincenza was reminded what a different person she had become since arriving in Los Angeles. No longer did she struggle in speaking with people she did not know.

It turned out that they were also originally from the Midwest. Employed in the industry in set construction, they were frequently off on locations. But, as they were both home, they were making it a practice to take the hike each day. Listening to them talking in their hushed, friendly tones, Vincenza was struck by how much genuine love they had for each other. She also, rather abruptly, realized that she had placed herself on a walk that would draw her along a series of bluffs overlooking the city. From any of these, you might fall to your death.

That thought made her twist her head, gazing about for the man following her. She had never really gotten a good look at him. He was just a sandy-haired figure in a car she had raced past. He might be beside her. She had reasonable confidence that she had escaped him, that she had lost herself in the mass, and she was attached to a couple who would notice if someone abruptly tried to shove her off a cliff-side. But she had no alternate plan or notion of where to go or what to do, and no idea which face might be his.

The walk was of increasing difficulty, and though Vincenza worked out on elliptical machines and attended yoga classes, this was a different sort of exertion. Inevitably, she found that she was flagging. Thankfully, the older couple, so accustomed to the stroll, relaxed their pace in order not to lose their new friend. The sun was coming out, and, as it exited a patch of clouds, she started to feel its power.

In passing, the woman mentioned that they sometimes liked to break from the path to the Observatory, hiking over to the Holly-wood sign. That was far to the north and west: a more treacherous route. By contrast, the one they were on was nothing more than a steep advance along a partially paved road. But, they assured her, they were going to the Observatory. This was the shorter route. Still, there were a few spots on it where a plunge was sure to be fatal.

She could not tell them her story: about Selva's death and that she believed she was in danger. What could she say? She had already volunteered that she was from Eagan and an actress. She had also proudly revealed that she had recently shot a film with Tom Selva, one she had produced. This name registered with them when she mentioned the car chase movies he starred in, and they gave her appreciative expressions which suggested that she might be a useful person.

Her training in acting classes was helpful in that these had taught her how to really listen, and she was able to do this as she scanned the faces around them, trying to identify the sandy-haired male. When a blonde man in jeans and a tank top edged closer, she shifted herself to the left of the husband. That placed her on the side of the path farthest from the precipice. To launch her off it, the blonde man would have to rush towards them and then shove her suddenly and swiftly past them.

"Do you have vertigo?" the wife asked.

Vincenza said that she did.

The talk with the couple—Gary and Fran—was remarkably unforced, so much that it surprised her. What concerned her as they began to reach the crest was another man with dirty yellow hair. He was walking quickly, gaining on them, wearing a T-shirt she knew as she owned one herself. It advertised membership in the Church of Life.

Then there was the matter of her clothes. They had not been picked out for a hike, and, while this had initially been a boon as they had protected her from the slight chill on a day at the end of February, they made her sweat. She noticed that Fran was sneaking a glance at her chest. This was something that she normally had an uncanny awareness of, a special radar that could detect sexual attraction coming from the ionosphere. But, preoccupied as she had been and more acute with regard to men, she was only belatedly recognizing that Fran had been conscious of it all the way up the slope. Had she greatly erred in her view of this happy pair?

The man with the Church T-shirt ambled past and disappeared. But the other blonde male continued to trail them at a distance of twenty feet. Pulling out his phone, he had tried on a number of occasions to make calls, but had given up each time, unable to gain a signal. Vincenza had the sense that he knew that she knew he was there for her, and, as such, she placed herself so close to Gary that he could place his arm around her.

As they came to the final hundred yards of the ascent, they moved onto a long ridge. It offered one of the best views of the city. To the left, it displayed the office towers of the downtown and beyond that, the barrios of East LA. On the right was the vastness of the basin of West LA, extending almost out to the ocean. Below was a drop of hundreds of feet. The path narrowed. Behind them were growing crowds.

Vincenza did not want to look down. From experience she knew what she would see: twisted branches and jagged pieces of stone sticking out from an almost straight line of rock face. There was no way to survive a fall from the crag.

As Gary and Fran paused, taking in the sight, Vincenza spun her head around. Her eyes stopped as they met with those of the man she suspected, and they exchanged expressions that suggested a shared knowledge. Whatever it was that he intended, each understood that he was being thwarted by the presence of the couple.

The strangeness of her situation grew as she listened to what they said next. Fran had done most of the talking on the way up, but as they drew within feet of the grounds of the Observatory, Gary took the lead. Like his wife, he appeared to be in his early fifties, but, as evidenced by his sinewy body, he was supremely fit. Of medium height, he had delicate features, a well-formed mouth, and a mottled, closely cropped, graying beard. Reflecting the time that the pair spent out of doors, his countenance was deeply tanned and heavily wrinkled. His eyes suggested a keen awareness of irony.

He seemed vaguely conscious of the man following them, and he stared him off, indicating a desire for privacy. Then he waited until when they were at a remove from anyone else. They had left the ridge and had reached the grass laid out in front of the Observatory, yet he gestured back towards the south and the tens of thousands of homes and buildings hazily visible below them. He began in what sounded like an innocuous fashion.

"I'm glad you came up with us, Vincenza," he said. "My wife and I like to make new friends. We particularly like making friends with people in the industry."

Vincenza could tell that he was about to make a pitch of some sort, and she assumed that it would be something to do with work. As he was expecting some hint of agreement from her, she bobbed her head without speaking. That was the prompt for him to go on.

"We like making friends with people in the industry because they're usually not so caught up in convention. *Religion*," he explained. Although he was grinning as he pronounced the last word, he said it with obvious distaste. Then, even before he spoke again, Vincenza understood what Gary was about to suggest. They wanted her for a threesome. They had picked her up. She listened as he began talking of the joint "delight" he and his wife "shared" for "beauty." With this, she asked herself what was most significant: her fear of those she believed were following her or her disgust for what was about to be proposed.

SHOULD SHE SIMPLY HAVE TRUSTED the men following her? Was David Clarkson someone she could believe? Vincenza was asking herself these questions, sitting in the rear of Gary and Fran's Saab. They were driving her back to their house, which was actually within walking distance of the park entrance. Without quite saying so, she had consented to their suggestion of a *ménage à trois*. Like the presence of Selva's corpse in her trunk, it seemed to her that it must represent an end-product, the result of some long train of missteps.

She knew it too well. Operating on not enough sleep, she stared at the clock on the car's dashboard. The LCD display told her it was just past one. In the morning she had to be at the dispensary for the start of another shift. She wasn't sure if she could return to her apartment or where she might wash and find clean clothes to replace those she'd hiked in if she didn't go back to her apartment. A lover was dead, and it was possible that others would think she had killed him.

To make matters still more difficult, they were driving away from her car, which remained where it was by Griffith Park. Conscious that her hands were shaking again and her heart was beating fast, she examined the pair. Sitting in the front seats with their eyes set on the road, they were beaming. They seemed already to have banked their achievement of persuading a young woman to come home with them and allow herself to be their plaything. But when they had settled her in the car's rear, they must have sensed her condition, must have realized that she was scattered and that there was something wrong, something motivating her willingness to get into their vehicle. Did they find that a turn-on?

The most bizarre aspect of the whole thing, of course, was the time of day. Who had casual sex with neighbors—even just one—at the lunch hour? And could she even be sure that regular sex—or as normal hanky-panky as one might engage in with an even number of partners—was what they intended? Was it possible that they planned to videotape the (so to speak) shebang and upload it to the internet? Or might they be sadists who wanted to manacle her and drip molten wax on her private parts as they asked her to call them master and mistress?

Seven years earlier she had gone down to the county courthouse to formalize her name change, to make it legal: Vincenza Morgan. She remembered thinking as she had done this what everyone in the city believed: Anything was possible in the City of the Angels. She had always assumed this was desirable. For the first time, reflecting on it, it struck her that it was like so many superficially welcome descriptive statements. "I will love you forever": that could be creepy. "We are a family, and families stay together": that one had caused her enormous pain.

Gazing into the rearview mirror, Vincenza noticed that one of the bronze minivans was thirty yards behind them. It occurred to her to tell them. What did she have to lose?

She was prompted in this by Fran, who had finally taken note that she was contemplating something other than that she was about to be stripped and impaled by people her mother's age.

"We're being followed. Or really, *I'm* being followed. That bronze minivan is tailing us." Saying this, she gestured towards the minivan.

"How do you know?"

"He followed me to the park. Then he followed us on the hike— all the way up to the Observatory and back down again. I'm not crazy. Drive in a circle, and you'll see."

As Vincenza said this, they came to an intersection, and Gary braked the Saab. The stop provided him with an interval in which to swing his head around to her. "You're in trouble with the police?"

"I'm in trouble, yes. But not with the police. As I say, drive in a circle. You'll see it's true."

They were moving west along Franklin Avenue. The streets bisecting it, running up the surrounding hillsides, were flanked by elegant, three-story homes. The greater number had sloping drive-ways with metal gates. Around those were entwined branches of bougainvillea and wisteria, or blossoming magnolias. But, taking Vincenza's suggestion, Gary turned south on North Bronson. This drew them through an underpass of the 101 freeway. Beneath it were tents and mattresses laid out by the homeless: mentally ill veterans and junkies, scrofulous people dressed in soiled sweatpants and ragged hoodies. One held up a tattered cardboard poster asking for money. Another shouted and gesticulated at no one. It was the most pointed demonstration and reminder that the city seemed only to admit of two outcomes: success or failure. She had the sense that triumph and attainment and honors and money and fame were just in front of her, almost beheld. Yet here she was, running away, possibly from the leaders of the Church to which she had devoted herself, and her heinie was placed on the leather seat of a car driven by sex freaks, squalor all about.

Jammed as the underpass was, they had to decelerate, and the minivan pulled up behind them. When the light flashed green, they turned onto Hollywood Boulevard. More homeless could be spotted crawling about, skulking in the alleyways around it, while on their left Vincenza saw a huge polyvinyl skull affixed to the front of a low-slung building: the Museum of Death. A notorious neighborhood tourist haunt, it was an exhibition space devoted to the activities of serial killers, the lowlight of the long block leading to North Gower. Vincenza watched as an obese couple parked on the street. Passing by the gaunt street people, they clambered out of their automobile with feverish looks of anticipation, rolling forward towards the museum's entrance. They were there to study its meticulous displays on the activities of cannibalistic murderers.

Nothing was said by Gary and Fran as they went by. They wanted to pretend that none of this existed. What was harder to ignore was the continued pursuit of the bronze minivan as they flipped back to the right, passing once more under the freeway, wending their way towards their home, which was on a hillside street off Franklin Avenue.

Fran was the one who spoke. "I guess you're right," she said. "He does seem to be following us. You have any idea why?"

Vincenza nodded, but did not explain.

"Are you in danger?"

"Maybe."

"You're running away from someone? Aside from your acting, are you..." Fran hesitated before asking the question.

Vincenza knew what her suspicion was and finished the sentence for her: "An escort?"

As Fran gave her a responsive if embarrassed expression, it occurred to her that this was a far more plausible explanation for her state of affairs than the actual one. If she were being hounded by a violent pimp, she was in a situation that might inspire their sympathetic offers of assistance, perverts though they were.

She did not even have time to confirm that this was the case before Fran planted both of her hands on her cheeks, taking in the horror of the imaginary predicament. "He beats you?"

Much as Vincenza had been hit by her stepfather, and well-trained as she was in the art of the memory exercise of "substitution," she had no trouble summoning real tears. Brushing these away with feigned shame, she looked at them as they parked in the driveway of their house. Her eyes said it all: They weren't really going to proceed with this tawdry scheme of theirs to make joint use of some combination of her orifices? They were going to help her, weren't they?

She watched as the couple exchanged looks with one another. They had mentioned on the climb up to the Observatory that they were vegans, and, like her, they worried greatly about climate change. Perhaps they were not the monsters that she feared. Their faces told her that they wanted very much to believe that they were good people. Yes, they would help her. They were obligated to. If there was disappointment that they were being deprived of what must have been akin to a seven-course gourmet tasting menu, there was an awareness that someone else was hungry and needed the meal more.

"We do think you're quite lovely, Vincenza. Exquisite, in fact," Gary said, "but perhaps this is not the moment for what we'd talked about."

Watching them smiling warmly at her, the actress had the odd sense that they felt it was important to affirm that they *wanted* to have the threesome with her as she *was* "exquisite." In their minds, it seemed, her confidence so needed bolstering that they had to let her down easy. They weren't rejecting her. They just wanted to focus on this first task of getting her free from her mack daddy.

"So," Fran said, extending a hand, placing it gently on her shoulder, "what can we do to get you away from him?"

She permitted the pair to engage in a mutual embrace, while wiping another droplet from her face. Then she composed herself and outlined a strategy to employ. The first matter was for her to get back her automobile. Then she had to go to a friend's place, somewhere safe she could stay for a day or two. In response to their complaisant expressions, she went on, explaining that they could return to Griffith Park to pick up her car, and then they could use the Saab to block the minivan as she drove away.

Moments later, she found herself an ecstatic observer of her own life. For the plan worked precisely. Yet, as she departed, what was most in her mind was something Gary said as she used her car keys to send the signal, opening its door locks.

"You should give us your number," he observed, "so that we can do *that*—assuming, of course, that we could work something out, and we wouldn't have to pay your regular rates. I mean, as we hadn't known that you charged."

She assured them that appreciative as she was for what they were doing that a discount was in order. Then she shook his hand and drove off. Once in the car, though, she began to wonder if she might have a bottle of hand sanitizer about.

CHAPTER 14

Todd Gelber suffered from an ailment that afflicted many male Hollywood executives. Through his power and rank he had managed to attract a woman of undeniable beauty, and all through their courtship she had shown him how much she worshipped him through passionate lovemaking. It was almost ceaseless, and on the nights when she was weary of intercourse or incapable of engaging in it, she took self-evident joy in pleasing him in other ways. He had never been so sated. Her eyes were always seducing him, thrilling him, intoxicating him, and when they went to restaurants or film premieres her hands were wrapped around him. If intellectually he understood that a woman might be drawn to him for his money and his position, he did not feel that with her. *She* adulated him. This marriage was going to be different. She didn't care about the home he lived in or the car he drove. He knew this for a fact.

But no sooner had they returned from their honeymoon then he had learned that she was pregnant, and from that point on sex was a scarce commodity. In a typical month they made love a single time during the first week, then once more towards the end. The number of her reasons for avoiding sex had proven to be as various as the positions in the Kama Sutra, if significantly less satisfying. In the winter she would refuse him if he had a cold, even one she had given him. In the summer, she was sickened by the air-conditioning. In the spring and fall, she had unbearable headaches. She did not work and had a maid and a cook, but she complained that she had no time. That compelled her to lodge herself away from the bedroom when he was about to go to sleep. Naturally, once he was unconscious, she was able to finish her vital tasks. Yet she was masterly at appearing to be an adoring spouse, and hardly anyone suspected the extent of his dissatisfaction.

Charles Tasker was one of the few friends whom Gelber felt comfortable talking with about this. A veteran director known for his trilogy of werewolf movies, he was someone Gelber could open up with as he had been the victim of an even worse confidence game. Tasker had married a notorious former fashion model and actress, a woman who had managed to earn a reputation for sleeping her way to the top in two industries. He had wed her with full awareness of how imperfect her past had been but with the absolute conviction that the wild adulterous sex they had on their film shoot would continue. The realization that he, too, had been placed on a starvation sex diet was galling. So Gelber felt less aggrieved when he was in Tasker's company. At least his wife was respectable and warm. Tasker's was a rancorous tramp.

They sat across from one another in a beloved Jewish delicatessen, one block from Rodeo Drive. Flanking them were bottles of cheap yellow mustard and Heinz ketchup, along with the most ordinary flatware and paper napkins. These were displayed on laminated imitation wood tables, bare of tablecloths. It was the sort of place whose sole appeal lay in its hominess and familiarity and its status as an industry landmark.

As they were both famished, they ripped into their dishes, eating as they gabbed, talking from the sides of their mouths. While Gelber felt that he could speak more frankly with his friend about his marriage, he had to be careful, even sneaky, with regard to his purpose in seeking out Tasker's presence: the Tom Selva indie picture which people were chattering about.

His plan was simple. He wanted to be in a position to buy the film before it hit the indie circuit, so that he could bury it. That would satisfy Selva's agent and perhaps the actor himself, when he saw it in its finished form. This would be a chit—or a blunt-force instrument—of undoubted value. But to gain hold of it he needed to employ a measure of stealth. For if others suspected his intentions they might bid on the movie as well.

To implement the plot he had to befriend one of the two women producing the film, winning her trust. Tasker knew her from the Church of Life. That was key. Gelber needed to use this connection. The aim would be to make Tasker believe that he wanted to be intro-duced to Vincenza as a potential mistress. Simply put, he had to seem like he wanted to screw Vincenza Morgan personally when what he wanted was to screw her professionally. Yet he couldn't have Tasker going around *saying* that he was finding mattress mates for him. This was the age of #MeToo, and he had gained his job because his prede-cessor had been ousted for making improper advances.

Regardless, he wondered: How did you go about indicating an interest in a struggling actress you did not know without tipping off your acquaintance regarding your real concern, her attempt at recre-ating a John Cassavetes's film from the days of wide ties and leisure suits? There had been times in meetings when Gelber had impressed himself by his talent for misdirection. This, though, required finesse and sleight of hand greater than that shown by a magician who hides a ballfield from the spectators sitting in it.

It seemed to him that the trick was to bring up Vincenza's chest in the context of a photo he had seen of Tasker standing alongside her at a Church function. He had known men who were connoisseurs of fake breasts. If he pretended to be such a character, then this could be the ploy by which to bring up his desire to meet Vincenza. Yet, granted the present temper of the business and the compact position of the tables in the delicatessen, he had to speak in a low voice.

To enter into the specifics of the matter, he told Tasker that he had seen Salma Hayek a few nights before, and he had been reminded of how beautiful her figure was—allowing that he was sure her breasts were enhanced. He said this leaning forward as he spoke, if taking care not to spit the corned beef hash he was wolfing down.

"I think someone told me they know her plastic surgeon, the one who did them," Tasker responded in a tone of considerable seriousness.

Apparently, this was not a matter to joke about.

"But this isn't anyone that Vera goes to?" Gelber said, referencing Tasker's werewolf-slaying spouse.

Tasker shook his head as he devoured part of a sunny-side egg. Then he glanced about to be sure no one was listening to them. "Vera's had hardly any work done. And hers are real. You know that."

Gelber smiled appreciatively in response. If nooky shortage was a refrain of their dialogues, he was compelled to acknowledge Tasker's wife's physical grace.

Pausing, Gelber stuffed his mouth with more of the hash. Then, having consumed the chunk, he entered into the matter which had inspired him to propose the meeting, which was not to listen to Tasker pitch him on a revival of his series of werewolf epics.

"I spotted you in a Church photo. You were alongside a gorgeous brunette, an actress, who must have had augmentation. I think her name was…" He hesitated, affecting uncertainty. "It was something funny. Vincentia, was it? No, *Vincenza*. You know her?"

Tasker blinked his eyes in agreement. "You want to meet her? I'm pretty sure she's single."

Gelber was surprised by how easy it had been. "I mean…*you* understand. We've talked about this. Sonya is *great* with the kids…

it's just that…of course, I can't and wouldn't do anything where I'm doing anything like offering parts. Or putting pressure on anyone."

"Of course. Naturally. I'll see what I can do. This isn't about business," Tasker said. "We're friends. You don't owe me anything."

The way Tasker said this reminded Gelber that he had no real friends in the business, and Tasker would be bound to remind him of the debt. He also had to bear in mind that the Church of Life could be a formidable enemy.

The rest of the breakfast was composed of Tasker's detailed descriptions of the plots of follow-up lycanthrope pictures and the part that his wife Vera might play in these movies. As Gelber listened, he was saddened by the awareness that Tasker was still in love with his wife, as shabbily as she treated him.

CHAPTER 15

"She had arranged to meet the people at Griffith Park. We don't know who they were yet or how she knew them. But she had obviously made plans to hook up with them there, and they talked the whole way up the mountain. They knew to keep us at a distance. After that they tried to slip away out on the roads. Then they cut us off when she went back to the park to pick up her car."

Clarkson was sitting in his seventeenth-floor office in Thai Town, and he was listening to a progress report from one of his aides, who was doing everything possible to avoid accepting blame for what had happened: For a second time, they had lost track of Vincenza.

The assistant was an embodiment of both the good and the bad of what he had to work with as the resident housecleaner of their new faith. On occasion, he had employed private detectives, the sort of people who specialize in surveilling unfaithful spouses and then filing reports on the co-respondents in divorce proceedings. These men— and they were always men—were usually competent, but you had no way of knowing what their ultimate intentions were. When you spoke with them, you felt their shiftiness. You sensed their absence of loyalty the moment they began talking and often before that. You saw it in their eyes and in the way they held themselves. You knew that they might be cooking up a scheme. And as he had so little confidence in their motives, Clarkson did not even feel comfortable permitting them in the Church headquarters building as he had the instinct when they walked around that they were sleuthing, eyeballing the site to some other purpose.

Of these aims, there were many, and you had to bear them in mind. Might they switch over to the role of extortionist? Would they feed a portion of what they learned in your employ to a website devoted to celebrity gossip? You could not be sure what they were up to. They would keep their own files on a case. They would not hand these over. What was more, there was only so far they would go for the Church. While Clarkson knew of at least one detective agency in Hollywood that had planted evidence and made threats on behalf of its movie actor and talent agency clients, his experience was that they would not perform these tasks for the Church—and couldn't be relied upon if they said that they would.

His assistants, on the other hand, were men of absolute fidelity. They were believers. What varied widely was their level of ability, how adroit they were. He had a team of seven—three men and four women—whose business was dealing with the reputations of those who left the Church and then criticized it. The greater part of their work consisted of media relations. There were many reporters who made use of what they provided them from their files. During Church counseling sessions, adherents frequently discussed their sexuality and the more unfortunate events of their childhood. This was enough to destroy many a tough guy actor. The growth of the #MeToo movement offered suitable material for decimating the reputation of directors, producers, and studio executives, and all of his aides employed in this area were adept. More than once, he had sat in on their conversations with journalists and thought to himself that he could not have done the work as well himself. They knew the arts of allurement, and there had been cases in which members of the team had moved past flattery and cajolery to the more explicit kind of seduction—and from that to blackmail of the reporters. They had used these techniques, as well, for manipulation of the tax authorities.

What he lacked was competent deputies who could handle duties like those required in Vincenza's case. These ranged from this mere task of keeping tabs on a woman so she might be confronted directly to less savory, but necessary, deeds. None of the four men he had for this category of activities had proven reliable.

The person addressing him was the least capable. Clarkson was struck by the fact that he spoke almost without pause, expressed himself precisely, and displayed a remarkably handsome face with dimpled cheeks and a manly jaw. If he had never gotten past playing the owner in a pet food commercial, he seemed on first glance as though he were born for leading-man parts in soap operas. His name, Cliff Stoop, fit. It was half-right, just as he always seemed to be. One reason he had not made it as an actor was his voice. Much too high, it made you wince. He sounded like a parakeet expertly imitating a man. The effect was made worse by his reflexive habit of smiling, trying to charm whomever he was speaking with as a cover for whatever ineptitude he had demonstrated.

Clarkson gestured for him to sit down in the seat opposite his in the hopes that this might cause Stoop to talk more slowly. Then Clarkson continued his questioning. "If what you say is true, why didn't they just cut you off the first time you were at the park? Why take her to their house and then back to the park?"

Stoop hesitated. It was obvious that this riddle had not occurred to him. "Admittedly, we don't know. That's a *good* question. Maybe they needed to get something."

"Did they go into their house, come out and give her something?"

"No. I suppose they didn't. Again, there's a lot we haven't figured out."

"When she left her car at the park, why didn't you think to check it? There were two of you there, yes?"

This last query caused Stoop to sit up straight as though he had been constipated and now had to rush to the bathroom. It was a matter that he had been dreading. "Well," he said, his voice rising an additional notch, "we were trying to keep communication with each other and to stay on Vincenza. You know that wasn't easy. You can't really get cell service in the park, and they were driving away from it like they were in a hurry to get somewhere. We had to keep up."

Clarkson tried not to roll his eyes. He had wanted to bring Vincenza in before he spoke to the Supreme Pilot. But affairs had reached a point at which he had to tell him what was happening, even though they were still without her.

Telling Stoop to keep one person outside Vincenza's apartment and another outside the marijuana dispensary at which she worked, Clarkson dismissed him. He watched as the actor left his office. Then he rose from his seat with the intention of heading up a flight to the mammoth, top-floor suite occupied by the Church's Supreme Pilot.

Two ATTRIBUTES DEFINE A CULT: Its members associate only with those within it, and they are not permitted to consort with anyone who departs from it. Vincenza had been dogged in her conviction that the Church was no cult. But as she drove away from Griffith Park, it struck her that this was how the Church functioned. You could not have contacts with those who had renounced the faith. She had supposed that this was a reasonable prophylactic. It was for your own protection, lest they contaminate you with their doubt.

What she had never thought much about was how circumscribed her range of contacts had become since she had entered the Church. When people asked her, she could recite a list of skeptics with whom she was friendly. This roll started with Sara, her co-star and producing partner. Driving away, she thought for the first time about how few other people there were with whom she spent time who were outside it. It was a shock to realize that for three months she had not gone out for a cup of coffee with anyone, aside from Sara and once with Todd Gelber, not in the Church. It was her charitable outlet. It was her place for prayer and counseling. It was where she found boyfriends. The only children she knew any longer were the offspring of members. She had not spoken with her mother in a decade. Could it be that she was a member of a cult?

Staring into her rearview mirror, she kept an eye out for anyone who might be following her. Several minutes went by before she saw that there was no one. Yet she was hardly free. She had no idea where she was going. In the morning she was supposed to be back at work. The Israeli brothers who owned the dispensary were gangsters, men who swaggered around with pistols at their hips. Did that make it safe?

She wanted to shower and change, but she doubted that she could go back to her own apartment, and whom did she know who was free of the Church's influence and in any respect trustworthy? Feeling overwhelmed, she stopped the car, parking in the lot of an overpriced supermarket. She unfastened her seat belt. She wanted to cry and would have done so but that she had wept the night before and then in telling Gary and Fran that her pimp was following her. She had had enough with the tears. Besides, she had little time.

Rolling down the window, she let in the air and lit up a cigarette. Though it had dropped to sixty degrees, she needed the ventilation. As she let the car's scents out and took in a mild breeze, a middle-aged man with a large gut waddled past her, pushing the groceries in his shopping cart. Seeing her face and hair and her enhanced bust, he gave her a leer. He seemed to want to approach her, so much so that she needed to stare him off. She noticed that he was wearing a wedding ring.

Her handbag lay on her passenger seat. Instinctively, she picked it up and began going through it, searching for her lipstick case and compact. She broke off with this when she noticed Billy Rosenberg's business card tucked inside. Abruptly she remembered something: Her mention of the Church had caused Billy to shift his glance. He was plainly no follower, if sufficiently respectful that he would not disparage her beliefs.

She began to ponder a subject which had been much on her mind: She was not yet thirty. Half a year would go by before she hit that yard-marker. Still, there were thoroughly untalented actresses she had met in her classes, women in their first year in Los Angeles, who had advanced more than she. In the run-up to the making of their film, she had begun to ask herself why she was still on the outside, not established, obtaining acting jobs only now and again, going to audition after audition but rarely booking jobs. One supposition revolved in her head. It percolated. It stewed. It weighed on her. Until she had gone to bed with Tom Selva, she had not selected a lover on the basis of what he could do for her. Even when she had dated a photographer, newly arrived, she had not asked him to aid her. She thought he was handsome. And she had passionately desired Selva.

Los Angeles had revealed her to be a different woman. She was freer. Far from Eagan and her mother and stepfather, in this place with its sunny days, she had discovered that she liked talking to people she did not know. It brightened things. It made her feel that the world was open and new. But she did not sleep with strangers or to get ahead. She didn't want to become that person she saw everywhere around her, the user, the game player, the woman who turned things that she desperately wanted—love, affection, intimacy—into something bare of these.

Who was the right man now? There was a time when she had been drawn to men who radiated their cockiness, projecting studied indifference. They had proven themselves coarse and callous. The reflection drew her back to Billy. Sitting next to him at the coffee shop, she had been struck by his shyness and lack of polish. Working on his filmscript, he had not noticed her before she had spoken to him. He appeared to be something different. If his voice was colored in doubt, it was tender. There was a respectfulness in the way he responded. Could she be attracted to him? His hairline was receding, his skin sallow, and, when he stood up, she saw that his height was largely in his torso. With her heels on, she was as tall as he.

The address on his card showed that he lived a single block away. She had supposed from his dress and manner that he was another man who could do nothing for her. Might it be that he could? He was at least the opposite of men like Selva. He presumed nothing.

Opening the driver's-side door, she picked out a building on the opposite corner: Billy's. Walking towards it, she realized that she could not tell him the truth, no more than Gray and Fran. He wouldn't believe it. This awareness prompted her to dawdle, and she walked past and around the structure twice before she placed herself at the entrance gate.

What reassured her was the sense of familiarity. The building had obviously been constructed by the same developer as the one she lived in. They were twins. Before her were the same beige cement walls, the birds of paradise planted outside and, peering inside, the pool. They were so much alike that she wondered if she should try her gate key. Yet she hesitated in pushing the buzzer on the wall with the tag reading "Rosenberg." Then, pressing it, she prepared herself to give a performance upon which her life depended.

CHAPTER 16

The Supreme Pilot did not like to be known by his given name, James Armstrong. What he liked was celebrities. To that end it had been his idea to open The Spas. Centers for recruitment, they focused on tending to the illustrious. The rationale was dual. First, leading figures in the entertainment industry served as advertisements for the Church. Beyond this, Armstrong supposed that those who gained prominence were gifted in some way, that ability to acquire fame was a marker of strength, the modern equivalent to Samson's forelocks.

David Clarkson knew this, and he understood equally well how incandescent the Supreme Pilot's rage could be. So Clarkson had no desire to tell Armstrong that Tom Selva was no more. Nor did he want to explain to him that they hadn't caught up with Vincenza. There was no longer a choice, though. Matters were at the point that he would be thought delinquent if he did not apprise him. This in mind, Clarkson paced from his office to the building's fire stairs, ascending these to the top floor.

The exit from the stairs led to a metal booth whose ceiling was made of a thick layer of clear plexiglass. Inside the booth were two guards and a woman in a gray woolen suit: Armstrong's secretary. They were the ones who could unlock the door to the Supreme Pilot's domain. An earlier phone call had told them of the urgency of his visit and with no more than a cursory glance, they opened it. Behind lay the chief executive's suite. No matter how often Clarkson came, it seemed strange. On one side, light streamed down through the plexiglass slats. But there were no windows along the walls, and the eastern half of it was illuminated by electronic imitations of wax candles. More, it had just a single chair, the Supreme Pilot's own, set on a mounted platform. Around this were silk pillows and mats. The design was such that all who came in to meet Armstrong were compelled to stretch their gaze up to see him shrouded in a vault of light.

The figure who shimmered in this way was small, at most five-foot-six, and, though he worked out frequently with weights, he had skinny arms and a concave chest. The lone parts of Armstrong that were large were his head and his eyes. These were enormous, and they were studying him, taking him in as he entered. Seated within the chair of his pulpit, Armstrong gestured with the back of one of his little hands for Clarkson to place himself on a pillow.

"This is about Vincenza?" His voice was soft and modulated. Clarkson knew that even when he was dangerously angry that it would remain so.

There was no point in trying to deceive him. "Yes, sir. I'm afraid we still haven't caught up with her. But there's something else. Tom Selva is dead."

"Really? *Really*? My goodness! What happened?"

Sitting cross-legged on a tasseled pillow, Clarkson could just make out Armstrong's glimmering head and shoulders. Dressed in a linen tunic, the customary day attire of the Supreme Pilot, he kept himself motionless. Was this a sign of calm or of controlled rage? The deputy was unsure.

"He seems to have been murdered. We have his body, which has a bullet hole where his left ventricle used to function. We found him at the beach cottage, the one in Malibu."

"And who do you think killed him?"

"Vincenza Morgan."

"Because…?"

"She placed the body there. In the garage. Footage on the security camera shows that."

"Was this related somehow to Tom and Vincenza Morgan's movie?"

"Not sure, sir."

"You haven't called the police?"

"Not yet."

"Why did she place the body in the garage?"

Clarkson shook his head to show that he did not know.

"You think she killed him somewhere else? Then she put the body there?"

"Possibly. Likely, it was some sort of jealous rage."

"You know, Tom said to me that he was concerned about her temper. Apparently, it was quite violent, and he knew she had taken a gun from the movie set." He paused. "My goodness. *Tragic.*"

"Yes, sir…. Do you think this is going to make us look bad?"

"It certainly could." The way Armstrong said this word was such that Clarkson had to fight the impulse to flinch. He pronounced it in a fashion that was seemingly mild but utterly devoid of connection. It was as though he were addressing a tongue depressor that a physician was sticking in his mouth. It baldly announced that his work in the matter had been less than satisfactory. "And you haven't gotten hold of her?"

"No, sir. We haven't. I'm sorry."

Clarkson watched as the tunic shifted, moving left to right and then right to left, as Armstrong silently contemplated this. The eyes, so green and so prominent, turned inward. Then they returned, bearing down on him.

"Well, even so, she's part of our Church. We must treat her with the respect she is due. But I'd rather, if I might, speak with her first."

"Yes, sir."

"And you'd better do some work on that videotape from the security camera at the beach cottage. Get rid of all but the last day of the tape. Can you do that? We don't want people to see that Tom was using it as a place for meeting his girlfriends." He paused. "I still can't get over that he's dead."

"I'm sorry, sir. Perhaps if I had brought her in earlier…"

"Don't blame yourself." Armstrong said this in a manner that plainly indicated that he ought to do just that. "I would like to see if we can get her to confess to us. Then you can go ahead and call the police."

"Yes, sir."

The Supreme Pilot paused and reflected. "Such a shame about Tom."

Clarkson was relieved. He was astonished by how calm Armstrong was: circumspect and impassive. This was the rational, calculating James Armstrong. It was the one Clarkson much preferred, and he listened then as the Supreme Pilot outlined his ideas about the funeral and how it would gather together the mightiest celebrities. The ritual cremation, he explained, would be on a giant pyre out of doors at a spot that television crews in helicopters might capture. There would be thousands of rose petals all about, and he, the Supreme Pilot, would address the crowd.

Pulling out a pocket notebook, Clarkson took down the ideas. What followed was about what Selva might have been. He had given the Church almost half a million dollars, Armstrong said, and there was much more that would have come. Then there was his name and his accomplishments and his commitment to the cause. They would talk about that, and they would have the widow and his child prominently placed in attendance, seated next to the Supreme Pilot.

Exiting, Clarkson passed the secretary and the two guards, went down the concrete steps, and returned to his office. Sitting back down at his desk, he eyed the screensaver he had placed on his computer screen. It was his personal motto: *To save the world you do what you have to.*

CHAPTER 17

Billy had an aunt who suffered from bipolar disorder. They had taken her in once after she had been released from the hospital. She was heavily medicated, and her face was blank. Still, she talked to him about the doctors and the food and how her delusions had seemed so real. Her hallucination had been that she had electric rays emanating from her eye sockets. These allowed her to control pigeons and dogs. There had been at least four of these psychotic episodes. In each of the others, the fantasies were slightly different. But all of them had been perverse, and they had ended with her institutionalization.

What to do with her, what could be done: These were topics of conversation with which Billy was familiar from childhood.

Consciousness that the illness ran in families had sometimes made him doubt his own sanity. Eventually, however, he had come to understand that while his acquaintance with the malady was of use, it was not with regard to identification of warning signs about his own mental state. In the entertainment industry you could not assume that people were just behaving dramatically when their actions were odd or theatrical. With artistic folk, all too often there were medical explanations.

This recollection was in his mind when he buzzed Vincenza in. After all, it was one thing to imagine himself inviting her over to his apartment on first meeting. It was quite another for her to appear on his doorstep unbidden. Necessarily, he drew up his checklist. There were five aspects to be on the watch for:

1. Did she seem like she hadn't been sleeping?
2. Was she inappropriately sexual?
3. Did she display signs of wild spending or drug use?
4. Was she paranoid?
5. Did her statements sound jumbled or confused?

The dark circles around her eyes affirmatively answered the first question. The way she showed off her figure provided a similar reading to the second. He had to listen intently to obtain an answer to the third, fourth, and fifth questions. His preference was to do this before she entered his apartment. But some mixture of politeness and attraction obliged him to bring her in, to sit her down on his couch, and to encourage her to set down her handbag before he could make a determination. What he noticed at once was that she was talking hastily and close to tears. She was embarrassed, she said. She didn't know whom to turn to. It was all her fault.

She began to sob.

A hug did not seem appropriate. He was seated across his coffee table from her, and he could not just glide over it to console her. In addition, her breasts were sufficiently rigid and large that he had the sense that he would be providing solace to them, rather than to her.

While it was upsetting to see her cry, he remained silent. Experience had taught him that it was best to listen, and he watched as she pulled out a handkerchief from her bag with which she mopped up the tears and blew her nose. She breathed in and gave him a gentle smile, if one that did not imply anything sexual. When she began talking once more, he noticed that the crying had drawn her voice down an octave.

The tale she began to tell him was of a boyfriend who had turned out to be a meth dealer. He was now in her apartment with his accomplices, and they had guns. As they were using the drugs themselves, she was afraid to go back, and she needed a place to stay for a few days. She knew how weird all this sounded, and she understood that he must suspect that she was a user. She asked him to consider her position. She was trying to make up her mind about calling the police, and she hoped that he could grasp her ambivalence—and fear—since a simple phone message would lead a man she had been involved with to a long term in prison. She knew it was horrible to ask a man to be a friend, nothing more, but she wasn't exactly in a place where she could take up with anyone else just yet.

Having said all this, she did one more thing. She asked him to come over and examine her teeth. She wanted to prove that she did not have meth mouth and wasn't a user.

Standing up, Billy nodded sympathetically. Before walking over, he ran through his list. She was terrified—that was to say, paranoid. She was trying to prove that she was not an addict, which was surely one of the most reliable proofs of enslavement. And she sounded supremely confounded and perplexed. Moreover, even if she were sane, his instinct should be to mistrust her and to offer her a small sum of money but not lodging. The city was filled, after all, with con artists, and there were plenty of actresses who were being thrown out of their apartments for unpaid rent. It was reasonable to assume that she was either deranged or seeking to prey upon and exploit him. Yet, for all this, he believed her. Her story was consistent, and it made sense. Granted that he wanted to get Claire back to his apartment as soon as possible, the timing could not have been worse. What she was saying sounded true, though, and, if it were, there was no way that he could refuse her. The persuasive aspect was seemingly trivial: her insistence that he take a gander at her teeth. It was the sort of nutty, earnest detail that no flimflammer would mention. Either it was so, or she had a much greater talent for invention than he possessed.

Reflecting on all this, he slid around the table. He had little doubt that she had neither seen nor guessed his thoughts. What she could perceive was that he was doing as she asked, making close perusal of a full set of bicuspids and molars, teeth which cigarettes had slightly tarnished. Determined to be a gentleman, he stipulated that she would sleep in his bed, while he would take the living room couch. A second requirement was that she had to smoke outside. The terms agreed upon and the bedsheets changed, he loaned her his second set of keys. Seeing how levelheaded she was discussing this, he told himself that he had done the right thing.

Then he listened as she explained that she was going to purchase a wig to disguise herself with. It was for when she headed to work, she said.

He was left wondering what he had gotten himself into.

THE BEST PLACE IN LOS ANGELES to go for wigs is the Miracle Mile area on Wilshire Boulevard. Along a three-block stretch, there are four stores that sell hairpieces. The merchants are between South Burnside and South Detroit. The customers are mostly Orthodox Jewish women who live in the neighborhood. This *klatsch* likes to hang about, socializing and gossiping, as they try on their *shaidles*. Typically, the women shun the costume designers and the stylists who, less frequently, came in to the shops. Having been to these vendors before, Vincenza was prepared for the expressions she would receive from the *yentas*.

On the way she had managed to stop by a Target outlet to pick up some inexpensive clothes. Normally, this would have occupied her thoughts. Her mind was elsewhere, though. She was not contemplating the garments she had purchased, nor the hair covering. And she was barely ruminating upon Billy. Instead, she was trying to remember the last night of her film shoot. Although this was only a few weeks before, it seemed as if it had happened much earlier. Like her arrival in the city twelve years prior, with wrenching suddenness it had transformed ordinary perceptions. Movie posters, taxi cabs, taco stands: Everything looked different.

How had she gotten in so much trouble? How had Selva's body wound up in her car's trunk? How had she gone from a devoted adherent of the International Church of Life to someone they were pursuing and not, it seemed, with welcome intentions?

These questions brought her back to the moment when she had acted out the film's climax. This was the scene in which her character, the *femme fatale*, shot and killed Selva. The payoff for the entire story, everyone on the set had been anticipating it.

Because they had been filming from midnight to eight in the morning, there were parts of the shoot which were blurry. It was in the nature of things that you focused less on the scenes you were not in, even, or perhaps especially, when you were producing. That compelled you to be busy every instant. So you couldn't always be watching when they attempted the fifth or sixth improvisatory rendering of a sequence. Yet there had been unforgettable moments, and, as she had been occupied through the past several weeks with editing the footage, some of these had grown more precise in her recollections, gaining rather than losing in fidelity.

Driving down Wilshire with the sun overhead and her car window rolled halfway down, she thought back to the scene. It had been preceded by the penultimate one. This was the segment in which Selva's character told her off. Explaining that he was returning to his wife, he had almost off-handedly informed her that she was one of those people that you not only didn't need but didn't want to hear from. She was good, he said, for giving head, no more. Her presence exhausted him, and he was bored. While Vincenza had never thought

110

much of Selva as an actor, as he gazed into her eyes and intoned the words, she had sensed his candor. It seemed that he was saying what he really felt. He spoke in a dead, cold voice, one void of emotion or a hint of tenderness. With that Selva pushed her away, tearing the sleeve of her blouse.

That moment offered them a chance to pause, and Selva and most of the other cast members had taken advantage of it, wandering off ever so briefly. But she could not. Her immediate concern was not what she was to say but the gun. The prop master had given it to her before they had begun, and she had it ready in her handbag. Because he could see that she was anxious, he had told her to practice in order to make sure that the gesture looked real. Hence, while the other actors were passing around a hip flask and joking and flirting, she had clasped the weapon with both hands, twice discharging the blanks.

The first shot frightened her. In spite of the prop master's warning, she had not anticipated how loud it was. Then the actors had come back, and a crowd formed. Everyone was there: the cameramen, the grips, the gaffer, the director, the producers, the makeup artist, the entire cast, and more than a few of their friends. As it was approaching dawn, the sky outside was turning pink. Inside, though, it was as it had been for the last few hours: a dim yellow-brown.

The two preceding days had been a blur as they had raced to catch up, striving to complete the required scenes. This urgency was apparent in the performances. What was to come was vital, though, not only for her, but for all of them. As the books on the art of screen-writing she had relied upon invariably noted, a movie could survive many faults, but it would never succeed without the third act: a satisfying conclusion.

The silence in the room reflected their nervousness, and throughout the lead-up to the scene, Sara, her co-producer, had been hovering and pacing. Chilly as it was in the restaurant that served as their set, a coat of sweat was visible, dripping down her forehead. Vincenza understood this. Her hands were clammy. Sara gazed at her, encouraging her. That was followed by the director's motion for her to begin.

This was the cue for her action, which was to culminate with Selva's death. But she had hesitated. She knew from her classes that she must not rush. Before she spoke in reply, the cameras had to capture her range of emotions: anger, confusion, and despair. Then, wiping away a tear, she changed her expression to something purposefully inscrutable. Asking Selva to stop and come closer, she announced that she had something for him. As he approached, she had reached into her bag, pulled out the gun, and, grabbing it with both hands, fired three times. His face registered shock and incredulity as the bullets struck. He fell awkwardly, almost hitting his head on the linoleum floor. She watched as, lying on the ground, he slowly bled out. Accompanied by the cameras, she crouched beside him and listened as, in a little voice, he asked her why had she done this? Pale-faced, he gazed up in bafflement. It was not only her revenge that stunned him but the fact of his death. The tormented look lingered in her mind.

Moments later, they were celebrating, as it was finished. Nonetheless, she remembered that a part of her felt let down. Was it how Selva had acted? He had not even glanced at her when he rose from the floor, and he remained aloof through the rest of the morning. He was cavalier and, as dismissive as he was, she had asked herself if his rejection of her in the scene they had played was sincere. He had spoken to almost everyone but her: There was a laughing, affectionate interchange with Sara, then one with the director and another with Hutchins. Later, he had exchanged meaningful expressions with Lorelei and the makeup woman who removed the white cream from his cheeks. These looks all but openly declared that they were his lovers.

Yet this was not the paramount matter. That was something she only realized later. In studying the footage, she saw something else: When she had dropped the gun and it landed on the floor, a woman's small-gloved hand reached out to snatch it up. That left it with two perfect sets of her own fingerprints.

She contemplated this as the hands that had first held the gun arranged the position of a countertop mirror in the shop on Wilshire. The hair covering she was about to buy was in the Marilyn Monroe style, as platinum blonde as her hair was jet. She could not but be amused, eyeing herself with it on in the store. Her hair had never been anything but black, and she felt as though she were gazing at someone else's face. Taking out her lipstick case, she applied a shimmering red hue. A sports car shade, it seemed to multiply the effect of the wig and her new nose and chest, and the religious Jewish women in the store were staring at her with unconcealed enmity. She was the *shiksa* homewrecker, the temptress who was going to steal their husbands or, more likely, one of their sons. They could barely look at her. Her appearance had the capacity to turn one into a pillar of salt—but not kosher salt.

To hold such power was delicious, and handing her credit card to the merchant, she made a point of casting the *yentas* a properly cutting glance in return. Then, having set them in their places, she strolled back to her car, started her engine, and headed back towards Hollywood.

The experience was hard to let go of, and each time she paused at a light, she found herself ruled by an involuntary impulse to examine herself in the driver's side mirror. Did she look bad or unsavory? The possibility reminded her that she might soon be a suspect in a murder, and there wasn't a soul in the world whom she could count on. Would her mother or stepfather come from Minnesota if she were arrested and charged? More likely, they would disparage her to the reporters who would camp out in their driveway. Her sole ex-boyfriend not in the Church would treat it as a press op, while her actress friends were more devoted to their diets than to her. It was shocking but true: The Israeli mobsters employing her might care the most.

Her reflections were cut short as she drew closer to her place of work, the dispensary. Pulling up to an empty spot half a block above Hollywood Boulevard, she inserted a credit card into an electronic meter, feeding it. Then she noticed the recognizable black-and-white, two-toned paint job of a county police cruiser. Holding her breath, she watched as the car idled on the opposite side of the street. When the officer guiding it picked up a call and sped off, she inhaled.

Then she trooped back down to the intersection. Tour buses passed by, and she could make out the amplified voice of one of the guides, pointing out various nearby landmarks, like Grauman's Chinese Theatre. Around the bus were the usual clumps of vacationers in pastel sport shirts and plaid shorts. They traipsed over handprints and gilded stars: the markers of the avenue's Walk of Fame. She watched as they made pit stops, gawking at the names on the sidewalk, marveling or else registering disapproval. Looking beyond them, she scanned the boulevard for a minivan, or someone standing and waiting. Common sense told her that if a man was outside the shop in a car, he would be half-asleep and unlikely to recognize her. Doubtless it would be someone who had never seen her before, someone trying to identify her from an old photo.

But she did not see any such person, and she threaded her way through the ranks of the visitors, eventually reaching the dispensary entrance. The expressions on the faces of her co-workers told her that they were confused, uncertain who she was. Then, recognizing her, they were eager to know the inspiration for her getup. The green glow of the plants, mirrored on some of the shelves, made everything seem unreal in the shop. The odd somehow became normal, and it was easy enough to explain that it was preparation for a role.

CHAPTER 18

Busy as the dispensary was that afternoon, there was a hardly a moment when Vincenza could stop to reflect. The flood of customers making purchases and asking questions held in check her impulse to muse upon the many fears preying on her. She was anxious to learn the result of the callback. Most of all, though, she wanted to find out what had happened, how Selva had actually died.

Continually staggering ahead, she felt as if she had been shoved forward by events from which she would soon awake were she not unsure of how to go about rousing herself from the dream. Yet the rush of people passing through occupied her. Still, whenever there was ten seconds free, she drew her phone out of her purse, checking it for texts or messages. Their absence was maddening.

At closing time, she changed clothes, exited through the rear, scanned the territory around her, and set off towards Billy's apartment. She was already halfway when she remembered that she had agreed not to smoke there. At the same time, she did not want to toke on the street in Hollywood. This was not just because it might lead to a ticket. There was also the possibility of attracting homeless people. As such, she made use of the stops triggered by traffic tie-ups. Reaching into the glove compartment, she pulled out her stash, mixing this with a portion of a cigarette, rolling herself a half-inch-thick blunt. Then, with the windows up, she switched on the car's ventilation system and drew in four tokes. The last of these came as she arrived at a parking spot a block from Billy's. As this was hardly enough to bring an end to the feeling that she was plummeting into an abyss, she remained in the car, peering about in the faltering light, gazing fearfully for the appearance of a police officer while inhaling deeply.

That prompted a bald man walking by to gesture at her as though he were about to approach. It took her a moment to realize that he was a would-be john. Eyeing herself in the mirror, she understood the problem and ceased being indignant. It was the combination of the blonde wig, the neighborhood, and the parked automobile. He thought she was a hooker. Worse, he took her dismissive glance as an attempt at bargaining. It required a middle finger salute to rid herself of his attentions.

The man's retreat reminded her that she had to get out of the car, especially as it was turning cold, and she once again had gone without sustenance. Reaching the apartment, she found that Billy was away. In the morning, she had politely refused his offer of the contents of the fridge. Now she was famished. Rummaging, she discerned, among its shelves, the ingredients for a sandwich. This served to satisfy her as she took off her sandals and her wig, changed into a fresh-out-of-the-package pair of flannel pajamas picked up at Target, and lay down in the bedroom, flipping on the TV. The controller brought her to what she needed: a black-and-white movie featuring Linda Darnell and Jeanne Crain. Among the great surprises that had awaited her in Hollywood was the discovery of how few people knew or cared about old films. It baffled her. Often she had asked herself how other actresses could arrive in the city with such fervent yearning for success but not be inspired by their example, nor even by their outfits.

The sound of the jiggling of keys at the door frightened her.

It was Billy. While it irked her to have to pause in watching, she understood that her role as a houseguest obliged her to come out to the living room to offer a degree of interest and sympathy in his tribulations. Even so, she had to be careful not to be too responsive. Nor, as much as she might like, could she share her Mary Jane. These were paths towards paying rent lying flat on her back.

Still, when she saw his face, there was no effort involved in feeling compassion. It displayed twice the fatigue and half the puffiness of the loser in a prize fight. Indeed, he was so deflated that he hardly took notice at first of her sleepwear.

"What happened?"

"Everything's great. Great," he said. "But thank you for asking."

With that he threw himself down on the couch he would be sleeping on, inviting her to recline on a chair across the coffee table from him. His head was perched on a pillow. He placed one arm around it as though he were seeking consolation from it.

"This is about a girlfriend?"

He ran his free hand through the thinning shock of hair above his temples. "Sort of."

She waited for him to explain, knowing he would.

"I mean, she's *sort of* a girlfriend."

"Yes...?"

"We slept together, but I'm not sure she's all that into me." Saying this, he paused and belatedly took note of her attire. With this, Vincenza realized the problem it presented. She had purchased a size small. This was equivalent to a woman's two or four. However, her bosom was not that of the typical woman who garbed herself in a two or a four. The result was loose around her waist, revealing a hint of her navel. Yet it bunched up at the top. This compelled him to pretend that he did not notice, even as he began shifting his body in a vain struggle to conceal a change in the outline of his trousers.

That did not, however, deter him from going on with his plaint. She understood that this was an effort at manners, such as the male of the species was capable.

"It's cool," he said. "It's not a big deal."

"...You were supposed to get together tonight?"

"Sort of.... She canceled at the last minute. I had an invite to a film screening and asked her to come along. I guess I shouldn't have invited her out so soon. We just slept together for the first time Tuesday morning."

"*Morning?*"

"We went home together, but we were very drunk. So not much happened. *Then.*" He paused. "We've known each other a while, actually. College."

"And you'd always had a crush on her."

"No, not really."

It was obvious that he was not ready to let her in on more of the details, and, in any event, she had done her duty. His expression told her that much, and she yawned in order to place a period on the conversation.

"I suppose you must be tired," he said.

Signaling that this was so, she headed back to his bedroom, deliberately trying not to sway or swivel or do anything else that might excite him. There was more involved than the fact that they were sharing a one-bedroom apartment. The situation he was in resonated with her. She knew too well what he was feeling, and unavoidably this drew her back to her last conversation with Selva.

The room she was in had a great many books and CDs but nothing in the way of color or refinement. She was surrounded by masses of black plastic. The material lined a computer, a vinyl border between the corner of the floor and the wall, and the shelving of the self-assembled furniture. Virtually the only personal touch evident was the framed photographs of his parents and a younger sister. This made it into a near-perfect opposite to the room she had been in with Selva. That one was devoid of pictures but filled with light and soft pastel shades.

The occasion was not at the end of the film shoot, but four days before Selva's death. Chatting about the movie and what ought to be done with it, they were lying in bed with one another at the beach cottage. Inevitably, she was rewinding the tape loop in her mind, trying to recall his precise words, what exactly he had said about the film, striving to summon this back even as she fixated on the best moments of their lovemaking and the sensation of his hands on her skin and the look in his eyes. The contents of that tape would have to wait to be unspooled though. For her phone had a text message she had been desperately waiting for. It was from Sara. She had not heard from her for two days. That was out of character.

CHAPTER 19

Todd Gelber wasn't from Westchester, and he hadn't gone to Northwestern, Swarthmore, or Wesleyan. He had grown up in Van Nuys back when it was mostly white, and he had barely graduated from Cal State, Northridge. Surrounded by the children of privilege, he was anything but. To the same degree, when he toweled himself off after showering each morning, he could not but observe that he had more hair on his chest than he did on the crown of his skull. He was not one of the beautiful people, and he had never been one. Like many growing up in Los Angeles, he had always thought of the entertainment industry in the way that Iowans regard farming. It was the local business. It was something you did. He did not think of the production of movies and television shows as any different from the manufacture of doughnuts.

This affected his relations with actresses. He regarded them not with fascination but wariness. He knew what he looked like, and he knew why they flirted. If he had a ready intellectual understanding that other movers and shakers took advantage of their status, routinely trading this for sex, a part of him had never grasped the logic of it. He wanted to know that a woman in bed with him cared. An awareness that someone he made love to secretly despised him was wounding.

For this reason, Gelber did not tell actresses that he could do something for them *if.* There was no *if.* Quite the opposite: He often said that he was not in a position to do favors, that his job was merely to act on behalf of his clients, most of whom were well-established figures, names that ordinary people knew or faces they had seen. It was, he insisted, to put together deals and to review contracts. That it involved far more than that—that it called for judgments, lies, negotiations, and trades of all sort—he did not explain.

This was not to say that he had never had an affair. There was, in fact, a minor actress, now past forty, that he sometimes got together with. She was an attractive, if not overwhelmingly glamorous, woman, and she treated him as much as a friend as a lover. His times in her company were largely spent not in the act of coitus but listening to her complaints and discussion of her cats, her wayward children, and the injustice of her divorce settlement. This was comforting. While he knew that at some point she would (and did) ask his assistance, he recognized that she saw him as a part of her life. And if his wife was increasingly withholding in the bedroom, she was present and responsive to him. They were not two separate people silently eating meals together. *She* was the one who demanded his conversation, the one who talked about taking ski trips together, the one who reached over and snatched his hand, seating it in her lap.

This sense that you had to maintain a core as a human, that you could not allow yourself or others to become commodities, served him. It helped supply him with the insight required to tell material that had heart from that which was devoid of it, assisting in his rise.

It had a determining influence on how his meetings with women went as well. It had become a virtual axiom of the business: All agents were gay until proven hetero. Part of the reason for this was that most of the successful ones provided actresses with something Gelber did: an unstated but welcome indication that overt sexuality was unwarranted. An encounter with him was a safe space, and it had been so since before the term existed.

That did not mean that every actress appreciated this immediately. Reflecting the joint influences of Southern California's weather and its principal industry, many reflexively incline towards brazen displays of sexuality when they meet anyone who can do anything for them, and it sometimes required some time in Gelber's presence before they realized that a recalibration was required.

One such instance of this was the occasion when he had met Vincenza. That was a week after the completion of principal photography of her movie and three and a half weeks before her headlong flight from the Church of Life. Through the entreaties of Gelber's director friend, they had been introduced at a press conference for a new series the streaming service was premiering. Gelber listened with seeming ignorance as she had told him about what she was doing, her movie, and, as though motivated exclusively by the benevolence expected of an industry veteran towards a tyro, he had suggested that they meet for coffee to talk about it. At the press conference she had been dressed in what might be called the uniform: a tight-fitting top and a miniskirt that almost displayed a fringe of her pubic hair.

But Gelber was gratified to see when they met for a second time that she had grasped it: Contrary to his friend's expectations, he was not trying to seduce her, and she was attired in more respectable garb.

His entry into the coffee shop did not go unnoticed. Nor did the disparity in their looks and ages. So it was a good thing that she was wearing pants, low heels, and a sleeveless sweater, and that they were opposite one another, displaying body language that would be hard for anyone to misconstrue.

Shaking hands, he gestured for her to remain seated and went to order coffee. Then he returned and smiled benignly, explaining that he sometimes felt impelled to lend a hand to a newcomer and, while he couldn't say if his firm could have any interest in a film like hers, he would be delighted if he could advise her.

"I didn't have a chance to look at your IMDb profile," he said. "So I confess that I don't know whether you've had big roles like this before."

The initials were a reference to the Internet Movie Database, which lists a person's screen credits. He had, of course, checked it and was waiting to see if she would overstate her negligible resume.

"*Starring* roles? I mean I've been up for things, but no, not a *lead*."

He nodded his head, turned it to the right to check on the progress of their beverages, and then gave her his attention once more. "And you wrote and produced this? And got Tom Selva and Tom Hutchins to be in it? I take my hat off to you. I do. So many people come here, Vincenza, and, one way or another, they never really follow their dreams. You know: They get sidetracked, and they forget about them. Do you know what I'm talking about?"

"Of course. Like, how we forget dreams we had when we were sleeping. Sure. People get into PR, and pretty soon they think maybe that was their goal in coming to LA."

Though it was not in Gelber's nature to allow himself to be charmed by actresses, it was hard not to be by Vincenza. Yet, staring at her, he wondered if her nose had been fixed, and, if it had been, whether the doctor responsible was the one who had done his teenage daughter's.

"And you are planning to submit it to the festivals?"

"Exactly."

"And how soon will it be till you have a rough cut? Something you can show people?"

"*You* would look at it?"

It was not every day that Gelber felt some remorse in what he was doing. But he had some then. She seemed as aware of her situation as a plankton in the mouth of a whale. Nonetheless, facts were facts. This was his job, and if he didn't do it, someone else would. What was more, he knew better than to agree when someone right off offered him what he was seeking. This was basic negotiating. You always tried to operate with the principle that by the time you left a car dealership, they should be paying you to take their best Mercedes off the lot.

So, hesitating, he stood up and walked to the counter to pick up their coffees. Bringing the cups back in a molded cardboard tray, he gave her a serious expression which indicated that she was asking too much of him. He was the head of production, after all.

"You are a friend of Charles's?" he asked, referencing their mutual acquaintance. "Perhaps I could have an assistant look at it, and I could then try to refer you to someone."

"You would do that?"

"Look," he said, nodding sheepishly. "I can't spend all my time being Mother Teresa. But if you're a friend of Charles…"

"The sound isn't properly mixed, and we're going to replace the music. But I guess—if my co-producer is OK with it—I could show you something now."

Gelber knew at this point that it was best to look at her but not to say anything. Instead, he sipped his overboiled coffee, giving her the pleasant but bland smile which he had perfected through twenty years of dealmaking. Inwardly, though, he was rubbing his hands together. That was how he became involved in the events surrounding Selva's death.

CHAPTER 20

Billy Rosenberg sometimes thought that if there were a talent for bad timing, he had it. When his novel sold, he had a girlfriend. This was the period in which the Tinder dating site was at the acme of its popularity. It was one of those brief moments in history when women accepted the practice of sleeping with men on first dates—or what were not even dates.

He had always felt slightly uneasy with random encounters. He sensed that most of the women engaged in them were actually seeking boyfriends, and, while he felt only so much guilt about their discomfiture, he desperately wanted to have a good opinion of himself. That presented an issue since there was an incompatibility between this wish to have pride in who he was and the practice of taking advantage of the momentary popularity of concepts like "friends with benefits" and Tinder hookups. So even when things with his girlfriend were at their shakiest, he told himself that he was right to stay clear of casual sex.

This conviction was buttressed by a recollection of what it had been like to be barely more than five feet tall as he entered high school. Still conscious of those unfortunate days, he did not wish for anyone to suffer the mistreatment and heedless disregard by the opposite sex that he had—even members of the opposite sex.

Nonetheless, when he had been studiously monogamous, it bothered him that his male friends were sexual adventurers, lubriciously exploring the wilds of Brooklyn and the vaginas of Santa Monica.

What came next showed his gift for bad timing. After his book had flopped and the publisher had turned down his follow-up, Billy had decamped to Los Angeles. Yet, as his girlfriend chose to stay in New York, they had broken up. This happened just as Tinder faded. The result was that his fantasies of exciting, wonderfully tacky sexual encounters were thwarted. That stamp would not go on his passport. The new dating apps coming into vogue promoted relatively chaste practices, and, partly in consequence, he had been through an extended dry spell. Indeed, his encounter with Claire had been his first sex in seven months, and that previous occasion in which he had gotten nooky took place on a weekend when an ex-girlfriend was in town, staying with him.

His meetups with women were putrid. He did not like to reflect on it, but on two occasions his dates had effectively ended when he had arrived to pick them up. Seeing his model of car and its age, they had started to make excuses, and in retrospect he wished they had called the evenings off. By the end of them, he envied substitute teachers. However much they were mocked, they got paid. He had picked up the checks.

Now things with Claire were headed in the wrong direction. He had decided to aim for a second meetup with Claire near her place. His supposition was that they would go back there afterwards. That had prompted his suggestion that she meet him at a film screening on West Pico, which was a short drive away. But even as he had made the proposal, he had sensed it was a mistake. Intellectually, he understood it: Given her hesitation, he would be best off not calling her for several days, keeping in touch by text. Yet, like a person who can't resist the itch to scratch a poison ivy rash, he had done what he knew he shouldn't.

Meanwhile, Vincenza's presence was driving him half-mad. He was suffering a potentially fatal case of the malady known as relegation to the friend category. While he genuinely enjoyed writing and rarely suffered from writer's block, no sooner had she departed in the morning than he had ceased composition. Where normally he risked injury to both hands from hours of typing, it was just the right hand which was afflicted by overuse. An instinctive belief that it would be bad form deterred him from going into his bedroom to peruse her things. He knew, in any event, that she had left her place with no more than a handbag worth of items. But he couldn't help reflecting upon them. At one point, this motivated him to set down a diary entry on his laptop. This read: "It's hard not to think about her perfume." Then, rereading it, he noticed that the second word in the sentence was too apt.

Her presence affected his sleep. Though only of average height, he was too tall to lay down easily on the couch. Consequently, his legs and back ached from being winched into it, and by two in the morning he was feeling particularly uncomfortable. Wide awake, he switched on a side table lamp, opened up his laptop, and tried to write.

Through a screen, he heard an occasional car passing. More infrequently, there were sounds of people on the street or an intermittent noise of the wind drifting down from the canyons. At the window, a soft flickering light reflected up from the building's pool. Eyeing this while listening to the low tones, Billy paused.

He was bothered, perturbed by a notion. A suspicion about Vincenza unsettled him. But contemplating it embarrassed him. What did it say that he had so little ability to trust someone who seemed to be the walking wounded? Yet the thought preyed on him, and, with his laptop open, he could not stop himself from typing in the words which Vincenza had recited about her meth dealer boyfriend, googling these to see if they might have come from a play or film.

Could this whole speech be an anthologized address, one that she might have memorized for an acting scene or an audition?

His cheeks turned brick-red as the screen of his computer returned a series of search entries connected to a movie called *Ozark Morning*. Wikipedia referred to it as a "critically acclaimed indie drama about a rural Arkansas family confronted by the brutal legacy of the meth trade." Elsewhere, it was described as "a hillbilly *Breaking Bad*." And sure enough, the affecting tale she had provided him was part of a collection, available through Amazon, called *Monologues For Future Stars*.

It was difficult not to feel it: What a dupe he had been! What a moron!

It was infuriating. Los Angeles is a place where everyone is nice, often aggressively so. Yet he could not but reflect: When you scratched beneath the surface, more often than not you discovered a scam. And all too often he was the one being hoodwinked.

Listening intently, he could almost make out the sound of her impressive chest, breathing in and out as she slept on his bed in his bedroom. He had put out his best sheets, freshly cleaned, for her. He had given her the toothbrush and mouthwash set, still in the package, from his last visit to the dentist. He had handed her his house keys and instructions about the pool, along with his beach towel. He had encouraged her to graze freely through his fridge and freezer. He had marked out a side where she might keep hygiene products and her makeup in the medicine cabinet.

Furious as he was, he was not about to march into the bedroom and wake her up in the middle of the night. He had seen the pink pajamas she wore, but it occurred to him that she had garbed herself in these in order to come into the living room. He was certainly going to throw her out, but he was not about to put this to her when she might be sleeping in the nude. She had looked bedraggled when she had popped up on his doorstep. Whatever was happening in her life, he would let her have one night of decent rest.

Regardless, he was on the clock with his *Arthur Rex* polish. That was due back with the production company in less than a fortnight, and, badly as he needed the money, he had to take advantage of any sleeplessness as time for labor. So, with this thought in mind, he went to work.

The rage, it turned out, inspired him. Every time he thought that he could make out her mouthfuls of air, he imagined the expansion of her already expanded bosom, and he typed faster. It wasn't until the sun was starting to peep in through the living room window that he finally went back to sleep.

During this time, he had prepared his own lengthy speech, a philippic the equal of Cato's addresses against Carthage. Everything about her was fake and phony. She was a cheat and a liar and a bad woman. She was a threat to goodness, and, inasmuch silicone was made from sand, she was a menace to the continued existence of the world's beaches.

Regrettably, the depth of his sleep nullified his carefully worked out plan of confrontation, and, by the time he awoke, she was gone. Entering the bedroom, he saw a bed, which had been made, and a few items sprawled out that were hers. Otherwise, there was little evidence that she had been present. It took him a moment to identify the one that might matter: She had left out the keys to her apartment.

WHILE BILLY WAS TRYING TO DECIDE what to do with the keys, Vincenza was getting ready for her meetup with her producing partner. That required a coffee run, one taking her into the shop where she had met Billy.

As it was just a few blocks from both of their apartments, she was walking to it. She was interrupted by a text from him. Taking off her sunglasses both to read it and to adjust to the light level she encountered inside, she read the message:

Know you are not involved with a meth dealer. Don't like being scammed and think we'd better talk.

The words immediately awakened her to the possibility—no, probability—that she was about to be tossed out. This was in her mind as she stepped to the counter and placed her order for a half-skim coffee, no sugar.

She had to ask herself: What else could go wrong?

Waiting at the side of the counter, she breathed in and glanced about. What she saw unnerved her. It was the "what else." Amidst the unfamiliar faces were two she knew: Gary and Fran. Worse, they appeared to be the only people who were not even momentarily fooled by her wig. With her sunglasses off, they recognized her and began speaking excitedly to one another. If it was too loud to hear their words, there was no point in pretending that they were strangers. The only alternative was to leave at once and stiff the store, which was her regular coffee spot.

There was nothing to do but hope for the best. She watched as they gestured for her to join them. When she demurred, indicating that she was waiting for her order, they failed to take the hint, got up and approached, smiling, leaving their mugs on their table. Wearing athletic attire that showed off their slim bodies, they came at her from opposite sides, hovering like open-mouthed fish. The friendly expressions on their faces made Vincenza even more uneasy.

Fran was the one who spoke first, poking her affectionately on the arm. "You look *so* much better now that you're away from him." She hesitated then. "You are free of him, yes?"

Vincenza wondered what the best way to be rid of them was. Instinctually defaulting to her habitual approach of being agreeable, she smiled back at them. "Yes, thanks. It's over. And I owe it to the two of you."

Hearing this, the couple gazed at one another. The glances that passed between them were soulful. Anyone who did not know them would have assumed that they were faithful high school sweethearts who took special pride in the honor-roll grades of their son in junior high and their prom-age daughter. It struck her then that a complaisant response was not the means to divest herself of their company. They were like Asperger's patients. They seemed unable to grasp subtext.

Thus, as clueless as his wife, Gary bared his rear teeth, grinning in carnivorous fashion. "By the way," he declared, letting her in on their happy secret, "we were both saying how much we love the wig. It really adds a quality of camp. Make-believe. That slightly hip, porno, flash-trash 1970s quality. We take it that it's something you use in your work."

"Actually, I was just trying to go incognito. What with the fight I've had with my man and all."

Vincenza saw that this declaration, informing them that they had misunderstood, didn't embarrass them in the slightest. They hadn't given up. In fact, they were even more determined. It was Fran who next took the lead, inching closer.

"We realized," she said, "that we should have said something that we didn't when we left you. So, permit us to say it now. We really believe in and support the cause of sex work, of those of you who *do* the work. We hope that you understand that if we didn't make it clear before."

Fran waited for her to digest this kernel before continuing.

"What that means is that whatever your rate is we're good with. We're professionals in *our* work, and we respect that *you're* a professional in *your* work. You don't owe us anything for what we did."

Vincenza was unsure what to do. Was the correct—one should not say proper—response to ask for an outrageous figure on the assumption that it would liberate her from their company? Or would that spark a negotiation regarding the terms? Or was the best tactic to explain, truthfully, that she had to be on her way? This last line of attack would leave her open to future entreaties. There was also the concern that she was likely soon to be flung out of her present abode. Were matters so grave that she was going to have to yield her skin to save her skin?

The arrival of the half-skim coffee gave her a moment's relief. But this was not freedom. She was distressed to see as she advanced to the counter and paid that Fran and Gary accompanied her. Their combination of persistent eagerness and toothy smiles unavoidably reminded her of pictures she had seen of a serial killer who moon-lighted as a clown at children's birthday parties.

Taking the change and putting two quarters in the tip jar, Vincenza picked up a stirrer with her cup. Then she nodded her head. While it was jarringly noisy in the shop, she did not feel comfort-able saying what she intended so close to the counter girl, and she began pacing towards the exit, confident that they would remain very much—literally—abreast.

"Why don't we talk about this later? As it happens, I have an appointment, and I have to be somewhere shortly."

This—and this alone—seemed to place them at more than arm's length, and with it Vincenza breathed a sigh of relief as she left the shop and stepped, cup in hand, towards her car.

Opening the door and sitting down in the front seat, she was struck by something anomalous. Though she was going through the most stressful week of her life, she was not experiencing a panic attack. This ran completely against what the Church had taught her. They had instructed her to come to them in times of trouble for their paid counseling sessions, and she had learned to rely upon them. Yet in some fashion it seemed as though she was getting stronger with each ordeal—and not with the aid of Church sessions, but by facing them herself and passing through them.

But she didn't have time to reflect on this. After all, were the traffic as dense as it appeared, she needed to focus on that, in order not to be late for her meeting with Sara. So, she reached for her purse before grabbing the steering wheel. Her intention was to send a text to Sara. She was stopped though by the sight of a text from the production company. It told her the outcome of her callback.

CHAPTER 21

David Clarkson had his calming rituals. One was to draw his index finger and thumb together while running them over the two sides of his lower lip. Another was to pace to the window and fiddle with the blinds. He had done both several times. Now he scrolled through emails. In five minutes, Vincenza was supposed to be arriving at Sara Kertesz's. That was the chance to pull her in, and he wished that he were there, not sitting in his office.

Was it the sympathetic tone of his voice that had persuaded Sara to tell them where to find Vincenza? Clarkson pondered this as he watched a light switch on, telling him to put on his headset. Through it, he heard his men, who were seated inside two vans outside Sara's apartment.

He thought about her. She had not proven to be as he expected. Vincenza had spoken of her on a number of occasions. What she said inclined him to be suspicious. The refrain of the conversations was Sarah's determined unwillingness to involve herself with the Church. Yet when he called looking for information on Vincenza's whereabouts she was not hostile or distant. In fact, he found that he had a natural rapport with her. Conscious that the Church was not an ideal subject, he had instead chatted with her about his years as an actor. That provided an opening.

It was a language he spoke fluently. The strange thing was that he couldn't talk with actors about many of their common experiences. Nonetheless, though it was unstated, this was part of the reason that he could serve the Church so ably—that he understood the indignities and knew this was something they concealed: the number of times every actor has been turned down for negligible roles, the struggles in obtaining auditions, that you had to put on a happy face and shut up about come-ons and solicitations. While he was more than glad those days were over in his life, that he had not forgotten them was apparent, and it made him part of their tribe. So it had not taken long for him to make Sara laugh and then to listen as she was happily interrupting him with her own stories.

Now his deputies were in their minivans along her street in Silver Lake. He tried not to gnash his teeth as he listened to their voices telling him that Vincenza was parking her car down the block. She was roughly thirty yards away, they said, from Sara's ground-floor apartment.

Earlier they had described the street: an ordinary residential block with wide sidewalks and few trees obstructing their sightlines. He had been a participant on calls like this before, and he was accustomed to the babble of voices that arose when a married reporter or a tax agent came into view beside his lover in a parked car. Then they had been waiting to take photographs. Those experiences had taught Clarkson patience. Consequently, he was not unnerved when the men began complaining that Vincenza was idling, not getting out of her sedan. The street, they noted, was relatively level with just a slight rise in grade moving towards them. Nothing was on it but two small schools at opposite ends, a parking lot adjoining one of the schools, and an apartment building and a handful of private homes in between.

One voice was especially familiar. It was Cliff Stoop's. He was pointed in saying that the schools were almost out of sight of Vincenza's car, and there was no one around. As Clarkson had always thought that Stoop was a toy soldier, he was quite astonished to realize what Stoop was suggesting: They ought not to wait for Vincenza to get out and go to Sara's house, which was shaded from view, before intercepting her there. Rather, they should approach her right on the street. This was precisely what Clarkson had told them not to do, fearful as he was of a scene that might attract attention.

Clarkson's first exposure to the Church had come through a fellow acting student who had explained that it might help him better understand himself and, through that, better grasp the art of acting. From the first, though, he had seen that it offered something more: The opportunity to save the people of a dying planet. Realizing that goal required a measure of ruthlessness. There was no shame in that. How could there be? The Church needed capable officers, and he had the skills and the willingness to do what others wouldn't. This logic applied equally to what they were doing with Vincenza. But though there was nothing *morally* wrong with their actions, as a lawyer he knew that none of it was quite legal. They hadn't killed Selva, and they were about to tell the police where his corpse was. More than that, they were going to try to persuade one of their adherents to confess. Still, Clarkson knew that just one of these acts could get him disbarred, and, taken together, they could lead him to a prison cell. His training made him list the offenses. The failure to duly report the discovery of the body was obstruction of justice, as was the destruction of part of the security tape from the beach cottage, and a clever prosecutor could even argue that trying to pick Vincenza up and interrogate her apart from the police made them accessories after the fact. So they had to be careful. They did not want anyone to see them approaching Vincenza, then asking her to come with them. The problem was that the Supreme Pilot had given them a measure of time in which to grab hold of Vincenza and that stretch of hours was running out, and though he could waste energy contemplating the dearth of resources available to him, a prompt solution was required.

A geosynchronous map and the accompanying pictures on his computer confirmed what his men had described. The parochial and public schools were at a remove from Sara's house, which was on a side street. Yet there was still a risk that a student might observe them or a driver might suddenly slow down, passing at a speed at which he might witness a scene taking place.

A minute went by as they watched her. Stoops's voice came in again then, announcing that she was texting and making a call, still not exiting her car. Then another quarter hour passed. The clock on Clarkson's computer showed that it was 11:45 a.m., fifteen minutes past the time when she was due at Sara's.

"There isn't any traffic. It's absolutely dead at the moment. We haven't seen a kid come out of either school. And no one's left the apartment complex." Stoops was speaking once more, making his case. Running his thumb around his lower lip, Clarkson gnashed his teeth. The risk was hard to calculate. Only if Vincenza really made a disturbance was anyone likely to notice men trying to accost her on the street. Was it so perilous to tell Stoops to go ahead and speak to her in open view about coming with them to the Church headquarters?

In her car, Vincenza was directly opposite the two minivans. Stoops was one of the two men in the front seats of the nearer vehicle, and, as she chatted away on her phone, she was gazing towards them. Clarkson knew the minivans, and he remembered that their front windows were composed of tinted glass. Bright as it was outside, was it possible that she was near enough even so to see them watching her? And might that be deterring her? Clarkson nudged the headset's microphone towards his lips. "Do you know if she can see you?"

"She's a hundred feet away. She'd have to have fantastic eyesight. We're using binoculars."

"In other words, you can't be sure?"

Stoops hesitated before answering. "Well, no," he said. "Not definitely."

CHAPTER 22

The front gate of the apartment building was identical to Billy's own. Now he placed Vincenza's key in its lock and turned the tumbler, opening it.

Finding her address wasn't hard. All that was required was a search of the internet. A site providing unknown phone numbers revealed not only where she lived but that they were the same age, each about to turn thirty.

As in his building, the front gate led out to a courtyard with a swimming pool and apartments formed into a rectangle flanked around it. Climbing a flight of steps, he approached her apartment on the second floor. While he had a high degree of certainty that there was no meth den and there were no armed drug dealers inside, he advanced with deliberate steps, and, reaching the door, he pressed his ear—and his nostrils—to it. These provided him with no peculiar scents and no noises from within. There was likewise no response to his knock.

He was discomfited by what he was doing. The inspiration for it was less a sense of grievance that he had been conned than curiosity. Who was she? Why had she done this to him?

The door was alike to his own. Painted a slate gray, it was surmounted with a pewter knocker. Beneath this was a pewter knob. His unease was partly assuaged by the feeling that he was opening his own door. He reminded himself that he had given her keys to his place, and she might well be examining his apartment. Setting a key into the lock, he unbolted her door. Behind it lay carpeting of the sort one encounters in beachfront cottages: a white cotton rug with a pattern of blue waves on it.

The room was ordinary: neither shockingly messy nor frighteningly tidy. It was lived in. There was a bookcase on one side and an armoire on the other. He remembered that when he had met Vincenza she had mentioned her involvement with the International Church of Life, and he noticed that its handbooks and therapeutic guides were among the volumes on the bookshelves. There were also coffee-table tomes on old Hollywood style, volumes on the environment and an assortment of cookbooks. Half-open, the armoire displayed an assortment of vintage dresses, blouses, and skirts.

On the wall beside her bed he spied a framed poster calling for a ban on whaling. Alongside this were DVDs of classic black-and-white movies from Hollywood's Golden Age and hardcovers on old-time actresses like Joan Blondell and Carole Lombard.

Something, he understood, was wrong. This was not the apartment of a grifter. Billy knew that the conventions of B-movies were false. A criminal didn't have fake passports and stacks of cash lying around. But a woman who was in the business of preying upon scuffling writers didn't live like this. For that matter, a *bona fide* fraudster—if such an oxymoronic concept existed—didn't target people like him. She went after celebrities or aging men with comb-overs who drove Bentleys. Her name was fake. That was proven by the website that had given him her address. Listed among her family members was a Martha Haines and a Peter Loehringer and several other relations in Minnesota, none of whom had the surname Morgan. There was also the matter of her augmented breasts and her exquisitely delicate nose. But these were the Los Angeles equivalent of what friends in New York had done, obtaining graduate degrees in writing. It was a normal, almost expected course of professional induction. That she had a few pretentions and grand ambitions was in no way out of the ordinary, and it did not explain either her apartment or her lies to him. Her possessions were not those of a person who identifies with the prowlers in stalker movies. Nor were there body parts in her refrigerator. There was store-brand mayonnaise and diet cola.

This left one last test. He was not about to open her desk or clothes drawers. But he was anxious to know what pill bottles were in her bathroom. Were there antipsychotics or drugs for bipolar disorder? Flicking on the light switch in her throne room, he was presented with a checkerboard tile pattern on the floor and brass faucets on the sink. Reaching forward and pulling aside the plate glass of the cabinets, he eyed a mess of toiletries. There was nothing in the way of prescriptions, though. There were not even antidepressants, a palliative as common in actress's medicine chests as chewable vitamins in dinosaur patterns are for Middle-American toddlers.

What did it all say? While he was perfectly aware that sexual attraction could make any man into a fool, the contents of the apartment seemed to tell one story: Vincenza was not mad. Whom—or what—she had cause to be apprehensive about, he could not say.

This was not altogether welcome news. Were he to tell her that he had entered her apartment, she would consider it a violation. Nor were his actions lawful, and he wanted her out as soon as possible so that he could have Claire over.

The sound of a dog barking in the apartment next to Vincenza's reminded him that he was taking a risk in being there, and it prompted his retreat.

He needed the money for his work on the *Arthur Rex* script, and it had to be completed, preferably to the production company's satisfaction, in days. But, even if he couldn't say why, he was worried about Vincenza, and no sooner was he out of the building then he took out his phone. The sun had come out, and it was turning into a warm day. Up on Franklin Avenue, he heard a car with a faulty muffler passing by. It was half past eleven when he dialed her number.

Knowing he was the one calling, she did not bother with a salutation. "I know you don't believe a word I'm saying, and I'm sorry. You have a right to be pissed. I'll leave whenever you want."

Her voice was typically husky, but she sounded scared and ashamed. There was something almost childlike in her intonation.

"I guess I was harsh. But why did you make up that story?" He listened as she paused, uncertain what she should reveal to him.

"I know you're not going to believe me, Billy. But I think I am in some trouble."

"Where are you?"

"Parked in a car on a street in Silver Lake. I know how crazy this sounds, but I think there are men watching me. In matching vans. I know you must think I'm delusional on top of everything. But it's true. I was afraid to go back to my place. That's why I came to you. I've been followed for several days."

He realized that she had the natural equipment to be an effective performer. She bled emotion. What was more, she had that ability to make people feel guilty for not fretting sufficiently about her.

"Why me?"

"You sounded honest, not like every other guy I know."

"You mean you weren't concerned that I'd try to get you high or drunk to have sex with you?"

"Well, that's part of it."

"And...? Did you do something? Or, should I say, what did you do?"

The way that she sighed told him as much as any words.

Anger had awakened an unexpected directness from Billy. It had made him sexy, transforming him from a supporting player into a leading man. Much too conscious of this, he wished that he could inscribe the impulse, that he could make himself into someone other than who he was. But he knew it too well: He was like a jazz pianist who had knocked out a few chords of an unfamiliar song in an unaccustomed style. Reflexively, he would return to the rhythms and melodies he was used to playing. Speaking with a woman he wanted to sleep with, he would avoid confrontation. No matter how much she yearned for a man who projected authority and determination, he was diffident, cautious, and restrained.

This was not helping Vincenza. The pause in which she had held off from telling him how she had gotten into trouble was running on, and although he recognized that he should go on pressing her, the disdainful rage that had pushed him to make her open up was gone. Now he felt fear and shame that he was about to make a woman cry.

"I'm sorry," he announced. "I shouldn't have said that."

He heard her hesitate once more, and he understood what it meant. She was disappointed in him. She felt that he was letting her down by not pushing her. Struggling to make up her mind about a decision, she wanted to be led to it.

Because it was his business to gauge what lay within another person, he sensed this and was humbled. The layers of feeling and instinct that he encountered in sensitive women were so many more than his own. When he wanted to eat a hamburger, he considered whether or not to garnish it with pickles. They weighed the moral ramifications of the act, the likely effects on the environment and their figure, and the retrograde motion of Jupiter.

"I can leave your place tomorrow, go back to my own. I hope you'll forgive me. I'm going to visit a friend. That's why I'm in Silver Lake. Maybe I can stay with her."

As much as this appealed to him, Billy was now the one who vacillated, asking himself what to say.

CHAPTER 23

"Villains are the heroes of their own lives."

Claire was fond of the phrase, and more than once she had written it at the top of her sheets of character notes. But she set it down with an ironic smile with respect to a role in a project that she had been trying to put together for over a year. Though the part was not one she would play, her pursuit of it was single-minded.

The character was Alex Forrest, the central female figure in *Fatal Attraction*. Watching the movie, Claire was fascinated by how caricatured and underwritten all the women in it were. This was especially true of Alex. She was said to be a publishing executive. Yet the audience was left with no sense of what she did in this job, although impressive as her office was, her work must have entailed meaningful duties which only a reasonably competent, levelheaded woman could perform. More strikingly, early on in the film her character makes a half-hearted suicide attempt in order to hold the hero's attention. When this fails to draw him in, she tells him that she is carrying their child, and she will not have an abortion. Finally, still consumed by the memory of a mere two nights of pleasure, she stalks the hero, desperate as she is for his love. In the end, he is saved by his adoring wife, who shoots the pregnant villainess in the chest.

What were paying customers being offered? A fantasy calculated to appeal to the male ego, plainly. Women's work was irrelevant, unintended conception was a device used to ensnare that could disappear through happenstance, and it was the female, not the male, who was prone to violence and fixation, engulfed by the power of sexual desire. The middle-aged hero was demonstrably potent, graced with a gorgeous and caring spouse and fundamentally decent. Wasn't a remake of the film, one that provided it with credibility and relevance, overdue?

In the version Claire aimed to produce, the Alex Forrest character was no villainess. The bad guy was the corporate lawyer who knocked her up, disappeared, and then stalked *her*. His threats and menacing came after she contacted him about a paternity lawsuit. It was the needed feminist retelling of the story, and an ideal role for a forty-something actress like Charlize Theron or Amy Adams.

Claire thought about this as she set down her notebook and switched on her interactive "mirror." Essentially a full-length, two-way video screen set on the wall, it was designed to offer guided, online exercise sessions in which a trainer provided live feedback. Hers was a yoga class, and for it she placed her mat half a dozen feet forward of her bed. Above her head, the sun was slicing through one of her windows, drenching the apartment in light, and at first she had difficulty making out the teacher appearing on the screen. But soon the angle of the sun shifted the square of light to a different patch on the wall. A familiar face, the yoga instructor was another Hollywood actress.

Setting herself down on the mat, Claire tried to empty her mind, knowing that the poses she was about to assume required utmost concentration. But it was in her nature to ruminate, and she was pressed to think about the extent of her privilege. The flip side of this was *noblesse oblige*. She hadn't gone to an Ivy League college and then through an MFA acting program to become one of these creatures she met so often, actresses who continually visited plastic surgeons so that they might get parts as the *love interest* or the *girlfriend of the hero*. She had to be better than that. She was sure of it: The word "part" had to mean more than a series of lines in a script. It had to be an instrument by which each performer took on a distinctive function in the work of reconstructing and renewing—mending—the world.

Setting herself into downward-facing dog, she contemplated what she was doing, her desire to create her own production company to tell stories that would be both commercial and significant. *Fatal Retraction*, as she liked to call it, was at the top of this list of projects, and, although her dream was to play the heroine, she understood that getting the movie financed and lensed was the goal.

Her consciousness of this was made more acute by the instructor guiding her into a handstand and the sun salutation. The teacher had not had a boob job, but the Botox on her forehead and the collagen in her lips were hard to miss, even through a video screen. Claire had looked her up on IMDb after her last session. That yielded a link to an acting reel displaying performances in slasher movies. Claire hoped that her face didn't tell her that she knew this was what the instructor acted in and she was pondering it.

What could be done? The question was hard to avoid. The instructor was drawing her through a range of positions: lotus, upward dog, *shavasana*. Claire listened to the class's soothing, new age music, but she could not help but remember the sounds in the teacher's movie. The contrast was unsettling. Unavoidably, Claire recalled the creepy, discordant music underscoring the action: low, rattling percussion beats. These were accompanied by screams. Now attired in fitness clothes, the teacher had been crawling around in panties as the killer took pleasure in cutting her arms and her butt cheeks with a switchblade. It was hard for Claire to get the images out of her head. Standing, she extended herself into more poses: chair, eagle, dolphin, half-moon, and finally warrior one and warrior two.

Finishing her session, she thanked the instructor and waved goodbye to her online classmates. With that she slumped over, spent. Now all she could do was think.

Was she making progress? Her parents doubted it. Whenever possible, they suggested that she was wasting her time in Los Angeles, chiding her and telling her that she should return to Seattle to work in the family business. But they did not understand what she was aiming to do or the number of steps required for it.

The short film she had made was a calling card. So, too, was the loft apartment. A recent purchase, it had been made possible by the terms of her trust fund, which gave her the greater portion of her wealth on her thirtieth birthday. Knowledge of the business had taught her that this was a way to advertise the money to get a project off the ground.

To that end she had recruited a top entertainment lawyer, then joined up with her former boss at the production company she had interned at. She had learned from him that one had to be cautious in talking about projects as ideas could be stolen, and she constantly tried to remind herself of his lesson that every person you were collaborating with had to believe that he was the focus of your plans.

She had managed to persuade one of the best-known showrunners in the business to attach herself to the *Fatal Attraction* remake, and she had gotten a famous friend to sign a letter of attachment to play the wife. The last step to rendering it into a saleable property was obtaining the rights to the original. This required the permission of Viacom, and she had just succeeded in setting up a meeting with the company to pitch them on the idea. She was so close, and such a success as a producer was sure to open up a thousand opportunities, including great ones for her as an actress. This was life-changing power. What made her doubt herself was what had happened with Billy Rosenberg. Why had she gotten drunk and slept with him?

She *had* a boyfriend. Yes, it was true that he was married, and, as such, she was in not a position of obligation. But he was her business partner and former boss, and hardly a day went by when he didn't speak of his intention of leaving his wife, of how they would work together and create projects expressly for her. Billy's script showed promise, great promise even. There was no denying that. But his name counted for little, and by itself that meant it was not easy to sell.

Full realization of the mistake she had made had not come with Billy's impotence. It had hit her when they had gone back to the Korean barbecue restaurant, and she had seen his car. Shabby and old, it announced his struggles in neon lights.

The class ahead of him at Dartmouth, she had once been in position to help decide if they would tap him, asking him to join her senior society, Casque and Gauntlet. She remembered the discussion. They had been formed into a circle in the living room of the group's old brick mansion. His name had arisen at the suggestion of a boy who thought that the intensity of Billy's intellectualism hinted at future achievement. Past members of the club included Theodore Geisel: Dr. Seuss. The boy speaking for him was convinced that Billy could become that sort of man someday. The girl intent on blackballing him asked if he had distinguished himself at the school, as Claire had through her memberships in the *a capella* singing group the Decibelles and in the Harlequins, the student musical society. Thinking he was an awkward personality, Claire had voted against.

Now she had to find a way to place a degree of distance between them, a space that wouldn't preclude her from working with him later on, however uncomfortable that might subsequently be. What she couldn't do was allow her idealistic goals to be crushed by something so foolish as an affair with a man who was incapable of helping her.

Pulling herself up, she strolled over to her armoire. She was stopped in the act of changing clothes by a worrisome thought. In the excitement with Billy she had not managed to get her diaphragm in properly, and they had made love near the height of her cycle. What if, like Alex Forrest, she was pregnant?

CHAPTER 24

Sara's initial text simply said: "Apologies. Have been in hiding. Will explain everything that's happened. Sorry to be out of touch. When can u please, please meet? 1000 times sorry. Love u." Alongside this was a big love emoji and another depicting a smiling cat.

That was her. Yet, like the texts that followed, it was scrupulous in not saying much. What did that mean?

Perhaps stranger was the idea that the Church was not what it appeared. While Vincenza had been toying with this notion, she found it difficult to accept. Almost since the hour she had come to Los Angeles, it was home. It helped her understand herself. It required sacrifice and alms from its members, and it was readying the planet for the day of leave-taking. Could it really be something so different from what she had supposed?

Rolling down her driver's side window, she lit up a cigarette, took a drag and tossed a few embers into her ashtray. This act often brought back memories. Now it drew her back to Mr. Anderson's honors eleventh-grade psych class.

The architecture of Burnsville High was an example of the most antiseptic modernism: high-ceilinged spaces inside and flat, monolithic walls outside. Much of the year its beige concrete exterior was partly draped in snow, and, large and frigid as the rooms were, the students liked to seat themselves by the ventilation ducts. In that long cold season, other girls wore short skirts, if keeping their parkas on. The scents returned. Not yet a regular smoker, she had been able to identify each cheap perfume and the odors of sweat and bar soap of the boys.

Mr. Anderson's favorite subject—his refrain—was how common mental illness was. You couldn't leave a class without doubting your sanity. Paranoia, obsessive-compulsive disorder, schizophrenia, kleptomania, gambling and drug addiction, psychopathy: They were all around us. It was just a matter of time before you had a breakdown, and the snakes slithered out. As he put it, there was only abnormal psychology.

Was this what had happened? She could rule out schizophrenia as she wasn't hearing voices. But might she be suffering from a manic episode or psychotic depression? The cigarette was real. So was the street she was on, and the two Church minivans on the opposite side of the street, curiously close to Sara's apartment. And Selva's corpse was beyond dispute.

But might she be suffering from a clinical bout of paranoia? Might the experience of driving around with the cadaver of a man she had been involved with have unhinged her? Was it possible that there was no one following her and years of competing for the entertainment industry's table scraps had left her vulnerable to a divorce from reality?

Letting go of Billy's call, she deposited the butt of her cigarette in the ashtray, clutched at her phone, and dialed Sara. She waited for her to pick up, keeping an eye on the vans opposite her and the men in the front seats, partially concealed by tinted glass. Then she turned on the phone setting, permitting her to make a recording of the conversation.

"It's great to hear from you," Sara allowed. "Are you nearby?"

Why did the words sound scripted? Was it her imagination that she sounded different, as Clarkson had somehow been forced and off?

"I'm sorry. I had some car trouble. I think I can be there soon." Vincenza paused. She realized that there was no point in delaying it.

"Great."

The way she said the word seemed to add extra syllables. Then she laughed and continued. "We need to talk, Vincenza. There's a lot to explain. How soon will you be here? I assure you it'll all be good once we've talked—the movie, everything."

One thing which had always attracted her to Sara was how natural and unaffected she was. Whether someone was beside her, listening in, or she was involved in some wild scheme, Sara did not seem that now. Vincenza's instincts screamed to her to drive away. The laugh was fake. The tone was false. This intuition was fortified by what she saw across the street.

The men in the van were getting out and marching towards her. This compelled her to drop the phone and press the ignition, starting the engine. Then she put her foot to the gas, made a U-turn, and flew towards Sunset Boulevard.

Could she return to Billy's? Was it safe to go to work at the dispensary? Should she call the police? The questions piled on top of another. But the last response was beginning to make the most sense.

She wondered if they would think she was insane. Her rearview mirror told her that she was not. The men who had left the vans were running back to them with the obvious intention of chasing after her. So, turning right on Sunset, she headed towards the downtown and the area south of Silver Lake. Typically congested as it was, she peered into the mirror to see if the van was behind her.

She had been avoiding the inevitable—the police—for two days. Her reasons went beyond the fact that she had transported Selva's body. That was terrifying. Still, because she had not killed him, a part of her was convinced that she could persuade others this was so.

Looking out, she observed what a glorious Los Angeles afternoon it was. A magnificent sun sat directly over her head. Yet she did not feel confident. One thing that particularly concerned her was the possibility that Sara was somehow involved in the murder and that this would tie up the film. Were that so, more than likely no one would come to know of her achievements as an actress or a writer. At best, she would have twelve seconds of fame on the gossip shows. And she would never get that small role, the two scenes in the Reese Witherspoon movie, which had been promised to her. If she avoided prison, she would nonetheless wind up a contestant on *Big Brother*, a D-list celebrity. She would write a memoir no one read and watch as a producer optioned her story with the hope of making a TV movie starring someone else.

That was not all. She had gone to great lengths to deny it to herself, but she had feelings for Selva, quite intense emotions, and going into a police station and revealing what she knew meant acknowledging the fact of his death.

Taking out a blunt from the glove compartment, she pressed the button to roll down her window, lit it up, and stared in the side mirror. She examined her face. It was prettier than she had once thought. Perhaps it was beautiful. But she could already see crow's feet around the eyes and a leathery texture appearing in the skin. Her lips were becoming thinner. Time was passing. The movie was her chance. Going to the police might toss that away.

Yet more disturbing was what she saw in the rear-view mirror: One of the vans was perhaps fifty yards behind her, weaving around cars and motorcycles, racing to catch up.

Directly in front of her was Sunset's intersection with Silver Lake Boulevard. Seeing this, she made a sharp left and swung onto it, dashing south towards the 101. Stopped by a traffic light, she searched on her phone for a police station. The nearest, it turned out, was on West 6th. With the van trailing her, she needed to reach it as soon as possible. There was no longer an alternative. Telling herself that she did not look stoned, she tossed what was left of the blunt out the window and pulled into the police station parking lot.

Gazing at the sign, she belatedly realized what she had done. The grotesque white concrete building in front of her was Rampart Station. Without thinking, she had brought herself to the nation's most infamous precinct house.

CHAPTER 25

Ray Chalmers was having a hard time believing his luck. His chances of promotion were largely dependent on the number of his collars—the arrests he made. And right around noon a beautiful actress had walked into the precinct house and asked to report her knowledge of a homicide. Her story was incredible. This was to say that he didn't think it was derived from events on planet Earth. But, if it were, then he had just heard her implicate herself in the biggest Los Angeles murder case since O.J. Simpson had decided that he needed to trim his child support payments. If Tom Selva had been shot to death, she was surely the perpetrator, and he was listening to one of the most damning statements imaginable.

It was one astonishing admission after another. It began with acknowledgment of her intimate, adulterous relationship with the deceased. Then there was her assertion that she had driven around with his corpse in her trunk, a body that she claimed to have dumped in the garage of a Malibu beach cottage.

He had been in the precinct for all ten of his years on the police force, and while he had not been present during the unpleasant period when the scandals with which the station house was known had taken place, he had seen a fair amount. An enormous quantity of paperwork, bureaucracy, institutional idiocy, and tedium had been matched by infrequent moments of terror.

Now he was listening to someone sexy, fascinating, and bizarre telling him a potentially life-altering tale. It was like discovering the entrance to a gold mine in the cracks of the asphalt at the edge of your driveway as you deposited the morning trash. Too good to be true as it was, throughout her account he had tried to maintain a steady, level gaze and a sympathetic expression while he let the video camera at the ridge of the ceiling record her words.

Three things worried him. The first and most obvious was that she was exactly what she appeared: a crazy, unemployed actress in desperate need of an audience—any audience—and that not a single word of it had happened. The second was that her story was true, but the cottage was just over the county line in Ventura, and their detectives and prosecutors would claim jurisdiction. The third was that a whack-job Liberal judge might toss her statement as it was not being made in the presence of an attorney.

The last concern was connected to a possible reason to disbelieve the lot of it. Her pupils were dilated, and the whites of her eyes were red in a month when seasonal allergies are unknown. She was more than a little stoned. This fit with something else she had said: She worked at a dispensary.

Chalmers knew that sufficient quantities of pot might induce a paranoid break in seemingly stable people, and she spoke in a wobbly tone of voice that told anyone paying attention that "stable" was not a term rightly applied to her, no more than to a teen idol in rehab. There were other telltale details that tallied with this inference. In particular, she kept speaking about men who were following her. She insisted that the latest among this number were in a van that had tailed her right up to the instant she had arrived at the station's parking lot.

At the same time, there was lucidity in her speech and an abundance of detail which suggested that some of it might be so. One particular fixation was the Church of Life. Her talk about Selva had repeatedly noted that he was something called an F.U.P., a designation of some sort within the cult.

Eager to believe that he was not wasting his time with a madwoman, Chalmers permitted her to pull a pack of cigarettes out of her bag and smoke as she talked, and he had even gone briefly to get her an ashtray. This was in spite of repeated memos instructing him that the interrogation rooms were no-smoking areas. These messages from his superiors about procedure went along with detailed correspondence and rule books on what qualified as a pensionable basis for absence, how officers were to be reimbursed for costs related to maintaining their uniforms, when and how to park on the street, permitted types of facial hair, and a thousand other minutiae. What higher-ups spent little time discussing was how to break important cases.

The room they were in looked like a thousand other interrogation rooms. The sides, painted a cool cream, were composed of cinder blocks. Fluorescent lights were fixed in the ceiling, and a wide chrome table was between the gunmetal chairs in which they rested. As is so often shown in detective series, there was a two-way mirror affixed to the wall on the side opposite to those being questioned. The only way in which the room defied clichés was in its scrupulous cleanliness and in the appearance of the men employed in it. Like so many Los Angeles police units, the squad was composed almost exclusively of officers, like Chalmers himself, who were notably fit.

As she had not been formally designated as a suspect, Chalmers was under no pressure to cinch the knot: to get her to sign a statement repeating her remarks and admitting her guilt. That would come. For now, he had to smile kindly and ask her to wait a moment. With that, he left her and went back to the detectives' room. This was where she had been brought after she had approached the desk officer with her story. What he needed to know was whether there was any means of corroboration. He contemplated this with a keen awareness that he was likely to be rebuked by his superior for wasting two valuable hours in her company—if there was nothing to her tale.

The detectives' room was down a corridor from the interrogation room. This hallway was unlike those in movies in that it was generally empty. There were no hookers kept there and no weary cat burglars waiting for their lawyers. Nor were many detectives present, as the precinct had never recovered from its scandals, and it was understaffed. Even in daylight hours it was a room almost forty feet wide, which typically had half a dozen unoccupied desks, and there were more of those than there usually were when Chalmers entered. That was because three of his fellow detectives—like him, men who had only recently been kicked up from patrol—were standing with their backs towards him. Eyes fixed upon a television placed on a stand that had been wheeled in, they were caught up in watching it. Approaching, he saw that the screen showed a dense crowd of reporters and cameraman outside what appeared to be a seaside cottage. Raised in Los Angeles, Chalmers knew that it was Malibu. With that recognition, Chalmers felt his heart beating quickly, as he was all too conscious that he had a chance to change his fortunes.

THE GENERAL RULE IN THE PRECINCT was "Eat what you kill." If you initiated the case, you performed the interrogation, took the statement, assisted the prosecutors, and testified in court. But this case, Chalmers knew, was different. The suspect had come to them, and the stakes were exceptionally high. Careers would be permanently marred if they failed to get a conviction.

He had just learned the timing of events: that the woman had entered the station house an hour before the news that Selva was dead and his body was lying in the garage of a Malibu beach cottage had appeared on television or reached the internet. So the detective had asked a co-worker to go and keep her company. They could definitely say now that she was a material witness, and they had the testimony that would form the basis for her indictment. With this in mind, he straightened his posture by lifting his head and throwing back his shoulders. Then he approached the lieutenant's desk.

Absorbing the information, Chalmers realized that he needed to scale down his goals, that he had to focus not on what he would get but what he might lose. He was in a nearly ideal position, and he needed to make sure that everything went properly, that he was not cockblocked, robbed of his share of the credit. Standard procedure was for two officers to take a statement in a homicide case. He needed to be one of this pair.

That depended on how he presented himself. Dressed in an unpressed tan suit which he had purchased in a discount store, he was self-conscious about his attire and unsure how he should hold his hands. He was grateful for the dearth of other detectives, that there were few men to choose from.

The sort who insisted upon being called by his first name and who liked to come across as a regular guy, one of *them*, the lieutenant wanted to be seen as fair and up-to-date: approachable. This had always bothered Chalmers as he recognized that if they were to screw up in a way that reflected on him, then he would not be any of these things. No, he would rapidly distance himself from them. More, he knew what the lieutenant was apt to be thinking: as he had only ceased with patrol two years ago, he was not an expert at the Reid technique, the prescribed nine-step process of interrogation.

Reminding himself that he must not smile, he stood before him, waiting for him to gaze up and yield him his attention. For now, he was staring at the seated lieutenant's bald spot.

"Yes?" It was exactly the friendly look that Chalmers had prepared himself for and to which he knew he must not respond with another grin. Drained by his session with the Morgan woman, he was able to not be affable, rather playing his part: serious and intent. This prompted a second, more serious "yes" from his superior.

"The Selva murder. The one on TV. I've been interrogating a woman for two hours who says she didn't kill him, but—get this—she had the body and dumped it at the place in Malibu. With the gun. Plus, she says she was his side dish. She started telling me all about it before the body was found. She knows everything."

Chalmers would remember the gaze returned to him for the rest of his life. It was the expression of a boy who has been told that his brother is grounded for a month, and he is free to ride his sibling's bike. The quality and amount of gratitude told him that he would be part of the two-person team charged with obtaining the signature on her statement.

Yet, as he readied himself for the task of breaking her, it occurred to him that they didn't even need it. After all, the woman's car was sitting right in their parking lot, and there was bound to be a trace amount of the victim's blood that she had not managed to clean from the floor of its trunk.

CHAPTER 26

As Vincenza waited for Ray Chalmers to return, she began to meditate on Sara, on the city, and on her life.

In speaking to the detective, she had felt that she was being listened to, and she had felt a bond of trust. He reminded her of the best of the Church of Life counselors. There was that intensity with which they gave you their attention, feasting on your words without making you conscious of attraction or desire. But she did not like the look of the second police officer, the one now keeping her company, and it dawned on her that her original reasons for evading the police had not fallen away. Sitting in a room of painted cinder blocks with only a mute, unsmiling officer beside her, her heart palpitations returned.

Her thoughts about Sara pulled her back to the occasion when they had first met. This had not been at her acting class. Nor had it been when she was working at the dispensary. Rather, it was in the parking lot behind it. Hesitating before going in for her job interview at the store, she had asked Sara for a light. Sara had been on her way inside as a customer.

What had struck her was how relaxed she was, how happy-go-lucky. It had been a typical Southern California afternoon: sunny and deliciously warm. But Vincenza was not calm. Part of her agitation had been spurred not by the interview but that she was walking into a dispensary. She had never smoked pot, not once, and, if she needed a job that offered flexible hours for auditioning, she was uncomfortable with the notion that others might see her entering. Sara was nearly her perfect opposite. Had any of the tourists strolling down the Walk of Fame have asked her, she would have happily posed for pictures outside the store. More, she would likely have grabbed a water pipe and let them shoot her holding that with the shop window behind them. Then she might have turned to their six-year-old and asked him in a seemingly sweet and sympathetic tone if he was someday going to be a habitual marijuana smoker.

Everything with Sara was chill. Everything was a scream. It was all sidesplitting and campy and a kick, and because of that her company was addictive. It was such a contrast with how she had been raised and, in a way, it matched the feeling that the city, at its best, provided. It was so unlike Eagan, Minnesota, and almost everywhere else Vincenza had been. It incarnated freedom: in its driving up into the hills and across its arroyos, in its uniformly warm afternoons, in the opportunity to be whomever you wanted, to imagine any future you sought. No one asked you if you were considering nursing school or teaching or whether your boyfriend had bought you a ring and how soon you would be having your first child. Whatever you were, whatever you wanted to be: That was it.

Yet she was not free, and, sitting in the interview room, she reached for her phone. On it was a text message from Sara. This confirmed her fears. It read: "Did u kill Tom? i don't understand. Wish u hadn't run away this morning. Wanted to hear u explain yr messages. Why he was missing. to talk. What's on the news—scary. Don't want to believe it. Love u still and thinking of u." There was another heart emoji after this.

Would they believe Vincenza when she said that she was innocent? Crushing the cigarette butt in the ashtray, she looked up to the first detective and another officer entering the room. Their faces told her everything. They were certain of her guilt. Chalmers had not believed her, and they were going to arrest her.

As the interrogation proceeded, it occurred to her that she could end it. Two hours had passed, and she was still in the room, repeating what she had said. They were just trying to catch her in inconsistencies in the hope that would lead her to a confession. When they weren't snide and insulting, they asked questions that contradicted their earlier ones. Thus, at one moment they demanded to know if she was angry that Selva had spurned her. Then they wondered if she had killed him because he was putting off leaving his wife. She was in love with him, yes? Or was it that she was enraged because he had pressured her into sex? There were incessant questions about where she had killed him. Then there were threats. They were going to open the trunk and find tiny flecks of remnant blood, they said. They had advanced tools for finding what she had not managed to remove with the water and the bleach. They also had tape of her dumping the body at the beach cottage. Didn't she want to confess? It would look better to a judge and jury if she did. But she had talked enough, and, weary as she was, she was not going to admit her guilt when there was none.

It was perverse.

When they told her she was being arrested, they had offered her the obligatory phone call. That had been the most painful moment as it brought home that it was real, even as it made her aware of how alone she was. She had no lawyer, and nearly all her friends were in the Church. Were she wrong about it, then the right thing was to call Clarkson. But, hard as it was to accept, she was convinced that she was not paranoid. For some reason the Church was against her. She had seen the minivans outside her house, at Sara's, and at the Church headquarters.

In fact, the Church was involved. There was no one else she could think of with the resources or a cause to follow her. That included

Todd Gelber's streaming service. Eagan was not much more than a twenty-minute drive to the 3M company headquarters in Saint Paul, and she had grown up alongside the children of its workers. She knew from them that big companies were not composed of the evil plotters depicted in B-movies, and that they weren't involved in Selva's murder.

This knowledge placed her in a further predicament. If she couldn't phone Clarkson for help, whom could she trust and might she want to call? Her mother was in Minnesota and would be bound to gloat, to enjoy the fact of her fall. Her agent was delinquent in returning messages that involved contracts and work; surely he would take his time getting back to a woman accused of killing one of the most successful actors in the world. Her beautiful co-worker at the dispensary was sweet but much too dim to rely upon. Gelber was powerful and kind, but he was busy with his streaming service and cautious. In any event, she hardly knew him. And Sara thought she was the killer, as would her other actress friends. That left only the Israeli brothers, Eilan and Binyamin, and Billy.

That was all.

The Israelis knew defense lawyers, but they were dubious characters. Who knew what legal troubles they were in themselves? Her habit of relying upon her gut had played a part in creating the situation she was in, and she was coming to be suspicious of the impulse. But instinct told her one thing. This was to dial Billy, and his was the number that she picked out on her phone.

In the back of her mind there was the thought that he would bail her out. Yet as the phone rang she realized that this was too much to ask. Likely he did not even have the money. What was comforting was the sound of his voice. It was gentle and warm, even when she told him that she had been arrested, that she was being held by the police, and she was to be charged with murder.

CHAPTER 27

The name of Vincenza's new home was the Lynwood. Or, at least, that is what the inhabitants of Los Angeles County's main jail for women call it.

Vincenza knew from the other inmates that it was located in one of the city's most dangerous neighborhoods, and, thick though its walls are, at night she heard the racket from the nearby freeway. But she had not seen this herself as she had been transported to it in a truck without windows. Manacled and pedacled, she was let out within. Then she was taken through a series of wide hallways broken up by two-inch-thick metal doors. These led to the space in which she was *processed*.

That took place in a giant, empty hall. There, alongside half a dozen other women, she was stripped naked and forced to undergo a body cavity search. A woman holding a flashlight approached her and made her display her anus and vagina. Deputies of both sexes watched as the woman checked to see that she was not transporting drugs. Then she was led with the other prisoners to the showers. Once she was dried off, she was put into her regulation jumpsuit—electric blue and made of something nearly as coarse as burlap. Printed in block letters on the uniform were the words, "Los Angeles Century Regional Detention

Facility." Then they were provided with shoes of the wrong size. Walking in them was like stepping about in clown shoes.

From the showers, they were next brought into a holding cell where they crouched or tried to sleep. Cold, crowded, and full of weird odors, it was composed of bare concrete. Hours passed. Then they were conveyed to the North Tower, a huge atrium that looked like the remains of a decayed spaceship. Nearly all its surfaces were bare metal: gray steel or scratched-up chrome. Incongruously, in delicate script, inspirational words had been spray-painted in foot-high lettering onto its I-beams: "Integrity," "Gratitude," "Beauty." Beneath these, tables with bolted chairs dotted the floor, and around them women played checkers or talked in screeching voices. Alongside them were other inmates charged with lesser crimes, who lay on cots, trying with varying degrees of success to sleep.

Above and around the floor, rising up in tiers, were layers of "pods." These were the cells in which the greater number of the prisoners spent the bulk of their time. Inside each was a toilet, a rusty sink without a mirror, a small TV set, and a pair of bunk beds attached to the walls. Because so many of the toilets did not flush, there was a stench of human waste.

The guards, who communicated with one another by old fashioned walkie-talkies strapped to their belts, kept them waiting there for twenty minutes. Then, finally, they received their directions, and Vincenza was separated from the other women. Three guards—two men and one woman—accompanied her. This attention was somehow taken as a sign that she was uppity, and inmates glowered at her as she was led past them.

Her own cell, she discovered, was separate and quieter. As a function of her newfound celebrity, she had been set outside "gen pop": the general population. Rather, she was housed in a tiny room near the commissary, and through its slim vertical window she could observe tattooed women filing past on their way to buy packs of chewing gum and candy. Her mattress was without a pillow. Instead, there was a thin, worn blanket and a torn, faded sheet.

The jail, she quickly learned, was a place of invariable routine. At intervals the guards came by with clipboards listing the names of the inmates on their ward. They were required to cross each off as present. In the early morning, there was a walk to the cafeteria for breakfast, which was usually sugary, processed cereal and milk, no matter that the large number of incarcerated Black and Asian women were lactose intolerant and threw the cartons out. Then, just after noon, they were marched back to receive their cardboard trays and sporks along with more predictably bland meals. Frequently this was instant mashed potatoes with overboiled string beans and tasteless strips of chicken. Most of it had a gelatinous appearance, whether it was cranberry sauce, poultry, or pudding.

No time was provided for the prison yard. This was something that the women sometimes saw, but which they were not permitted to visit. To make matters worse, the clatter was unending. Easily a third of the women were disturbed, and more than a few were unmedicated and prone to wailing or chattering with nonexistent acquaintances. There were also loud arguments among the cellmates, and cackling insults directed towards the guards.

Those expected to remain in the facility for longer stays were obligated to take classes. These were meant to prepare them for jobs working as kitchen aides, seamstresses, or beauticians. There was instruction in reading, writing, and arithmetic, nutrition, and simple use of computers. The prison doctors and nurses used the absence of cellmates to check on the many pregnant women in the jail while psychiatrists went to see the deranged.

Sexual predation took various forms. One involved a male guard on the ward. In the middle of the night, he would let a woman down the hall out, bringing her to the cell of her lover. The price for their lovemaking was that he watched.

Few of the women were hardened criminals. Many were incarcerated for drug possession, drunken driving, or even driving without a license or insurance. Yet there were a few manifestly predatory butch toughs. Shot callers, they were accustomed to having their way with attractive young flesh. On trips to the cafeteria Vincenza came to realize that she had not even escaped #MeToo in prison! As grotesque as any producers she had met, these shot callers were eyeing her when she ate and when she showered. She was grateful—more appreciative than she could have imagined—that the guards were keeping a special watch on her. She had no doubt that in the paired cells women were molested at night, forced to masturbate or to orally please their companions.

The nights at the Lynwood were long, and it wasn't merely the sounds that kept her up or the sense that something within her was being swallowed up. Some of the inmates hated her, and she was more tired from lack of sleep than she had ever been in her life. If she went to bed at nine, she was up by eleven. If she fell asleep at one, she was wide awake at three.

Little things made her angry. This included the slogans on the walls—"Hope," "Determination," "Family." Those put her into a particular rage, and though she had received books through the mail and enjoyed reading, she sometimes found herself staring vacantly at the pages. It was as though the letters could become momentarily unintelligible, like hieroglyphics. It took her some time to identify a portion of the problem, that she was suffering through a double withdrawal: nicotine and pot. Wouldn't that make anyone crabby and restless?

The tiredness reached its peak at the hours when visitors arrived. For most this was their children, and it was heartbreaking. The images etched themselves in Vincenza's mind: a little Hispanic girl with tiny fingers pressing her hand on the plexiglass divider, unwilling to be led away; a skinny Black boy with pale green eyes and clunky plastic glasses tearing up at the sight of his mother's face.

Her own trips to the visiting room were mostly for conferences with her would-be attorneys. This was because two of her assumptions had proved false. There was no bail. The "people"—meaning the prosecutors—had asked for remand, refusal of her release based on the claim that she was a flight risk, and without hesitation the judge had agreed. At the same time, her difficulty was not in paying for counsel but in selecting one. Every lawyer in Los Angeles, it seemed, wanted to be chosen and was eager to take her case on *pro bono*. There were flashy defense lawyers with pinkie rings and wide ties, law professors from USC, radical public defenders with goatees and turtleneck sweaters, "activists" with political aspirations, and those aiming to be TV talk show hosts. There were, in fact, more requests than time for those she could meet with.

There were also bags and bags of mail, much of it scurrilous. If Selva had not managed to make it at the box office with teenage girls when he was alive, he now had legions of them as admirers, and nearly all wanted horrible things to happen to her. There were men, too—presumably missing teeth—who wrote to express their love for Vincenza. Often accompanying these expressions of undying affection were dick pics.

While she was a local story, she was much more. As the rejected mistress who had killed Tom Selva in what was presumed to have been a jealous rage, she was someone of note. For however long the case played out, she was as worthy of attention as J. Lo or Beyoncé.

This did not mean that the press's treatment of her was favorable. Although it violated the basic provisions of the law for prosecutors to leak pertinent details in the hope of prejudicing the public and the prospective pool of jurors, they had done nothing but this for a week. In this way, the *Los Angeles Times* and the *Orange County Register* each had "broken" aspects of the story, offering readers and viewers some latest detail that seemed to demonstrate her guilt.

They were not alone. The *New York Times* had flown a prized reporter out, choosing not to rely upon a stringer. There were likewise writers from *The New Yorker, Time, The Star, OK, Entertainment Weekly, In Touch, Hello!, Paris Match, Life & Style, People,* and each of the networks. Even *Vanity Fair* and *Vogue* had assigned correspondents. The local TV channels were assessing the case through "team" coverage, and although she could not see it, Vincenza had heard that there were never fewer than half a dozen news trucks camped out in front of the jail. Yes, she was at last famous, or, to put it more accurately, notorious.

Prepared and articulate, Clarkson was among her visitors. He was altogether too slick. Like a bad tap dancer, he grinned incessantly. As a child Vincenza had been fascinated by beauty pageants, and she had learned from them to distinguish between the contestants' smiles. There was one kind in which they flashed their molars. That was the fake sort. Then there were the unaffected ones. His were the first kind, and when she had asked him why anonymous sources within the Church were suggesting that she was an apostate, he said that he had no idea how that might have occurred. Then he had informed her that they could handle her legal needs, and, in fact, he was a lawyer himself.

Billy, on the other hand, was different. Yet it was not his gentleness nor his sincerity that meant the most to her. It was a question that he asked, one that gave her hope.

CHAPTER 28

The two days that followed the announcements of Selva's death and Vincenza's arrest were the most hectic that Clarkson had known since the days before his bar exam. While nearly the whole leadership of the Church had been thrown into the funeral preparations, it was nonetheless a colossal undertaking.

In its brief history, the Church had managed to establish a number of conventions for memorial services. These rites offered them an outline. This included the reverent words to be spoken, and the alcohol-free libations to be served. After this, Armstrong would point to a spot in the sky, the location of the planet where they would latterly trek, and there would be the lighting of the fire.

What was unfamiliar was planning a service for a celebrity so young at the height of his fame. The last time they had arranged a send-off so magnificent was a quarter century earlier when the Church's founder had passed on. Necessarily, they had scanned old file cabinets for information on how that had been performed.

The unknowns included basic matters related to presentation. How were they to get that much lumber for the pyre, how was it to be assembled, and where was it to be set? How many rose petals were required and where were they to be strewn? Where was the teleprompter from which Armstrong would read his eulogy to be placed, who would compose the speech, and what would it say? Where should Selva's mother and where should his wife and infant son be? How were they to lay out two thousand folding chairs and what should they do in the event of rain, always a possibility in February in Los Angeles? Where was a good location for the reporters and the cameras, one that did not obstruct the views of the mourners? What transportation should there be for the eulogists? What advice should be given to the cosmetologist who would work on Selva's corpse, and should it be set out within or alongside the kindling? Should mourners be allowed to pay their respects by approaching the body? Many of Selva's friends wished to offer eulogies. Which should be permitted to do so and how much time should each be allotted?

In addition to these, there were hundreds of other questions which they had not immediately anticipated. Was it reasonable to give prominent seating for Selva's pets? What sort of accelerant for a fire so large was safe and what should they do if there were a downpour? How many fire marshals needed to be present? The president had sent his condolences. Should these be read by his wife or by Armstrong?

Vincenza was among their biggest concerns. As far as the law was concerned, the Church had a blanket protection. Nothing in Vincenza's files could be subpoenaed or read in court, and no Church counselor could be compelled to testify. While this was a shield, it was not a sword. They could not lawfully use the files to portray her as a disturbed woman attacking the Church. The best they could do was to leak pages to friends at the gossip magazines in order to convince the public that she was an unhinged antagonist.

Some of their plans had been complicated by the Supreme Pilot's inspirations. At one point he had summoned them to the top floor to suggest that they ought to move the event to a larger venue than the one for which it had been planned, the Church's outdoor assembly space in Encino. Could the Staples Center, the Hollywood Bowl, or the Los Angeles Coliseum be rented out on short notice? Each notion had to be investigated.

Finally, though, it was the afternoon of the service. A playing space for the musicians—an orchestra pit—had been set below the raised podium upon which the guests of honor sat. Behind them was the pyre and the corpse, and on the stage were the tens of thousands of pink, white, and red rose petals. Selva's wife had asked that he be mounted upon his favorite Harley-Davidson, and they had worked to prop him up in a heroic posture on this metal steed. That had required use of ligatures and a tightly bound corset underneath his blue suit. They had watched, then, as the early arriving guests formed into a line to see him and pay their respects. Made up as heavily as Selva was, he looked a bit like a trans member of the Hells Angels.

Still, the sky had cleared, and, as the dais had been laid out facing southeast, the sunlight was coming in from a favorable angle from the southwest. Armstrong was to speak last. Tom Hutchins was first. Well aware of his fondness for pot, Clarkson had taken time out to meet with him and to emphasize the need for sobriety. They had also reviewed his speech beforehand and set it in the teleprompter.

None of this mattered.

His pupils were the size of walnuts. Initially he tried to read from the monitor, but it gradually became apparent that he was nearsighted and without his glasses and unable to concentrate. He therefore began ad-libbing, chattering about the filming of the movie and how he and Selva had been imbibing Wild Turkey in between scenes. One moment he would speak haltingly. Then he would spit out his words, saying that he envied Selva for his wife's beauty and all the other "fine trim" he had enjoyed in his short life. With that expression, the sound engineer cut off the mic, and they escorted Hutchins unwillingly back to his seat. They were fortunate when he shoved a security officer that the guard managed to avoid tumbling over the edge of the stage down the eight feet into the orchestra pit.

The speakers who followed were not high. The difficulty was that nearly all were intent on ignoring time limits, and, just as at the Academy Awards, the musicians were repeatedly called upon to cut in on them and drown them out when they ran on. They rambled. They said that Selva was almost their dearest friend. They talked about their rank in the Church. They pumped their upcoming releases. One even managed to mention his agent and his manager.

Close to ninety minutes of this preceded Selva's mother and his wife, both of whom spoke with genuine feeling about their recollections and their grief. Then, at last, it was time for Armstrong. Dressed in his white tunic, he had a satin shawl draped around his shoulders. The lights had been arrayed to create a subtle glow around his forehead, and the musicians cued him to the podium with a low bass melody that was solemn but portentous.

He began to speak. Behind him the sky had turned gray and a wind had picked up. Still, it was not raining, and in some respect the weather suited the occasion. Clarkson and the other pilots below Armstrong had tested the speech by reading it aloud and counting the words. They were quite sure that it was fifteen minutes long. Yet Armstrong expressed himself with a wealth of pauses. Each word was declaimed with special emphasis. Moreover, in the middle of the address he stopped, seemingly battling back tears. Then he commenced once more with a grand sigh and moist eyes. Selva represented everything that was best about the Church and its followers. The movie he had just completed proved what they all knew: He was potentially among the greatest actors of their time. He was talented, beautiful, committed, magnanimous, and devoted to his spouse and the Church. When Armstrong said this, a mic located beneath Selva's wife was boosted so the audience could hear her sobbing.

Large as the crowd was, two huge television screens had been set up, left and right. These showed the faces of the speakers, or they flashed to celebrities. Those arranging the choice of images switched then to a split screen that contained both Armstrong's countenance and that of Selva's much affected widow and his child, whom she held in her arms.

At that point church volunteers present passed out small paper cups to the rows of mourners. These were filled with grape juice, and the Supreme Pilot lifted his to eye level, indicating for others to imitate the gesture. Then, he toasted Selva, reading the Church's traditional incantation:

> You have lived among mortals but are now immortal. You were upon the ground but are now in the sky. You fought to save the planet and are now saved. Great is your glory, mighty pilot, space voyager!

Armstrong pointed into the heavens and swallowed from his cup. Above them, the crowd could see the helicopters filming the scene, as they, too, downed the nearly flavorless liquid.

Lorelei was next called to the stage to warble the "Hymn of Journey." Its lyrics, which referred to the Church's founder, went:

> *The day is long,*
> *But the hour is nigh;*
> *We sing this song;*
> *You did not die.*
>
> *You live in memory,*
> *And will travel far;*
> *Through Denton we are free*
> *To visit a nearby star.*

As many in the crowd were Church members, they sang along in a wide range of keys. In Lorelei's own take on the threnody, several notes were held to astonishing length. As she drew these out, she swayed in such fashion as to demonstrate that she was not wearing a bra and had taped up her breasts. These sashayed, just outside the plunging v-line of her blouse.

Thanked for her fine rendition, Lorelei was brought back to her seat as Armstrong returned to the lectern for a last bit of preaching. Here he commanded his listeners to reflect upon the moment, reminding them that they could preserve the planet, improve their spirit, and possibly even aid their careers by doing what Selva had in joining the Church. With that message pronounced, he called for assistants. The handlers reached for Selva's body. Detached from the Harley, which was wheeled from the stage, Selva's remains were set neatly under the pyre. The late actor's wife and mother were then escorted to Armstrong, whence they joined him in grasping lit torches, soaked in kerosene, to start the conflagration.

Then they retreated. It was dry enough that the flames climbed rapidly. Towering as it soon was, the helicopters were compelled to draw back, and those on the stage felt the heat. It was as though they had opened an oven, setting a choice pot roast inside it.

Clarkson could not but be aware of the irony. Each breath of smoke, after all, was meant to declare the faith's unbending opposition to destruction of the earth, its water, and its air. Even so, he could not but be thrilled and touched. The fire was magnificent. The pyre roared up sixteen feet high, and the flames shot half a dozen feet above that with embers reaching out into the firmament as Selva's body was incinerated. The whole was glorious. The only question was how it would play on TV.

By the next afternoon, they had their answer.

On the internet, Hutchins's eulogy had gone viral. Tens of thousands of tweets mocked him and his stoner expressions. But the TV and radio reports politely skipped over this, instead focusing on Lorelei's performance and the faces of the famous actors and actresses present on the stage and in the crowd. That was unwelcome. For what was not being shown was the Supreme Pilot. And he was furious.

CHAPTER 29

In some ways jail was alike to a cruise ship. You tried to make friends. You were sickened by the food. You couldn't jump out the windows.

Obviously in jail you sought out alliances warily. Still, no woman entering into the embrace of the state correctional system did not desire attachments, and Vincenza did not sit by herself when she went to the cafeteria or to hairstyling class. Consequently, within the first week she had managed to make a number of new acquaintances, and as the women's jail did not have the strict racial demarcations of the men's facilities, these relationships crossed color lines.

It was apparent that the Black women she befriended knew some of the ins and outs of the system. One turned out to have been a South Central madam, while another had been the lookout for a drug gang. So, sleep-deprived though she was, she listened intently to their suggestions regarding lawyers. Aware that she was auditioning attorneys, they instructed her to select a former public defender who had just switched over to working as a criminal defense lawyer. Their reasoning was that an established defense lawyer would be extremely busy with his other cases, and his focus would not be on winning but on using the trial to get on television as frequently as possible. By contrast, a recent public defender, they said, was apt to be someone who was fervently hostile to the police and the prosecutors, and he would be determined to get her off in order to establish himself.

This comported with what she saw in her meetings with counselors. The big-name criminal defense lawyers were a little too polished and cocky, and she wanted someone geeky, impassioned, and eager. More, she sought someone who didn't just say that he believed her account but who seemed open to the possibility of her innocence.

This was a pretty good description of the man she picked: Jerry D'Allesandro. His suspicion of the prosecutors and the police was palpable. Unashamed to tell her that he had been on the law review at USC, he had turned down corporate jobs to go work for $32,000 per year as a public defender. Now he was trying to pay a few bills, he said. Even so, he hadn't lost his radical beliefs, and his clothes didn't quite fit. An enormous man, he had the same body type though not the skin tone of a Polynesian football player. He also had the sort of easy, natural smile that Vincenza associated with people from the South Seas. That was matched to mild hyperactivity. He didn't smile when she told him her story, but he nodded intently, occasionally interrupting, often out of sheer nervous energy.

They met once each week in a windowless room with chairs that had been bolted into the floor. Guards escorted her to meet him, and then they closed the door shut so that the conference was private. Alongside the chairs was a long table which had a peculiar scent that she only managed to identify at their second meeting: the odor of vaginal fluid. This was further demonstration of the absence of hygiene in the jail. It also reminded her that the injustice inside was not so different from what many an actress faced on the outside.

The smell cued her thoughts as well to her lawyer's desire for her, and as much as she yearned for the touch of a man's fingers she had begun fantasizing about him. It required willpower not to flirt. Yet, in spite of his manifest attraction, he was professional, and within ten minutes of the beginning of their first conversation he had taken out a yellow legal pad and begun asking her questions, scrupulously logging her answers. Those queries brought her back to something Billy had asked her: Didn't the dispensary have video cameras that recorded the times she was there? Didn't her apartment building have security equipment?

D'Allesandro was pointed in emphasizing it: They had to create a precise timeline of her activities in the hours leading up to Selva's death. The coroner's office, he explained, said that Selva's body had been studied for *algor mortis* and *rigor mortis*. These tests of body temperature and stiffening were complicated by the range of environments in which the body had been kept. Forensic investigators had concluded that he had been slain inside the beach cottage and moved to Vincenza's trunk. It had then been taken out and dropped upon the garage floor. The first and last of these environments were chilly, though one was dry and the other damp. The range of these factors made it hard to come up with an exact time of death. But the medical examiner was reasonably certain that he had been killed between eighteen and thirty-two hours prior to the time when she had left the corpse in the garage. That meant the latest he might have been shot was around dawn on the morning of her first audition for the Reese Witherspoon movie, while the earliest conceivable time was during the evening the previous night.

D'Allesandro hadn't been able to get the prosecutor's office to provide him with the time-stamped videotape that showed her driving up to the beach cottage. That might just be the normal tardiness of the pre-trial discovery process, he explained. Nonetheless, it complicated their efforts as it deprived them of the ability to craft a separate time-line in the hours when the killing might have happened for each of those they had identified who had been to the beach house.

Vincenza had a clear idea how her own timeline set up. That commenced at the dispensary. On the day before the audition, she had worked there from 11:00 a.m. to 7:00 p.m. with an hour off for lunch. Then she had headed home, changed clothes, made herself up, and met for drinks with a Tinder date in Los Feliz. That was around nine. That ended forty minutes later, and she drove back to her apartment by Franklin Canyon, returning at 10:15 p.m. or so. In bed by 10:45 or 11:00 p.m., she had woken up around seven, rehearsed, and walked over to the coffee shop where she had met Billy. That was around 9:30 or 10:00 a.m. This seemed to cover the whole of the time, and it included two different alibis placing her in Hollywood. Even in the early hours of the morning that was more than an hour's drive from Solromar, the stretch of Malibu where the beach cottage lay. Getting there required two hours round trip, and while her phone showed that she had called Selva during her lunch hour, the message had gone straight to voicemail.

That brought up the matter of her phone records, and the video from the apartment building and the dispensary. As it turned out, the apartment building's garage security cameras were props. They recorded nothing. But the dispensary's cameras proved that she had been at work during the daylight hours prior to the murder, and this was further substantiated by her co-workers and by the company's time logs.

Then there were the phone records. These showed that she had "pinged" cell towers in the neighborhoods around her—Hollywood, Franklin Canyon, the Downtown, and Los Feliz—and no other areas through most of the time when Selva was believed to have been murdered. Granted how long it would take to reach the stretch of Malibu where the beach cottage was, this proved that the only window in which she could have met with him and killed him there was between midnight and eight a.m. To do that she would need to have agreed earlier in the day to an assignation with him, driven there, shot him in the beach cottage's foyer, dragged him out to the garage, somehow managed to lift his body into the trunk of her car, sped away from the crime scene, spent a day wheeling around Los

Angeles with the body in her trunk, and then returned that night to place the corpse and the gun near where she had previously shot and killed him.

This wasn't just wildly implausible. It also depended upon the idea that Selva might have been out past midnight with a mistress when his wife was breastfeeding their infant son. The transcripts from the official investigators' interviews with Selva's widow did not answer the question of whether he was ever out so late. But D'Allesandro assured her that he had a meeting set up to ask her about this.

Obtaining statements from Gary and Fran was more difficult. They could testify that she had been followed by a bronze minivan. But they were not answering their telephone, and D'Allesandro said that he couldn't get a response when he stopped by and knocked at the door of their home.

They would soon have a copy of the message she had left on Selva's phone. That could provide further evidence that she had not made any arrangement to meet him late that night at the beach cottage.

D'Allesandro—Jerry, as he insisted upon being called—had told her about the cell phone records at their second formal meeting. It was a step out from the darkness she was in. The worst part of this wasn't the anguish, but the fear that she could not escape it. Grief had an end and a significance. This was without place or meaning. It was as though you were in a huge abyss, a void without walls to grasp or to climb. If she were convicted and spent the next twenty years in prison and everyone assumed she was guilty, then what had her life meant? The news that she might be able to prove her innocence was sunlight. The long, sleepless hours of the night were times to think, and they had compelled her to examine things as she had not since high school.

The conferences with Jerry were limited to seventy-five minutes. They were among the few moments of the week that passed rapidly.

The desire for pot had turned to aversion. It had not happened at once, but over the course of weeks she began to realize that her worst

180

mistakes had been made when she was high. Not calling the police when she first saw the corpse fell into that category, and continuing her affair with Selva did as well.

He was the subject women in the prison asked her about most. What was he like? How had they become involved? What was he like as a lover? She brushed off the questions, then fixated on them at night. Yet, at the same time, the longer she was in the jail, the more she realized that it might be possible for a woman to seduce her there, and she even found herself considering the more *femme* inmates. The actuality of that was complicated, however, by the speed with which women were shifted about. Between the frequent releases from the jail, the appearance of new prisoners, and the institution's goal of deterring attachments, not a day went by when a woman on the floor wasn't being moved somewhere else.

Three weeks went by like this. It was the hardest twenty-one days of her life.

CHAPTER 30

The refrigerator was along the back wall of the detective's room. Chalmers had placed his lunch inside it. But it wasn't there. This was among the many things that weren't right.

Generally, the precinct divided into two groups: The married men and the women were different in their eating habits from the unmarried men. The lawfully attached males and the female officers brought bag lunches, which they housed in the precinct refrigerator. The never-wed and divorced men ordered in, or else they stopped into local restaurants. Although Chalmers did not have children, he did have an ex, and usually he fell in with the second set and rarely packed a lunch. However, he had woken up early and with nothing better to do and an abundance of credit card bills, he had flipped on a morning sports show and made himself a sandwich, which he had stowed in the departmental icebox. Yet someone had decided to clean the refrigerator up and had tossed the sandwich out.

It was one more annoyance. This was on top of the vexation he felt about the case. When a witness provided a statement as damning as Vincenza Morgan's, ordinarily it was easy to find evidence demonstrating her guilt. Yet there didn't seem to be much.

He thought about this as he braked an unmarked sedan he was driving. In front of him was the car he was tailing. The person of interest was a writer whom other detectives had interrogated a week before. This was more reason to be peeved: The case had more than fifteen officers assigned to it, and he was getting the least important tasks. Senior detectives, men presumed to have more delicacy, had been sent to meet with the leader of the Church of Life. He had been left with the business of keeping watch on someone who had no criminal record—none whatever.

In fairness, there was some logic to the idea that solving the case required observation of the man he was following. Although the Rosenberg character did not seem like much of a physical specimen, it was obvious that he was strong enough to have moved Tom Selva's body into the trunk of Vincenza Morgan's car. This was especially true if he had her help. Moreover, that he was visiting her in jail and that she admitted to staying with him pointed to an obvious interpretation: As her lover he had either committed the crime himself or he had assisted her. That would explain a number of inconsistencies.

These started with the many movements of the cadaver. After it had been found, the investigators in Solromar had searched the beach cottage. Inside they had discovered the remains of the crime scene. Because it had been ineptly cleaned up, they had no trouble finding bits of blood splatter in the foyer, and there were trace amounts of gunpowder residue. But that made little sense. It was highly unlikely, after all, that Vincenza could have dragged Selva's corpse to the trunk and lifted the body into it on her own, and, in any event, why would she have done that and then returned to deposit it there later?

Then there was the issue of the tape that showed her arriving at the beach cottage. There was nothing on it from before the morning of the crime. It appeared to have been wiped clean.

This confusion was complicating already complicated departmental politics. Initially, it had seemed that the Ventura County prosecutors wanted the case, as it was so notable and this was where the crime had occurred. Then they seemed to be backing off.

The response of the chiefs in the LAPD paralleled this. Some said that the commissioner wanted to avoid it because there were officers and patrolmen who had joined the Church of Life, and he didn't want to antagonize it. Others in the precinct insisted that the opposite was true, and the department's top officials were eager to take on the case in order to show that the Church was not to be trusted. That would be the basis for a purge. Whichever of these versions was true, it was apparent that they and the prosecutors were wary. So Chalmers had no way of knowing if he would get the credit due to him.

In the meantime, he had been charged with looking into the "minor" details. Through these he had managed to develop additional leads. Each represented a chit. They were proofs that he could handle an important project.

He had uncovered one useful piece of information by poring through the records of the homeowners in Franklin Canyon. That had led him to a Garrison and Frances Hodgson, the couple who Vincenza said had picked her up. In their account of meeting her, she was a hooker who had tried to reel them in as paying customers.

Now it was two in the afternoon, and he was driving along West 6th Street, trying to keep a distance between his car and the jalopy of this Billy Rosenberg. When he parked in a lot near Pershing Square, Chalmers circled past him. The detective then exceeded the miracle of the fishes and the loaves by securing a spot on the street a block away.

Parking, Chalmers walked slowly back. Rosenberg was in sight, but so preoccupied that it was questionable if he even noticed the hint of rain in the air or the darkening clouds above them. Halting, Rosenberg gazed into the window of one jewelry shop and then another. They were in the downtown's diamond district and the display cases featured engagement rings. Was he going to buy a square cut sparkler for Vincenza?

Chalmers stepped past the store. Out of the corner of his eye he saw what was happening: Rosenberg was inspecting rings while talking excitedly with the diamond salesman behind the counter. Watching him enter one of the shops, Chalmers felt a sense of elation. The pieces of the puzzle, he concluded, were finally beginning to fit together. If Rosenberg had participated in the killing of Selva and he persuaded Vincenza to marry him, then they could claim spousal privilege and refuse to testify against each other.

The detective's thoughts returned to the process of interrogation they would employ. Would it be helpful in breaking Rosenberg if they waited before springing on him the fact that his would-be fiancée was a call girl who solicited couples in Griffith Park? Or was it even possible that Rosenberg was her pimp? The detective considered the idea. He certainly didn't look the type.

CHAPTER 31

Two hours later Billy Rosenberg was standing outside the front door of a luxurious Mid-City apartment building. Pressing a buzzer, he was waiting for Claire Hesper to respond and let him in.

Yet she wasn't expecting him, and she hadn't seen him in three weeks. She was, however, expecting. Or that was what the at-home pregnancy kit she had bought at her neighborhood drug store told her.

When she had gotten the news five days earlier, she had immediately called Billy and left a voicemail emphasizing her certainty that he was the father. Then, a few minutes afterwards, she phoned him back. This time he managed to pick up. He had not yet gotten the first message when she abruptly declared that she was confused and that she needed time to figure everything out. It took him a minute to puzzle out what she was saying.

The moment was awkward. But, once he understood, he had told her that he was happy, that he was crazy about her, and that he wanted to see her at once and wished to hold her in his arms; though, if she needed time, of course he totally understood. Nonetheless, he had not immediately assumed that there would be a bris or a christening, and he had not purchased a ring at the diamond store off South Olive Street. Rather, he had been there to get some sense of the price of an

186

appropriate bauble. If he had not known that pregnancy testing had advanced to the point that only a week after you missed your period you could find out why you were late for $8.99 plus tax, he did know that the tests could result in false positives, and that there was a great likelihood of a miscarriage within the first ten weeks. More, he knew that abortion was not just an option for a rich girl in Los Angeles pursuing an acting career. No, it was almost a given that at some point or other such a young lady might choose to flatten a bump that was a bump in the road.

Still, the news prompted reflection. This focused upon his respective feelings for Vincenza, Claire, and his ex in New York. Intellectually, he grasped that it was absurd to be thinking about Vincenza. How could he be? They had never so much as kissed, and he had no reason to think she was interested in him. More, they had nothing in common in terms of education or background, and even if she weren't accused of murder her appearance would repel his parents. Between the pneumatic bosom and the Bettie Page haircut and stockings, they would consider her not just *traif* but *déclassé*. They would find her stomach-turning, something out of a reality show—a threat to the health, happiness, and, most of all, the bank account of their son.

Nor was his ex much of an option. The day before Claire's call he had seen the news of her engagement announced on Facebook. This was painful, far more than he wished to admit.

Claire, however, made sense. He was approaching thirty. He was often lonely. His younger brother already had two kids. Marrying Claire was stepping up. She was smart and beautiful, elegant and ambitious. And rich. At the same time, she was obviously quite unsure about him, and the request that he give her time was more proof of this.

The spring equinox was a week off, and the weather was glorious. The air was dry and largely free of smog. The temperature was just above seventy, and the sky was cloudless. He was dressed in a nice pair of pants and wearing an expensive dress shirt and newly purchased loafers. He had taken the time to iron the shirt, and he had gotten a haircut. He also had a bouquet of freshly cut roses in his left hand. He could not but be aware of the irony: He was there to court a woman he had knocked up.

Was it a mistake to turn up in the middle of the afternoon when she had expressly told him to stay clear? His heart beat rapidly. His throat was dry. Fearful of pressing the buzzer a second time, he shifted his feet back and forth, waiting for her to respond, hopeful that she was at home. While he did not have a ring with him, he did have the flowers. More than that: He had news.

"Who is it? Is this the UPS?" Claire's voice was unmistakable. The tone reminded him of her well-honed ability to assign everyone—lovers, friends, and furniture movers equally—to the role of the hired hand.

"Billy. I'm on my way back from the studio. Forgive me. They just told me that they're buying my pilot script. I wanted to tell you. I figured I'd stop by. That your apartment was on my way home."

She hesitated. "Oh, that's wonderful. Naturally, you did, yes. But I'm afraid I can't talk right now. Can I call you later?"

For a second time, Billy was made conscious: Matters were askew. He felt like he was going to throw up. It was as though he were experiencing her morning sickness by proxy. Her manner of speaking was that of someone on a business call discussing a rental car. The possibility that someone was with her was hard was to ignore.

Shifting his feet again, he held his hand more firmly on the button that permitted him to speak. He noticed then what he had not before: He was visible to her from the doorway camera. There he was in his nice outfit holding the roses. He had even added a dab of Brylcreem to his hair in order to make his bangs look fuller.

"How does six o'clock sound? I think I can talk to you then," she said.

People told Billy that he excelled at writing subtext but that he was not as good at reading it. Even so, he was able to grasp one possible meaning: She was trying to get rid of him before the person with her walked over and saw the man outside her building holding the posy. Realizing this, he grunted out an acknowledgement and smiled into the camera. Thoroughly deflated, he started walking away, staring more at the pavement than the automobiles swiftly moving in both directions over it.

As his own car was on the opposite side of the street, he did not have far to go. But he hesitated when he reached it. He was stopped by a perverse notion. It was a virtual certainty that she had seen the flowers through the little monitor in her kitchen showing him at the doorway. The idea was simple enough: Why not walk back and act as though he were unaware of this, then mentioning the roses and asking to come up to give them to her so that she might put them in water? If what he thought was happening was taking place, then by appearing with the bouquet, he would be taking a bulldozer and ramming it into the structure of her relationship with the other man.

Placing the flowers on the hood of the car, he tried to think, watching as vehicles flashed past. More even than when he was writing, he had to pause and reflect. What would be the effect of doing this? Would it get him Claire, and, if she was with someone else, was he right to want her? Contemplating this, he was unnerved by a dark notion. Might it be that she was trying to pass his child off as someone else's? It was hard to believe that she was so neurotic that she just didn't want to see him.

Sighing, Billy turned his head about and scanned the street, wondering what he had gotten himself into. He was puzzled by what he saw. Quite plainly, there was a man half a block away watching him.

CHAPTER 32

"The roses aren't for you."

"I didn't think they were."

"You're a reporter or a police officer?"

"If I was a reporter, wouldn't I just have walked up to you with a pen or the mic?"

"What's your name?"

"Chalmers. *Ray.*"

"Do I need a lawyer since I'm answering your questions?"

"You haven't been answering my questions. I've been answering yours."

Billy had to smile. The detective had a point. Still holding the flowers, he had crossed the street, advancing to the police officer, who was sitting in the front seat of his unmarked beige sedan.

"Why are you following me?"

"Is it so hard to figure out? You're a person of interest in the biggest homicide case this country has seen in years. You and the Morgan girl both tell us that she met you the morning of the murder and a day later she's living with you. And you've been stopping by the Lynnwood to say hi. It's an hour wait to get into the jail, an hour to get there, another hour back to Hollywood. But you say your dick has never been closer to her than to Mother Teresa in her grave. Would you believe that story?"

"I can tell you it's true. Aren't you supposed to read me a Miranda warning or something?"

Chalmers rolled his eyes. Impressively, he still had not gotten out of the car. He was perfectly comfortable carrying on the conversation, it seemed, with Billy standing outside the vehicle, in the path of the traffic. Chalmers's right forearm was perched on the wheel and his left arm was dangling outside the car with the window rolled down. "We don't have to do that until we make an arrest. You're not even officially a suspect."

"But unofficially...?"

"Why don't you come around to the passenger side and get in? If you get hit by a car, I'm going to have to write multiple reports, and I hate typing."

In the past, lawyers had told Billy not to talk to police officers without an attorney present, but curiosity had the better of him, and he came around, opened the passenger-side door, and sat down next to the detective. He could smell spilled coffee on the imitation leather seat.

Chalmers gazed at him. "Who are the flowers for? Boyfriend or girlfriend?"

"Sort of a girlfriend."

"She hadn't invited you over, but you show up with roses? Some people would call that stalking."

"OK."

"You boned her?"

"Let's just say I have more knowledge of her anatomy than yours."

"You know that the Morgan girl turned tricks?"

"I know on the detective shows that police lie to people they're interrogating. And I understand the courts say that's permissible."

"I heard it from a pair she tried to work. A couple."

"I thought that the tough-guy thing was just TV, but that really is how most of you are?"

Chalmers smiled back at him, amused. "We see a lot of shit. Can't but affect you." He paused. As is often the case on especially beautiful Southern California afternoons, it was hard to be in a hurry. "She didn't want to see you and didn't take the flowers, huh? Why do you think that was?"

The car they were sitting in had an LCD clock on its black vinyl dashboard. The timepiece told Billy that it was a quarter past four. The sun lay behind them, and the people approaching them on the sidewalk were trailed by long shadows. Half a block forward was the entranceway to Claire's building. The area in between was empty even of palm trees, and Billy was close enough that he could make out a man dressed in California formal—blue jeans, sneakers, a linen shirt, and a fancy blue blazer—exiting from the doorway that he had been standing in front of a few minutes earlier. As the man drew nearer, Billy received an answer to the question. From an internet search, he knew that the figure was the same one Claire had worked for. His name often appeared on movie screens before the main title. It showed up as part of the designation *A Mike Fruchtman Production*. It would then be followed by the director's name with the required description that the motion picture was *A Peter Kenyon Film*.

Intently as Billy watched Fruchtman advance, he realized that Chalmers was reading his eyes and that he understood what was taking place. Billy could even catch Fruchtman's self-assured self-absorption and his vague sense in walking past them that they must be a discontented gay couple, granted their silent discomfiture with one another and the presence of the bouquet, which was resting on the passenger side of the car's dashboard.

"I get it. Totally," Chalmers said, once Fruchtman had passed them by before seating himself in his Bentley, which was parked directly behind them. "I'm sorry. I could say that I've been there, Billy. But I don't think I have."

CHAPTER 33

Just after seven o'clock, Claire picked up her phone and searched it for Billy's number.

She was wearing a chic bias-cut dress that showed off her legs and more than a hint of her small bosom. The outfit was in a 1970s style that seemed at once vintage and classic. She had taken considerable time with her makeup and her hair, but she had not yet strapped on her heels. Half-standing, her feet were on the floor and her buttocks were propped on her bed.

The time spent making herself look presentable had been a welcome distraction as the preceding three hours had been among the longest of her life. There had been a solid twenty minutes of sobbing. Then there was time spent with cold compresses and ice under her eyelids. These were employed to diminish the swelling induced by the tears.

Fruchtman had known she was pregnant for four days. During that period they had not spoken for very long. Mostly they had communicated through text messages. He was in pre-production for a film and working grueling hours, and, as he explained, this was much too serious to talk about over the phone. He needed to see her. He was thrilled, and he was crazy about her. That was what he kept saying.

She had told herself that this must mean that he was shopping for a suitable ring and that they would do what they had generally avoided: meeting at a very public, fancy spot. More than likely, it seemed to her, he would make the proposal somewhere like Spago.

Waiting, she had engaged in a considerable amount of preparation. This wasn't just anticipation of how she should react when she saw the size of the diamond. She was quite sure that she was hard-headed and realistic, and horrid as his marriage was, she knew that he still had fears and objections about freeing himself from it. Doubtless he was anxious about the cost of the divorce, and, although he had rarely spoken of it, she knew that he dreaded the effect it might have on his children. So she had run through what she needed to say if he engaged in more temporizing. She could point out that her trust fund and her future inheritance constituted a backstop of sorts and that it guaranteed that they wouldn't have to move into a smaller house in a shabby part of town. She would make abundantly clear to him that she loved little ones and that she would be a good step-mother to the children he already had—as good as she would be a mother to their children.

She had been thrown off when he had said that he would stop by. But his voice was comforting and warm as ever, and when he turned up he looked as joyful as could be. A wonderful dresser, he was wearing a snazzy blazer and a baby blue linen shirt that was almost impossibly unwrinkled. His expression was adoring, and he took her in his arms.

The first thing he said threw her off, though. It was a winking declaration that they could finally make love without a condom. With that he drew her back, past the island in her kitchen, all the way back through the long, open room to her bed. Not sure what else she was to do, she proceeded to let him ravish her again, rapidly removing the clothes that she had spent an hour carefully draping herself in, and, as he was not a selfish lover and she was always taken by his slimness, his height, and his cologne, it was satisfying. Then they were in bed, and there was no way to avoid it. They had to talk.

He gazed at her expectantly and placed his hand on her belly where a convexity would soon be. "This won't be simple," he said.

"I understand."

"We'll have to wait. Until we're sure he—or she—is all right. They say not to tell anyone until you get past the twelfth week, you know."

She nodded. "I suppose in a way that it will make things easier for you, though. I mean your wife can't refuse you a divorce if she knows I'm expecting. In fact, she'll probably throw you out."

"So you're sure you want to have it?"

"What do you mean?"

There was a pause. He smiled, and his head bobbed thoughtfully as he took his hand off her abdomen and ran a knuckle over his deeply tanned chin. "That would make for a very ugly divorce. And expensive. But if you had an abortion and then we tried again in a year…"

From there things got ugly quickly. It astonished Claire at how easily the rage and the screaming came to her, and when he noted that he didn't even have any way of knowing it was his and he had been exceedingly careful, she grew more inflamed. She really hadn't ever been so angry in her adult life. How could he make such an accusation? She had been a compliant mistress for more than a year, almost never going out with him in public, not asking anything in return, patiently listening again and again to his claims that his marriage was over and that he hated his wife and to his promises that the papers would be filed any day, and now he all but said that she was passing off another man's child as his, trying to trick him into wedlock? She was reminded of the violent feelings she had as a girl, the kind where your face turned scarlet and you spat as you talked.

In the midst of this, the buzzer had rung, and she had thrown her blouse back on, quickly brushing her hair, before walking back to the opposite end of the loft to pick up the receiver and stare into the monitor showing who it was. The image of Billy, nervous and holding a bouquet, was terrifying. She could only chalk it up to her acting training that she was able to affect calm, responding in a tone of flawless indifference. When Mike asked her who it was, she hit the mute and casually informed him that it was the superintendent. Then she assured Billy that she would call him later and hung up.

The interruption momentarily pulled her up short, reminding her that Mike was not the father. But, if that was so as a matter of strict fact, it was not *emotionally* true. She did want it to be his baby, and it was appalling for him to say what he had. He had been leading her on. He had lied to her. He was not ready to leave his spouse. He was using her.

It was as though she were on a narrow mountain pass, and she had just gained her footing. To recognize what he said was to step downwards onto a spot where it was impossible to maintain your balance and you would be tossed over. With this in mind she went back to fulminating, roaring, and bawling. This alternated with attempts to pound her fists upon his chest. She had the advantage, and she was not going to concede it. She had spent so much time fantasizing about their future together, a life in which he worked to make her dreams come true, to just let it go. In any case, it was his fault. He had been scrupulous about protection. If he hadn't, she would have conceived long before. It was pure selfishness. She was yielding him her eggs and getting nothing in return. A friend had once said to her that there were many unplanned pregnancies but there were few unintended ones. The remark had baffled Claire when she had heard it. But as time had gone by, she had come to understand it. The aim of bringing them together through a child was just and right, and she had it in mind for months. Her only error had been in getting pregnant by the wrong man, and as her heart was in the right place that shouldn't be held against her.

In retrospect, she saw that she had done the only thing she could by becoming hysterical. Incessantly assailing him, she had established what their positions were, marking out how much she was owed, and she had watched as he skulked out, guiltily insisting once more that he would talk to his lawyer and his wife.

Then she broke down again. For some time, she lay on the bed with the covers around her. In a strange way, the intensity of the emotion was soothing. It was so absolute that it enveloped her and made her feel alive. Then there was simply grief. The sorrow was accompanied by a conviction or an inmost knowledge that the world was a place of indiscriminate injustice, but that others lacked access to this fundamental truth. That she alone saw the full spitefulness made her yet more conscious of how abandoned she was.

The high windows of the loft threw large shafts of light onto the floor. These patterns seemed suggestive and meaningful. Gradually they crept forward until they were on top of her. Two hours passed. She needed to prepare herself for a party, and she had to decide what to do about Billy. No longer could he be summarily written off, not if she were to actually have the child. The news that he had just sold a script was heartening. It needed to be investigated.

She had to compose herself. It was dark outside and turning colder, and she switched on the lights and the heat. Then she walked to the bathroom and examined her visage in the mirror. From there she went to the kitchen and put ice in a plastic bag which she alternated in setting on the two sides of her face. Could she go out like this? Jeff Bridges was supposed to be attending the affair, and she hoped to talk with him about the role of the lead actress's father in her *Fatal Attraction* remake. The host had said that he would make a point of introducing her in the most flattering terms. Her meeting with Viacom had been a success, and it seemed she would obtain the rights.

One thing she couldn't do was bring Billy to the party. Because he was—strictly literally—the father of what was inside her, he would be bound to act in a proprietary way, and she couldn't risk having word of that get back to Mike. For now, that relationship would need to be somewhat *profil bas. Discret.*

Setting the improvised ice pack down, she went and took a long hot shower, toweled herself off, and began making herself up. When she was not unhappy with the results, she dressed and got out her cell phone.

But, on this day, it seemed her timing was singularly off. No sooner was she ready to make the call then she felt a wave of nausea. It took her a moment to realize what the queasiness was: a first bout of morning sickness. She was standing by one of Mike's T-shirts, and it was bathed in his scents. These had triggered something, and she barely had time to get to the toilet bowl before she started retching. While she felt better after, the vomiting and the moistness around her eyes compelled her to do her makeup a second time and then to gargle mouthwash. Staring, she observed a curious side-effect of the puking: The dehydration had counterbalanced the tears, slimming her face and bringing her cheekbones back to their customary prominence. Even so, where she normally relied upon the natural whiteness of her skin, she caked on a layer of base. She seemed to be breaking out, and she felt that she was in need of a mask in order to leave the house.

Billy's voice had a false cheerfulness. He did not sound like someone who had just sold a pilot script. Nor did he even come across as so eager to speak with her. Rather, there was a resentful, almost icy edge in the way he talked, and when she put down the phone it struck her once more that she was in a wolf's den. This was the father of the child, a nerd whom they had blackballed from her senior society, and even he was full of himself and declaring his importance as a *significant novelist*, acting as though he didn't really need *her*! Where in God's name did it end? The men in Hollywood: They were *unbelievable*. The egos! The self-importance!

CHAPTER 34

There are few gates separating USC's campus from the South Central neighborhood around it. Martha Greaves had this in mind when she showed up for her first day at Gould. That is the name of the school of law.

She had dressed as though she were heading to a job at a downtown law firm. She was in a mid-calf rayon print dress, and she was holding a shiny leather satchel. It was her way of telling the guards—most of them African-American—that she was a student and not some demented local wandering off South Figueroa onto the campus.

The school made a big deal about its "diverse" representation and everyone bent over backwards to talk about concern for "people of color." It had been incessantly, annoyingly PC. Yet she knew all too well that if she attired herself the way the other students did—in a patched-up jean jacket and sweats—that she would get sidewise looks from security. The school brochures pointedly said that the school was 24 percent minority. That seemed to mean almost everything but black. Of the 121 members of her class, there were four brothers and sisters, and two were mulatto. They were café au lait, not black coffee.

The sense that she was a lone voyager carried with her to the county prosecutor's office. It felt at times as though Noah had filled his ark, and she was the sole parakeet in a hold full of carnivores: jackals and dogs and cats of every size staring avidly at her, anxious to tear her apart, hungrily eyeing the flesh beneath her bright plumage.

Friends told her that the junior entertainment industry talent agents were going to great lengths to sign up ex-pat Nigerian directors and British-Jamaican writers. And she saw African-American businessmen opening up art galleries and restaurants, hair salons and fashion labels. But, in the business of enforcing the law, she remained not just a minority in name but in fact. That had made her election as chief prosecutor all the harder. If the greatest number of the city's residents were impoverished immigrants in the barrios of East LA who had come from Mexico and Guatemala, Honduras and El Salvador, the top ranks of the police department and the attorneys' office still resembled a jury panel from the 1940s. They were male and white, paler than milk fat. She hadn't seen so much blonde hair on a trip to Stockholm. The impossible to pronounce last names announced their Midwestern German roots: Hoffmeister, Braugel, Dieterschmidt. And she knew they resented her. When she had been selected as Deputy Prosecutor, she was seen as a "minority choice," protection against another Watts Riot. She was an instrument, a means to keep a lid on "the ghetto." Her record of convictions was, it seemed, incidental. No matter how many cases she won, she was the choice of *other people*, the voters in South Central and Baldwin, Maywood and City Terrace.

There was no way to ignore this. Her office lay in one of the ugliest monoliths of the 1970s. Although it had been renamed, it is still known among those who work in it as "Criminal Courts." Set above a concourse at the top of Bunker Hill, it's across from the old ziggurat-shaped City Hall, just east of the warped metal of the Disney Concert Hall and the concrete bunker of the Mark Taper Forum. On its north side, Criminal Courts has a view of the packed line of cars on the 101 freeway. Within is the public defender's office, the prosecutor's division, a huge police unit, and the courts themselves. Necessarily, you see everyone you work with and against in the elevators and the bathrooms. You brush up against them when you're purchasing a candy bar in the lobby, and when you get your car from the garage at night. You see their sidewise glances, and you hear their snarling. She knew what they thought. She wasn't one of them. She was Black, a woman, a politician, and now she was confronted by the most talked-about murder they had ever afforded her, the Selva case. And the full extent of their fuck-up was gradually becoming apparent. She had been raised not to use expletives. Her mother was pointed about this. Theirs was a Christian home. But time among the police and in the attorneys' office had worn off on her, and in this instance the words were altogether apt. It *was* a shit show. The detectives in the Rampart precinct house who had provided her with the case did appear to be fumblers and screwups, blowhard incompetents to the nth degree. She knew the name that other cops would have applied: cocksuckers. They were goddamn, fucktard, piece of shit cocksuckers.

Yet the case was hers. The attorneys' office in Ventura was quite sensibly keeping its distance, though properly it should have been theirs: Vincenza's statement showed that she knew about the crime before the body had been recovered, she admitted that she had had dumped the corpse, and they had videotape confirming this. But if there was a conspiracy to commit the crime and acts in furtherance to it that had been perpetrated in Los Angeles County, the homicide had occurred in Ventura. More, while the most plausible explanation of events was that Vincenza was a party to the crime, they had no admission of that. Under normal circumstances, she—like all prosecutors—dreaded the Brady Rule. This is the requirement that exculpatory evidence must be peremptorily provided to the defense. In this case, that might have been helpful so that they could be rid of it. But they did not have that. Rather, they merely had evidence that she had not acted alone.

There appeared to be three or four directions they could go with the prosecution. Perhaps the Morgan woman's co-conspirators were figures in the Church of Life. There was also her association with the Israeli gangsters who ran the dispensary she worked in. Then there was the theory of the Rampart Village precinct that she had acted with the man she had been staying with, Billy Rosenberg. Some in the press had even implied that Vincenza had committed the crime in concert with his widow, though there seemed to be no evidence the two women had even met.

The need for answers had brought her to a corridor in the Lynwood—this and knowledge that her career and her next election might be decided by the case's outcome. She would not be asking the questions. But she wanted to watch through the two-way mirrored window when Vincenza was brought in.

She did not wish to greet her lawyer. She knew what Jerry D'Allesandro thought of her as she had been opposite him in court. While a number of the rank-and-file cops doubtless called her a spade when they were driving about in their prowlers, to D'Allesandro she was an Aunt Thomasina. She was the servant and the toy of the mighty: a race traitor. That the person who regarded her as such was white vexed her to no end. He had not had to live as a Black woman, yet he judged her. There really was no way to win. The balancing act required to do her job and protect the public—minority women especially—was beyond Olympic gymnasts.

Watching through the window, she folded her arms over her chest as her assistants stepped into the interview room, seating themselves around the interview table. D'Allesandro and the Morgan woman were there already in their clashing attire: he in his rumpled blue suit, she in the prison jumps. Greaves had forgotten how cold the jail was. She was shivering, and bothered by the odor rising up from the floor. Beside her were the warden, two jailers, and two more aides.

Staring ahead, she tried to make out Vincenza's condition. There were giant circles under her eyes, and her hair was a tousled mess. Yet she seemed defiant.

The district attorney listened as her assistants began not by asking Vincenza questions but by noting the contradictions in the case. They tried to sound modulated. They smiled. They offered her coffee. There was no good cop/bad cop act. They wanted her to be comfortable. Then they paused and asked her ever-so-gently if she had something she wanted to get off her sizeable chest.

As she looked to D'Allesandro and did not speak, they laid the situation out for her. It was simple enough. They knew she was a party to the crime, and they could give her a much-reduced sentence if she would tell them the truth, revealing to them what had actually happened and who it involved, and if she would testify against the guilty parties.

Martha watched as Vincenza shook her head in exasperation. Her loud insistence upon her innocence was hard to read. Was this the histrionics of a professional actress or was there something else at work? Undeterred, the assistants repeated the offer and turned to D'Allesandro, seeking his aid.

But Vincenza was determined. Her only crime, she kept saying, was in not calling the police when she found the body. And on one matter she was particularly unrelenting: The Church of Life had been following her, she said, and that was where they needed to look. What did this mean? Two decades as a prosecutor had taught her that there were immensely convincing liars, and there were truth-tellers who were no more persuasive than the average failed school board candidate.

Some details suggested that Vincenza was either mad or gifted at deception. She claimed that, as a woman, she had feminine intuition. She had this, she said, to an unusual degree, and they ought to listen to her as she was not getting high and could remember all the suspicious things she had previously ignored or missed. While she had been an adherent of the Church, she knew that their fixer, David Clarkson, had plotted the murder. They absolutely had to speak with him, she said.

This was not what Martha Greaves wanted to hear. Getting to her position had required brains, diligence, and shrewdness. The smarts and the doggedness she had always had, and skill in the courtroom came with experience. Yet you had to be watchful. To fight for those without power you had to be judicious in picking fights with those who possessed it. It was not until the #MeToo movement broke into the public consciousness that she had dared to go after Weinstein. She knew that they and their friends could raise the money to finance a campaign to replace her. While justice had to be present, it was hard to make use of her services when she was actually blindfolded.

All this told her that she needed to proceed haltingly. The Church of Life was a dangerous enemy. She had heard it said: James Armstrong was a combination of boa constrictor and rattler. He could squeeze the life out of you, and, if you kicked his tail, his bite was poisonous.

The Lynwood was equally full of women who ought to be let go and those who merited long sentences. To realize those ends, Martha Greaves needed to keep her job, and if everything was pointing one way, she had to walk towards it with tact and prudence. How was she to do that?

The newspapers were saying that she had been too slow to move on Weinstein. Was it time for her to pick a big target? To display her toughness, should she challenge the biggest hombre in the bar? Listening to the fervent way that Vincenza spoke, she ruminated on the idea. Was she someone who would be intimidated, a typical politician focused merely upon the acquisition of power? She did not think so.

CHAPTER 35

There was a sense in which Los Angeles was more like Johannes-burg than New York or Chicago. Abril Fernandez knew this.

The realization had dawned upon her gradually. Initially she had thought Los Angeles was *los Estados Unidos*. Should the rest of the country differ, she supposed that this was a function of the weather or the topography. Surely, she thought, all of *El Norte* must be like the city.

Abril had arrived with her parents as an eleven-year-old. They lived in the one-bedroom apartment of her aunt and uncle in West-lake. For two years, there were seven people in their two rooms. She, her parents, and her younger brother and sister slept on mattresses in the living room, and she had to hopscotch her way to the bathroom if she awoke in the middle of the night. The heating was poor, and in the winter it was cold and damp.

When her mother became pregnant again, they moved down the block. Her parents worked long hours, and she had to watch the little ones in the afternoon and sometimes in the evenings, too. In the morning, *mamacita* awoke early, fed them, and then got onto buses that delivered her to empty street corners. From these she walked to the homes of the *Anglos* who employed her as a maid. Sometimes

206

these were far off, whether to the west by the ocean or north into the Valley. Her father hung out among a crowd of itinerant workers who congregated around a home supply store. There he waited to be called to perform odd jobs: painting walls, grouting bath tiles, trimming hedges.

It seemed to her unimaginably wonderful. It was so much better than their *barrio* in Guatemala City. There, in *El Limón*, they lived in a concrete hovel without hot water or a toilet that flushed. A frequent sound was gunshots. Here they were in walking distance of the mansions of Hancock Park.

In the middle of their neighborhood was MacArthur Park. On one side was a meadow with a soccer field where she and her brother and sister played. On the other there was a small lake with sailboats. Beneath a pair of palm trees, men drifted in and out. They kept an eye out for the police as their business was selling counterfeit social security cards. When her father managed to obtain one of these, it allowed him to move up to employment as a dishwasher. In addition, it permitted them to get food stamps, and rather suddenly they had more in the cupboards. Down by Pico-Union, they could stroll into a bodega and purchase anything, from bags of *chicharrones* to corn masa and yuca and satchels of rice. There were also American staples like Ring Dings and breakfast cereal and tubs of margarine. There was every kind of plantain.

Her school in Los Angeles sprawled onto what had once been a parking lot and a basketball court. Prefab buildings had been tacked onto an older structure, dating to the 1930s. The English-language classes were mostly filled by Korean children. But there were also a great many Blacks, Mexicans, Lebanese, El Salvadorans, and her fellow Guatemalans. That she had been assigned to Spanish-language instruction was a mixed blessing as her first language—the one she used most often at home—was K'iche: Mayan. That her English-language instruction did not commence until she was in her first year of high school and that she was an illegal: These sidelined any chance of college, even were it something she might have seen as a real possibility for herself. But who wanted to spend years more in school when there was work and a life for yourself to be had?

That life soon focused upon another, as in her senior year she had gotten pregnant and given birth to her son. She had been surprised by how relaxed her parents were that she was moving in with her boyfriend, though the two were not wed. It was many years before she understood that they were gratified to have more space and one fewer mouth to feed.

That her boyfriend was unreliable was not obvious. He had a job that paid well. And not only was he naturally skilled as a mechanic and gifted with charm, but he was also operating his own garage within a few years. Over time, though, it became apparent that he liked to drink, whether it was tequila or beer. Yet his love for her was real, and still greater was his affection for their son and the daughter who soon followed.

Her own work was what her mother's had been. As her English was so much better, she did not need to go off to distant parts of the city to clean people's homes. There were innumerable families in Hancock Park who wanted her as a maid. This entailed cleaning but also picking up and dropping off children at school, going for their laundry, and setting out the baby carrots and the cheese plates when guests came over. Sometimes it meant walking the dog.

Her boyfriend's business supplied them with cars. He made money fixing them up, and so in addition to the two they relied upon, there were usually three or four others available. They had cable television and an air conditioner for the occasional sweltering evening.

The weather was the most miraculous thing. If you bought a space heater and a decent blanket, you were armed for the chill winds that came in the winter. Then, week after week passed when all you knew was bright sun, warm air, and cloudless skies.

Was there reason to be resentful? She was startled and amazed by how palatial some of the homes the Anglos lived in were and she was conscious that while the mayor was of her own kind, the wealth and the power was in other hands.

Still, theirs was a good life, and you had to be a fool to want to part with it, to go back to the chaos and the poverty and the violence of home. She was not put off by the obstacles that were being thrown up against the college plans of those, like herself, who were without papers. She had her life. But the danger of being identified by the ICE agents was not imaginary.

All this had become relevant because of something she had observed by chance. Not all those who employed her were well-off. There was status in having a maid and many of the Anglos had grown resistant to toil. Because of this, there was always extra work if you wanted it, and that winter she had elected to take some. That brought her to an apartment on Golden Gate Avenue. The job called for three hours each on successive Sundays, and the woman hiring her was sufficiently desperate that she was not only paying her twenty-five dollars per hour—five dollars more than her regular pay—but she was also giving her money for gas and a takeout lunch. The boss was an actress and first-time movie producer.

It seemed that the woman was planning for a big party to celebrate the sale of the movie she had helped make and star in. She was bubbly and effusive in speaking of it. Indeed, it was hard to get her to stop chattering about it so Abril could get an explanation of what it was she wanted done.

Part of that was dealing with the kitty litter. But there was lots else. There was caked-up dirt and cat hair on the baseboards and in the corners and under the bed. That last spot was where she had come upon something she had not expected: a gun. Tucked artfully away beneath the mattress, it had a distinctive smell that drew her attention. Were it not for that, she would have missed it, hidden as it was. It was a scent Abril knew from her childhood in *El Limón*: the odor of gunpowder. Yet when she searched for it upon her return the following Sunday—spurred by an unhealthy curiosity—it was missing.

The woman's picture was frequently on the news over the weeks that followed, and she asked herself what she should do. She had always taken a secret delight in the fact that her *indio* face, pretty though she knew it was, escaped the notice of the Anglos. That had kept her safe..

CHAPTER 36

Billy Rosenberg was finding that the ballyhooed sale of his novel had been a much smaller boost to his career than the Selva case was. Overnight, he had become a minor figure of fascination. In some versions, he was a dashing ladies' man and seducer. In others, he was a soulless killer, a writer who was at once the instigator, the man behind a compelling true crime, if also its eventual recorder.

Nearly every story in the press began its discussion of him by implying that he was Vincenza's lover. She had been staying with him, hadn't she? Inevitably, pictures of him arriving to see her, standing outside the Lynwood, were reported on with the dewy-eyed concern usually reserved for accounts of the death of Princess Diana. On some days, it was suggested that he and Vincenza were sweethearts who had plotted murder together. On others, it was intimated that they were perhaps both innocent, victims of an unkind fate, as deserving of sympathy as Heloise and Abelard.

Because his name was so often mentioned in the articles and TV reports about the Selva case, his pilot script had finally been read, and then it had been passed on to a veteran showrunner who attached himself to the project. With that it was sold to one of the broadcast networks, and between the purchase of his bounty hunter pilot and the fee for his revision of *Arthur Rex*, he was not only out of debt but flush. More, he could not get out from under the flood of dinner party, cocktail party, and barbecue invites he was receiving. At these, he was surrounded, pressed with queries about Vincenza and his role in the affair. Slyly, he would claim that he had been advised that it was best if he spoke reservedly about Vincenza and the case, then noting his own innocence. This tease only whetted the curiosity of his interrogators, even as it made him seem mysterious and beguiling. Meantime, his motion picture agent was circulating the environmental dystopia script he had written, and his book agent in New York was prodding him to send along revised opening chapters from his unpublished second novel.

Then there was Claire. Was it the pictures of Vincenza that were all over the internet that had reawakened her interest? Some showed Vincenza in a string bikini. In the photo you could not only see how large her chest was but the small waist and the toned abdominals. Or was it that matters were flatlining between Claire and Mike Fruchtman? Whatever the cause was, his baby mama was now calling him, eager to talk. Indeed, she was finally coming over to his place— and at eight in the evening, no less!

Billy had told himself that he must not spend too much time following press reports of the case. This was impossible. He was a *homo sapiens*, and when your name was cropping up on hundreds of websites, in Reddit posts, and in manifold TMZ stories you wanted to know what was said. In addition, he was eager to learn whatever he could about Vincenza and whether she might actually be guilty. And while his awareness that he was prospectively a father had deterred him from sleeping with other women, he was curious to know what thoughts were being expressed about him by floozies taken with his fame.

This led to frequent halts in his workday. He would start writing, knock out a few lines, and then persuade himself that he needed to take another break to see how many times his name was cropping up on Twitter, or whether he had been mentioned by one of the networks. These were ever-present preoccupations. Pausing in making dinner for Claire, he went to his computer and typed in a Google request. This one told him that his name had come up in 1114 stories and blog posts that day. 309 had appeared just in the four hours since he had last checked.

One was of particular interest. It was the lead article on the *Los Angeles Times* website. It began:

In a surprise announcement, Los Angeles County prosecutor Martha Greaves said this afternoon that her office was transferring accused killer Vincenza Morgan to the custody of the Ventura County Sheriff's Office. Ms. Morgan, 29, is charged in the death of movie actor Tom Selva, star of *The Dangerous Race* movies.

In a prepared statement, Ms. Greaves, who is running for reelection in November, commented: "It is with considerable regret that this office chooses to reassign the case. However, there can be little doubt but that the crime took place in Ventura, and this office is well-aware that it must always have as its aim the true administration of justice. This can best be served by its adjudication in its proper locale. I wish to emphasize that I did not assume this post in order to use it as a stepping stone, and, extraordinary as the interest in the matter is, I wish rather to focus, to the greatest extent possible, on my long-stated goals. These are, as they have been, bail and criminal justice reform along with effective prosecution of the most heinous acts unlawfully committed against the people of Los Angeles, poor as well as rich."

Responding briefly to follow-up questions, Greaves refused to speculate on the further progress of the case. However, the two-term prosecutor, dressed in one of her familiar pleated dresses, did say that she was "in regular and faithful contact with the authorities in Ventura County, and that our city and county police will, of course, continue to assist with the investigation." She also reported that Ms. Morgan is now in a prosecutor's office vehicle bringing her into the custody of Ventura County. She insisted that the investigation was proceeding as anticipated and denied reports of concerns within her office over the strength of the case.

The last words especially caught Billy's attention. That the case was beginning to look tatty and infirm was increasingly hinted at in the press. He did not have time to process this, though, as no sooner had he read it then he saw a text from Claire, announcing that she was stuck in traffic and she wouldn't be arriving for another thirty-five minutes. This reminded him of how little time he had to get the brussels sprouts finished, the wild rice out of the pot, and the *mise en place* arrayed for the ginger swordfish he would be sautéing.

After she buzzed him from downstairs, he combed his hair once more, gazing into one of the sheets of plate glass covering the closets of his apartment. Then he tried to remind himself to be cheery and not to allow thoughts about Mike Fruchtman to inspire dyspeptic looks.

Opening the door, he saw a woman in a thin, cream-colored dress. She was not yet at the point of showing. Quite the opposite: It appeared that she had been struggling with morning sickness, and she had lost weight. She was gaunt but smiling and very beautiful. Her skin was especially pale, and her eyes were particularly green. She had been careful not to wear too much makeup. Her appearance plainly was meant to contrast with Vincenza, and the dress seemed to be a dry run—or a suggestion—for another white outfit, one she might attire herself in on a later, more formal occasion.

He was not sure, though: Was he supposed to kiss her passionately on the lips? The cheek she offered him told him that while she had been calling him, he was still auditioning for a role.

Bringing her in, he set her down on his couch. He had hired a maid to clean the place thoroughly, and he had spent the morning putting books and papers in boxes and cabinets, fluffing the pillows, changing the sheets, and washing the floors of the bathroom for a second time after the maid had departed. He knew that the room was still apt to seem less than wonderful when the competition was a producer who lived in Bel Air and his visitor had been raised by people who owned hotels. Mixing them both nonalcoholic drinks, he discovered, however, that it was not his drapes that were being queried but his connection with Vincenza.

The line between text and subtext was blurry. As he worked in the kitchenette on their meal, he noticed, gazing back to her, that for once she was not crossing her legs to show them off. She wanted answers. Careful not to seem hostile, she was intent on finding out: Had he been sleeping with Vincenza when they had gone to the Korean barbecue restaurant? Had Vincenza moved in with him prior to her arrest?

He understood that there was no way to be artful. He saw, too, that it would look almost as bad in Claire's eyes to admit that he had taken a stray, mangy creature in off the street as to say that Vincenza had been in his bed. Nor could he make note of what he knew—or at least strongly suspected—about Claire's relationship with the other man whom she was presumably trying to sell on the notion that he was the father of her child.

There was no way around it. He had to be what his time in Los Angeles had taught him never to be: honest. So, slowly, then, he told her what had happened. He followed this up by sharing the details on all of his recent good fortune: how his agent had invited him to a party at the agency where he had been introduced to the firm's founder, his meeting with the successful showrunner he might work with on his bounty hunter series and their work on the show's "bible," the industry veterans who were asking him to lunch. He noticed that she was not listening as intently as he might have hoped. She was sleepy.

Still, the account seemed to have its intended effect. Curling herself up on the couch, she kicked off her heels, showing off her calves. Yet, when he set down the meal, she sat back up and the movement seemed to return her to full alertness, and, as she began eating, she commenced a string of inquiries. First, she wanted to know more about the bounty hunter show. If the pilot were ordered, she asked, would he arrange for her to audition for it? Perhaps even for the lead, supposing that a name had not been attached to play it? Did he see them as a team?

Billy knew the correct answers, but he was dismayed by the questions. She had not even told him about her latest doctor visit. Nor had she informed him of her views on his cooking. She smiled and flirted, but the rawness of the ambition frightened him and made him wonder: Would a future with Claire be a succession of such negotiations? Would there ever be a moment when they were just going to the beach with their child? Or would it always be intruded upon by discussion of when he would prod his agent on her behalf or whether he had managed to flesh out her character's motivation in the script's third act? Would it be one of those entertainment industry marriages where once she had gotten when she wanted—paternity established and a helping hand in her career—that he would be dispensed with? It was impossible not to be aware of her toughness.

These fears battled with his attraction. Before she had arrived, he had told himself that he was no simp. He had a new level of confidence. He was the one being talked about, and she was carrying his child. He would be master of the situation. But no sooner did she enter than he was conscious again of his old feelings of desire for her and the power of her beauty and her poised assurance.

She ate deliberately. It was difficult. He watched as she dispensed with her swordfish cutlet and put down her fork. This was her way of telling him that she would reveal what she had learned about the fetus from her gynecologist. The big "takeaway," she said, was that a fetal heartbeat had been detected, and she was in her sixth week. Given her age, that meant the likelihood of miscarriage was below 5 percent. The doctor said not to announce it generally yet, but, more than likely, they were having a child. However, they would not know the sex for another two months.

Did he prefer a girl or a boy?

When they went to his bedroom for their second occasion of lovemaking, he was aware that she was not fully in the moment, that she was performing for him and investigating him. He had felt more openness from Chalmers when he had been questioned by him in the car outside her apartment.

Still, Billy was tender as he could be, determined to show his passion for her and not to harm the child. He kissed her all over face and her neck with light little pats of his lips. He ran his hands down her legs and back, slowly stroking them. In turn, she was set on showing him that she could focus on his pleasure—at the very least until he had gone back to the diamond district for an appropriate ring.

CHAPTER 37

Claire arose early and wrote a note which she placed on Billy's coffee table. It thanked him for dinner and the lovemaking, and it ended with the word love, the letter C, and a big heart sign.

Though she had to be back at her apartment to wash and change and ready herself for Mike Fruchtman, the note was not insincere. Billy's sweetness touched her. She was acutely sensitive to the difference in the treatment she received from the men in her life. Mike had offered her a deal, although it had not been presented as a transaction. Nothing with Mike ever was depicted that way, and as much and as long as she had pinned her hopes on him and as deep as her sexual attachment was, she did not want to admit to herself how completely fooled she had been. But, as she drove back to her Mid-City apartment, she saw things as they were, and she knew that there were only two paths open. One was to marry Billy if he would propose to her. The other was to have the child on her own. For as it grew day by day within her, her revulsion for the thought of abortion grew.

This surprised her. It astonished her. Her credit card was charged each month for her Planned Parenthood donations, and for years she had loudly insisted to anyone who would listen that a fetus was not a baby and anyone who supposed it was hadn't taken biology and didn't know that during gestation there was a period when it had *gills*. But this was not some random person's fetus. This was her child, and it was growing, fed from her blood and bones.

The arrangement that Mike had proposed—professing that one thing need not go with the other—was that he would take her to her gynecologist for an abortion. One week later they would meet with Todd Gelber about their *Fatal Attraction* remake. Then, in a year, he would have a more affordable settlement with his wife, and they would try again.

If she had misled herself about his intentions for many months, she was not deluded now. He was not leaving his wife, not for her. It struck her that what had happened to her was in its own way worse than what Weinstein had done. It was #MeToo raised to a higher power. Weinstein had pressured women for sex in return for parts. Mike was pressuring her to kill her fetus and then to go back to being his mistress. It was an offer of professional help for one abortion and fifty or sixty subsequent sex acts, depending on how these fit into his schedule.

She had left Billy's apartment by Franklin Canyon just after seven, and the roads back to her place were empty. It was the sort of morning when the day began with gray clouds, ones that would burn off: ideal weather for thinking.

It struck her that perhaps Mike was not as smart as he imagined. After all, he was relying upon her truthfulness, and if he had taught her anything, he had taught her to get it on paper. Yet they did not have a contract on *Fatal Attraction*. He had simply assumed that as she was his lover that she couldn't push him off the deal.

Desperately hungry, she was both too nervous and too nauseated to eat, and she went straight to her bathroom, once she had opened her door. There she took a shower. Afterwards, she prepared herself, taking her time. At nine Mike would be parked on the street outside her building. He would be there to pick her up and drive her to the obstetrics clinic, which was in Brentwood. This was his idea of being a gentleman: taking her. Brushing her hair, she was moved to a perception regarding conception: Fathers attend births, but no man is present at the abortion.

From within her armoire, she selected a black cashmere sweater-set. It was sexy but also appropriately mournful. Examining herself in the mirror, she saw that it was perfect. The outfit would entice him. At the same time, it sold the idea that she was going to go through with it.

Once in his car, she added to the ledger by breaking down in tears, hinting that maybe she wouldn't be able to do it. Cruelly as he had taken advantage of her, she delighted in watching him squirm, begging her to trust him. Then she blotted the tears with a handkerchief, made herself up again in the passenger side mirror, and watched as he pulled out into traffic. If she had ever doubted her talents as an actress, she did not any longer. She was inspired, and she knew it. Streep, Davis, Hepburn: How often had they been so brilliant? She felt a small sadness that one of her greatest performances would perish without record.

The silence they drove in would have frightened a mime.

THE CLINIC, WHICH LISTED ITSELF AS ON WILSHIRE, was actually a block south, just past the 405. It looked like any other Los Angeles medical office: There were orchids in the lobby, and a gay man, an aspiring actor, was at the front desk. Mike sat on a leather sofa in the waiting area, fidgeting, almost shaking, as she went to see her doctor, Irina Shepero, an attractive, solidly built blonde woman who spoke with a slight Russian accent.

She had not told Irina that she was supposed to be having an abortion. But it occurred to her that her meeting had to seem longer than what it was: just a routine drop-by to chat with her gynecologist. So, after she had spoken with her once more, Claire walked to a bathroom, made herself up, and briefly played a video game on her phone, checking her watch until forty-five minutes had elapsed.

Then she walked back to the waiting area. She was dismayed to see that Mike had signed the receipt, and a sinking feeling came over her. But then, in examining it, she saw that it merely offered the anodyne "gynecological services" as an explanation and that the charge was $450. Thus, the bill fit the bill. With that recognition, she stepped towards him.

"That was very brave," he said.

"It certainly wasn't easy."

"I'm proud of you. We should talk about how many we are going to have, once we can do this the right way." He stopped. "I mean having a family, of course."

"I understood."

As he drove her back, she had the weird sense that he thought he was being generous in returning her to Mid-City when he had so much work. That consciousness motivated her towards the *coup de grace*.

When he arrived outside her building, she suggested that he park the Bentley on the street. Then she began crying again. Removing her seatbelt, she leaned to her left, placing her head on his chest. She knew what effect this and the black cashmere sweater-set would have, and she waited until she observed his erection. Then she pulled it out and used a memory exercise to recall a noisome odor. This did the trick as she barfed the remains of her brussels sprouts and ginger swordfish into his lap.

She feigned great shame in apologizing. When he asked tamely if he might wash up in her apartment, she explained that she needed time now, after the procedure, to be by herself. *To heal.* Didn't he understand?

"I'm sorry about the smell. That it will stay in your car. I know how much you love it."

Saying this, she retreated from the automobile as he rather submissively accepted her apology, reminding her that he would see her again the following week at the streaming service for their conference with Todd Gelber.

CHAPTER 38

When Jerry D'Allesandro heard the phone message saved on Tom Selva's phone, he knew at once why the Los Angeles prosecutor's office had dumped the case on Ventura County.

They could say it wasn't cause for a Brady disclosure. But you could also claim that the moon is under an hour's drive from the Earth or that French fries are a health food item. The message he heard, which had been left on Selva's cell phone, was from "James." James was informing Selva that he might be delayed because of traffic. Vincenza's obsessed chatter about the Church of Life had prompted D'Allesandro to hunt for tapes of James Armstrong's speeches. The first of these to turn up on the internet was his memorial address at Selva's funeral. The bass voice was unmistakable.

There could be no doubt that Martha Greaves knew this, and that she didn't want to tangle with the Church. No one did. They had blackmailed the head of the IRS, and they had tarnished the reputation of many others. Those who had left and criticized them found themselves accused of sexual assault or child molestation or being in the closet. They had real dirt, and they also knew how to manufacture it when it was absent.

The audio recording from Selva's phone strongly hinted that Armstrong had been present when the murder had taken place while his client insisted that she had not been there. They had confirmation that she had been followed by Church operatives, and the Church had been busily leaking salacious material about Vincenza taken from their files. It was suggested that she had left Eagan because her mother had come to see her as a rival and competitor for her stepfather's affections. Her addiction to marijuana and her work at the dispensary were prominently mentioned, as were her past affairs with other performers and with a well-known photographer. Her lack of education was commented upon. Then there was the imputation that she was in love with Selva, and that he had gone back on a promise to leave his wife for her. There was the fact that she had been in possession of the body and the gun that killed him. All this was coming as much from the Church as from the prosecutors down in Criminal Courts. The Church was set on her conviction.

Yet what was lacking was a logical sequence of events explaining not only her guilt but the *existence* of the body, to say nothing of its placement in her trunk. If someone else had shot Selva, why hadn't they buried the corpse or thrown it along with a weight into the ocean or obliterated it by burning the cottage down. That was the most puzzling aspect of the case. These were all far easier and surer methods of evading the law.

While it is a convention of TV shows and movies that someone has been "framed," in real life this happens in but one of two ways: false witness identification or, more rarely, prosecutorial misconduct. D'Allesandro knew this. He knew it from many years of his own experience and a hundred conversations with other defense lawyers. And yet, rather than destroy the cadaver, someone had moved it in order to incriminate Vincenza.

Why?

That there was a corpse strongly implied Armstrong was not the killer. After all, the Church immolated its dead, as it had Selva. If he had murdered Selva, there was little reason for him not to torch the beach cottage. The only conceivable motivation was that they were the beneficiaries for the insurance policy on the house and that an arson might waken additional interest on the part of claims investigators. In any event, Selva was a prize asset for promoting the faith.

Determined to resolve the question, D'Allesandro was again watching the movie that Vincenza had made. It was his fourth viewing of the film. On each occasion, he had scribbled extensive notes on one of his yellow legal pads. He had stopped the tape repeatedly to study Selva's on-screen shooting. Then he had scrutinized it—and its various outtake reels—with increasing zeal and frustration. He had watched the main titles and the end titles for clues. He had hunted for possible discrepancies between the story treatment and the finished film. He had studied the multiple improvisations of certain key scenes. He saw nothing meaningful or relevant.

His arrangement with Vincenza called for him to handle the case *pro bono*. His only profit would come from a future sale of a memoir. An irony that had occurred to him more than once was that he stood to lose by proving her innocence before the trial took place as it would mean that he would not be the trial lawyer whom the nation saw on TV. Nonetheless, he was determined. He was going to win. He wanted to demolish them, and he believed her.

It was past ten o'clock at night, and he was seated in the storefront office he had rented in South Central. Outside he heard the sounds of the neighborhood: sirens of passing ambulances, people talking loudly, laughing and arguing, car horns going off, and a beatbox playing. A box of fried chicken from a local joint was on his desk. It was nearly finished and cold, yet he was famished.

Stopping the tape, he walked to his office's front window and gazed at the faces on the street: young African-American couples walking together, teenagers in groups. They weren't working. They were enjoying themselves. For all the difficulty and oppression that they faced, at the moment they were living as they wanted.

That insight abruptly spurred another one, and quite suddenly D'Allesandro came to a surmise that told him why Selva's body might not have been destroyed and who had killed him.

CHAPTER 39

There were certain things about *El Norte*—the United States—that never ceased to befuddle Abril.

One was the priests. Why were they all gay? In Guatemala, there were three faiths. There were Moravians, Pentecostals, and Catholics, and at different times she had encountered ministers from each sect. While she had been a girl and not attuned as a woman is, none had struck her as effeminate. The Pentecostal ministers in particular tended to be macho. When she had reached adulthood, she had asked her mother if she were mistaken or if there was a difference between a pastor in Guatemala City and a man of the cloth in Los Angeles. Her mother had assured her that she was not in error.

This did not bother her. It was just odd. Why was it that every time she entered the confessional she was presented with someone who talked in an almost caricatured fashion? They were good men. They were kind and thoughtful. She felt that. She heard it in the way they spoke to her. Never once did they tell her not to take communion because she and her boyfriend were unmarried. Never once did they scold her when they offered her absolution for her sins. They didn't ask her if she was putting money into the contributions case. Before Christmas one year, a priest made her a present of one of the

remaining trees that they hadn't managed to sell. They had not solicited donations from her after either of her children's baptisms. Yet each
time she went into the box she found herself wondering: Would she
ever encounter a straight priest, one whose voice made her conjure
up the image of a handsome actor, the sort you saw in Telenovelas?

This was on her mind one morning as she gazed through the
screen. As always, it was hard to see the priest clearly. But she knew that
it was not the one who gave the homilies for the Sunday afternoon
services. This was someone different. While his accent told her that he
spoke Spanish, his voice was deep and commanding. She could see
from where his head was placed that he was tall, and she could make
out a square line to the jaw. She could see, too, that he was young. The
hair was thick and of that deep black shade that's almost blue. Though
she loved the father of her two children, she could not deny it: She
was aroused. She experienced it in her loins. He was sexy as could be.

She had come for guidance about the Tom Selva murder case.
Was it right to allow a woman to face prosecution for a crime—
the most serious—when she knew of evidence that cast guilt upon
someone else?

When Abril said this, the priest stopped her. He had that quality
of presence, manliness which she felt immediately. His breathing and
the movements of his chest conveyed his intentions, and she paused,
waiting for his words.

"You're concerned because you're not legal? Worried about going
to the police? That's what you mean?"

She had spent years imagining a priest who spoke like this. She
could even make out his scent, which was clean and welcoming.
Notes of bar soap mingled with something just a touch musky.

"That's right, father. I could be deported. We're not married,
and even if we were, they say that I could be denied a green card
because I've been here illegally. Thirteen years. They say I would
have to go through something called consular processing. I'd have to

leave my children with him and return to Guatemala. And it could take me up to ten years waiting there before I could come back with a green card."

"I'm glad you came to me. I can tell you: They've changed the law. In California, you can testify in court, and they can't question you about your immigration status."

"I understand. But it's the Selva case. There are so many reporters. People will want to know who I am. It would be hard for them not to find out. And then…"

She could vaguely make out his lips. They seemed to purse as he weighed what she was telling him.

"You speak Kaqchikel?"

"K'iche, father. Close enough. How did you know?"

"It's my own dialect. I had a sense." She watched as the position of his mouth shifted again. She knew he was smiling at the connection between them. She had heard that the church was bringing in a new priest to translate the services into some of the Mayan dialects, and she realized that he was the minister assigned to this task. "The Tom Selva case?"

"Yes, father. As I say, I cleaned the home of one of the women in the case. I not only saw the gun—where it was placed beneath her bed—I could smell that it had been used. Recently."

She sensed that he was still pondering some idea. The rumination provided her a moment to reflect upon her life. She and Alejandro—her Alex—had made love whenever they could up until the time she had gotten pregnant, even though she was in high school and living with her parents. But once their son was born and they had moved in together, she was focused on the baby, and it had become less frequent. She knew that he resented this, yet it seemed the problem grew worse with their daughter. When she wanted it, he didn't. When he did, she was tired, and then the children were always fighting to have her breast. She felt guilty for her attraction to the priest. His vow of celibacy was the least of what was wrong about it. But what was his suggestion?

She wondered what the priest was thinking. She had the sense that he might be playing with his thumbs or fingers. But overall she had a feeling of stillness. The church was nearly empty, and the only noise was a mop that was running over a distant stretch of floor. The minister's placement in the confessional set him in profile. She knew that his focus was upon her. This was not a priest who was somewhere else. He was with her. Still, it took some time for him to collect his thoughts. His voice then was very gentle, almost hushed. It was the sort of tone that she had used herself when she was talking to her children as they were falling asleep.

"You're married?"

"We're not."

"But he's a citizen?"

"As are the children."

"I know something about this consular processing. My mother had to go through it."

"She did?"

Although it was impossible to see him nodding through the screen, small as the gesture must have been, she had the vague awareness of it.

"This case is important. I suppose you know that the whole country is following it. I know someone in the government who might be able to help. I can talk with him. But I would like you to do something first."

"Alex and I have to marry?"

"You don't *have to*. I'll help you either way."

"You would like me to?

"It is a sacrament…Would you like me to officiate?"

She could not say no. Quite suddenly, then, her thoughts shifted away from the priest and the wooden closet she was in. It was as though she had been supernaturally transported outside the box, passing from shadow to light, as she began to daydream about the dress she would be wearing.

CHAPTER 40

Billy wasn't angry when he realized that Claire was gone. He was in a state of exultation. More even than when he had first slept with her, he was intoxicated.

He understood that she was guarded and often self-centered. There were concerns, too, about the child. Was it his? If it was, had she tried to exhibit it as another Mike Fruchtman production? Yet these questions hardly seemed to matter. She was Claire Hesper, and she had gone to bed with him. It had happened a second time. He was really in the running to be her boyfriend or husband. It was as though the Swiss Guards in the Vatican had successfully planned a moon landing. Or, rather, given his ancestry, it was as though an Israeli was standing on the top step when they were awarding the medals after the hundred-meter race at the Olympics. It was incredible. A shaft of light peeked in through a window and reflected from the plate glass on the cabinets and closets. It made the objects in his living room shine: the chair, the floor, the plastic covers of the DVDs. Outside, the sky was perfectly blue, the air devoid of smog. It did not seem possible.

Even so, he was not heading that morning to Claire's place. He was fulfilling a very public obligation by driving to the women's detention section of a jail in Santa Paula, California. This was where Vincenza had been transferred.

The best that could be said of the trek was that it was against the flow of traffic. The 101 North took him past the modernist mansions of Coldwater Canyon. There he had picked up the 405. That brought him onto the old I-5 with its innumerable gas station and diner exits. Turning onto one of these, he plunged into the undulating course of the 127 West. Then, ninety minutes after he had started out in Hollywood, he was parking his car at the Todd Road Jail, a horizontal line of windowless buildings within which Ventura County housed its women detainees.

Just two news vans and not more than a dozen reporters were in the lot. This absence of a crowd seemed to Billy an elegantly neat solution to an old philosophical question: When a tree falls past the Los Angeles county line, has it really happened? As his view nonetheless continued to be that it had, he posed for pictures, refused to answer the reporters' questions, and then entered the main structure, signing in at the visitors' desk. There he found that he was compelled to wait far longer than he had at Lynwood. Vincenza had a meeting with her lawyer that was to take precedence. It was uncertain how long that would take, and because the jail required him to give up his electronic devices and all reading materials, there was nothing for him to do but ponder and look about. Still, he was cheery. Claire had even tried to focus on his pleasure. Was this a herald, a portent full of wonder, a miraculous event presaging a future sex life with her in which she considered his satisfaction?

He was conscious of how much he was smiling, and he worried that he was out of place or that his keenness might be irksome. Yet, as he gazed about, he saw the faces around him were markedly different from those he had eyed at the Lynwood. Even the lawyers in the visitors' room seemed jaunty and optimistic. Plain as it was that they knew each other, he watched as they bantered.

Brightly lit, the room reverberated with expectant chatter. Because the jail housed inmates of both sexes, along with the mentally ill and those awaiting bail, there were girlfriends with unrinsed hair and tattoos and the well-dressed parents of deranged offspring. There were even a few married men there for their wives. Most, though, appeared to fall into just two categories: lawyers and mothers of the accused.

The attorneys were dressed in flashy suits matched to highly polished dress shoes. The striking thing about the matriarchs was their thin hair. Almost without exception and regardless of their race, they displayed bright patches of scalp on the tops of their round heads.

The one attorney not part of the fraternity was Vincenza's own, Jerry D'Allesandro. While they had only spoken on the phone, Billy recognized his face from his frequent appearances on TV. In these, he persistently lambasted the prosecutor's office for leaking details of the case, insisting upon Vincenza's innocence. During these moments, he projected a mix of righteous fervor and arch self-awareness.

Like Billy himself, he had driven up from LA, and, noticing him, he approached, introducing himself and offering Billy a hand. He was a head taller than Billy, easily twice his weight, and smelled of greasy food. His hand swallowed Billy's own as a boy's is enveloped by his father's. Yet avuncular as D'Allesandro was, Billy was neither intimidated nor threatened. That the attorney loved engaging with people was hard to miss. He gestured towards a leather satchel around his shoulder. "I've got the stuff to get the case dismissed. Or I think I can get it," he said.

"I believe you. And I believe her."

"But...?

"Well, I mean, everyone is wondering: How did the body wind up in her trunk?"

D'Allesandro beamed. His expression told Billy that there was a perfectly reasonable answer and that he wanted to say what it was, but that he couldn't just yet. Still, Billy realized that the lawyer had a specific aim in mind that he had come over to offer him his hand.

"You want something of me, don't you?"

"Yes, I do," he allowed. "There's a way you can help her that may not be obvious."

"Go ahead."

While there was something comforting in D'Allesandro's manner, Billy did not like the way he was hovering over him. Nor was he drawn in by the pungent odor of fried food glazed onto D'Allesandro, and Billy motioned for him to sit down and speak more quietly so that they would not be overheard. Taking the cue, D'Allesandro rested himself on a plastic seat at his side, hunching forward.

"I think you know that leaving a cult is one of the hardest things a person can do," he said. "You lose all your friends. You lose your identity. You lose your sense of purpose. You even lose your past. What did the last ten years of your life mean without it? It's probably easier to accept divorce or the death of a parent."

"I'm sure you're right."

"Vincenza knows that the Church played some role in this. But she needs to really part herself from them—in order to open up and give me some additional things I need. *Details*." He paused. "It seems you're one of the few people right now she's even in touch with, who's speaking to her. And I think she respects you. Can you help me? Make her see that she has to tell me everything there is about them? Including about their leader? The man she's followed for the last decade?"

"I'm sorry I lied to you. About the meth gang and everything. You're one of the few guys who's treated me decent. That means something. A lot, actually."

Billy shrugged in response. He and Vincenza were sitting side by side in the visiting area. She was not looking her best. Her hair was stringy, and she was sleep deprived. Then, of course, there was the absence of makeup and the shapeless jumpsuit. Four sizes too large, it concealed her figure. Still, it was hard not to notice the delicacy of her features and the radiant, almost cobalt shade of her eyes. Even without mascara, the black of her eyelashes contrasted and complemented with their deep blue.

Because D'Allesandro's presence had meant more waiting, it had been almost two hours from the moment that Billy had arrived at the jail until he was beside her. The process of getting to see her had not only been lengthy but elaborate. He had been searched, and he had given up his identification. He had signed an assortment of forms, and then he had passed through a series of hallways divided by heavy, metal security doors.

The room they were in was at least seventy feet long, and it had the vaulted ceiling of a high school gym. Beneath were forty or fifty people. Perhaps a third were inmates. Around them were small children happy to see their incarcerated parents. As they tossed themselves into their mothers' laps, the hair-deprived grandmothers gave them stern looks. This variety of sounds and voices served to make his and Vincenza's private. Now, as Billy gazed at her, she smiled back.

"I think I've kind of been leading my life wrong," she said.

"The dispensary?"

"Not just the pot." She looked at him with an expression that was hard not to understand. It all but asked him why he hadn't made a pass at her when she had been staying with him. Then, perhaps embarrassed by this, she turned her head and stared off into space. What she said, though, continued the thought. "Are you involved with anyone?"

"Would you be asking me that if you weren't in jail?" He did not say this in an accusatory way. Nonetheless, he was grateful that she was amused and not offended by the question.

"I notice you didn't answer my question—which I guess is an answer."

236

"Since you were arrested, yes, something sort of happened. My sort-of girlfriend."

She took this news in without rancor. Sitting side by side, they were alternating between looking at one another and the other inmates. Now she turned to him once more. "You thought I was just being a flirt when I introduced myself? In the coffee shop?"

"Honestly?"

"Well, you're wrong. You looked different. I guess I was already aware that I had to do things different. My life, I mean."

"Thanks."

"You have a question?"

Billy took this as his cue. Nodding, he accepted what she was saying. Then he made her the pitch that had been requested of him. "Your lawyer spoke to me back in the waiting area—"

"He thinks this—what happened—is connected to the Church? And wants me to tell him everything about that?"

"James Armstrong. You know what he's talking about?"

Her eyes told him that she did.

While the jail permitted the inmates nearly unlimited time for attorney conferences, it allowed just two thirty-minute meetings each week for other visitors, and they knew that their time would soon be up. So they talked then of more mundane topics and not again with such intimacy. Even so, as he was leaving, they glanced at each other as people do when they share a secret.

CHAPTER 41

They had a plan. He had laid it out to her. They had agreed upon it. He would do most of the talking.

A Mike Fruchtman production was not nothing, and he had been in many of these meetings. He had known Todd Gelber for seventeen years. On several occasions, he had been to Gelber's home, and he had often negotiated with him. Back when Gelber was a talent agent, he had once gotten a phone call: One of Gelber's clients needed to leave a production a week early. As a favor, he had reversed the order for the shooting of several scenes of a movie they were making so that the actress could fly to Vancouver to be on another set.

Yet what had happened? Almost as soon as they were seated on the couch in Gelber's huge office, Claire had hijacked the meeting, turning it into her pitch for her remake of *Fatal Attraction*.

Part of the problem was the angle. Because it was supposed to be woman-oriented and feminist, it did seem natural for her to explain it. Then there was the abortion. Somehow that gave her a sort of moral immunity. He was beholden. And as they went down in the elevator afterwards and he gradually processed what had happened, he couldn't but be aware of what had occurred. Though they had gotten the greenlight, she was going to try and screw him out of a credit and a producer's fee. He was taken back to his first days in the business and the fashion in which he had been cheated out of a credit on a Denzel picture.

It was the one essential thing he had taught her, the immutable and eternal principle of the business: Get it in writing. She now had an option on the property. He didn't. That was all there was to it. It had simply never occurred to him that this seemingly harmless little blonde with her pale skin and her delicate calves could be capable of such treachery.

The worst thing was that his longtime acquaintance with Gelber meant nothing. He could see it: Gelber had a schedule to fill, and the *Fatal Attraction* remake made sense. It would sell service subscriptions. He could imagine it already. Before the day was out, Gelber or one of his assistants would be calling Claire—not him—to hash out the terms. Then they would work with her to find out what Anne Hathaway's availability was. Or was it Sarah Paulson? Laura Dern? Might they even aim for Nicole Kidman? Reese? But he had set the meeting up! He had used his industry capital to arrange things!

He could feel it in the way she was standing in the elevator. She was being perfectly pleasant. Yet he sensed it: her assurance, her smugness. She had gotten what she wanted. She had used him. The smile was insufferable. After all he had done for her, introducing people to her, explaining the finer points of contracts, mentoring her!

Leaving the elevator, pacing back to their cars, they began the post-mortem. But for her it was no post-mortem. It was living, breathing. She was glowing and radiant. The closer they got to their cars—his Bentley, her leased BMW—the more annoyed he became. Here, in the parking garage, they were out of earshot of the streaming service's staff. That meant he could be direct, and it struck him that if he were to put a stop to her scheme that he had to do it at once. With Gelber's approval, a project like this would gather momentum quickly, moving rapidly ahead without him. It was the old cliché about how once the train left the station and you weren't on it, there was no way to get on. Yet he had trained her in how to keep him off the choo-choo!

Knowing he had to do something, he grabbed her by the arm. It was not a violent grip, but it startled her. Then she stared at him. The expression said it all. It declared her superiority, asking him what he was doing and who he thought he was, and, rather meekly, he let go.

"Sorry. I'm *sorry*, Claire."

"OK."

"I just…"

She did not even speak to him in reply. Rather, he watched as she began to march away, shaking her head. Conscious that her car was all the way on the opposite side of the garage, he gave her an intense gaze that demanded she stop.

"Yes?"

"You're trying to cut me out?"

"What do you mean?" The way she said it reminded Fruchtman of her limitations as an actress.

"I can call him and put a stop to this. I've known him for twenty years almost."

"Did you have an abortion for him?" She paused, letting that sink in.

"Claire, I want for us to be together. I love you. I am getting a divorce. You just have to be patient."

Her eyes were full of hate. He could see that she knew that he was lying, and she waited a moment before speaking again. Her sense of control and authority was frightening. As much as anything else, it astonished him in that he had not suspected it in her. He had thought she was a mouse. "You don't believe me?"

She indicated her lack of faith by staring at him. Her body was still. She did not need to shake her head. Instead, she smiled, silently.

"Fine. But I'm not going to let you screw me out of this credit. Or the money."

The light in the underground garage was shadowy, and she was standing at least ten feet away from him. Yet he could see the not-quite-concealed quality of pleasure in her face when she responded. "I want you to work on this, Mike. I'm grateful for what you've done for me. We'll talk."

"Can I stop by your place? How's later today?"

Her face expressed the impossibility of the notion.

"Well, what about tomorrow?"

She nodded vaguely and then began searching for her car keys in her bag. "The next few days might be tricky, but obviously we'll be in touch."

It was incredible. Did she actually think she could get away with it?

"Don't try to screw me, Claire. You don't know all I can do."

This last comment caused her to hesitate momentarily. She gazed back at him more thoughtfully then. "You do know," she said, "that you signed for my abortion with your credit card. I have the bill." She did not need to complete the thought: She could forward a copy to his wife.

He was screwed. Thinking back to when he had first spotted her in the building lobby that morning, he realized that he should have known what was coming from her attire. Though it was just professional enough to be appropriate, the skirt was short enough to really show off her legs. The purpose was obvious: to get Gelber aroused. Would she now try to move on to him as her next target?

That women in the business were decrying their mistreatment: It was rich! He was the one who had been taken advantage of. He had tutored her. He had been her supporter and guide and counsel, and this was how his selflessness was repaid. He watched, then, as she strode away, displaying her graceful posterior and those trim legs. The injustice of it rankled. It was just wrong.

CHAPTER 42

Todd Road was different.

The Los Angeles County jail system was a colossal, frightening collection of fractious communities. The Lynnwood held 2000 women by itself. That was almost twice the number in the entire Ventura County jail system. Of these, 200 were at Todd Road. Thus, within a few weeks it was possible to memorize the names of every woman prisoner in the facility, and Vincenza had managed to learn at least half in a few days.

Naturally, all of them knew who she was. This wasn't simply a function of her celebrity. Her appearance was singular. Without her fishnets and her pointy-toed heels and her dark red lipstick and hair arranged in its Bettie Page, she still looked to be from another planet. Her trained voice sounded peculiarly gracious, and, though absent of the usual painting on her nails, her hands stood out for being slimmer, finer, and less callused. She weighed half as much as the typical female inmate, and she walked with a slinkiness, a daintiness that was as distinctive as the plumage of a macaw among a murder of crows. Even more than at the Lynnwood, she was fresh meat. Whether their visitors were boyfriends or girlfriends, she sensed how much they desired her. It was a rough-looking crew.

Still, in the smaller space, she felt safer. There was more of an effort to keep them busy, whether in the GED classes or the vocational ones. The latter focused on teaching them the art of printing, and a great many of the inmates spent their days arranging for the manufacture of county instructional bulletins. There was a prison yard, and, bland as the cafeteria's food was, it was palatable. The beef patties resembled the ones on the griddle at chain restaurants. The mashed potatoes were mostly absent of unidentifiable splotches. It was warmer in the jail, too. You could sleep at night.

The restorative power of the shut-eye came gradually. She had accumulated a sleep debt akin to the financial obligations of Bolivia, and it was not going to be paid back quickly. Still, as one good night of rest followed the next, she saw a healthy color returning to her cheeks and the circles under her eyes began to fade away.

The move from Los Angeles had shortened the list of those who wanted to meet with her. At the Lynwood, she had gotten dozens of requests every day. In addition to the lawyers, there had been scores of reporters, both from the print and the electronic media. That number had been cut with her remove to Todd Road. But she continued to resist the impulse to speak with them. She wanted to have her story heard, but she understood the reasoning behind her lawyer's entreaty to stay clear of them. She did not need to provide extra material for the prosecutors.

The absence of one name from the list of those who wished to visit was noticeable. Sara Kertesz had tried to see her once at the Lynwood. But she had been in conference with her lawyer when she had come, and they had missed each other. There had been no effort since. Was Sara emailing her? Lacking access to her email account, Vincenza did not know. But she was more than a little intrigued by what D'Allesandro told her in his second trip to Todd Road: The police had raided Sara's apartment. Displaying a search warrant, they had entered and stayed for hours, combing through it for evidence.

Scuttlebutt was that they had relied upon a tip from an illegal. Whatever it was that had inspired their inspection, they had something, some reason to think that she was involved in the crime, and D'Allesandro—Jerry—wanted Vincenza to tell him more. His theory about why the body had turned up in her car's trunk made a sort of terrible sense. The question was how Sara might have become entangled with the Church. That was hard to fathom.

Yet it was becoming harder and harder to deny that there was a connection between the two. It had taken the police some time to find and analyze Tom Selva's phone, and it had taken them even longer to provide its contents to the defense. It offered more exculpatory evidence. Just as Vincenza had said all along, she had not spoken with Selva on the day of his death. No, the last two people he had called were Sara and James Armstrong. He had phoned them from his house in West Hollywood, and then he had received a call from Sara at the beach cottage around 7:00 p.m. This last call came from a nearby road in Malibu. Was she on her way to meet him there for an assignation? That was what the phone records implied.

But what did Vincenza *know*?

"Well, he had always told me that I was the only one. Other than his wife. But it seemed that something happened with Lorelei during the shoot. And maybe our makeup girl. I was very angry with him. He denied it, of course. I was awfully ashamed that I was sleeping with him given he was married. As you know, a father, too."

Because no one—not even lawyers—was permitted to bring recording devices into the jail, Jerry was rapidly scribbling, taking down what she said on a yellow legal pad. Stopping, he looked up with an expression whose sensitivity almost matched its seriousness. "The phone records confirm the affair with Lorelei, Vincenza. They show that they were meeting at the beach cottage as well. Quite a few times, I'm afraid."

"Anyone else?"

"It seems a waitress. Maybe a dancer." D'Allesandro paused. "I'm sorry."

"I feel stupid. What's there to say? I believed him. I wanted to believe him. I felt sort of special when I was with him. And God knows he was handsome. Beautiful, actually. Does that sound stupid? I knew it wasn't going anywhere."

D'Allesandro had an unusually deep voice, and he loved to talk. But he knew not to. Instead, he smiled sympathetically and waited for her to go on.

"Then there was our connection through the Church. That's what you want me to tell you about? And Armstrong?"

Once more, he remained quiet. But now she hesitated. This led to an awkward silence, and, as they were not out in the visitors' area but in a conference room reserved for lawyer-client meetings, the only other noises were those of steps in the adjoining corridor. She listened as a prisoner walked past with what sounded like two others. The tread was heavy, either that of a man or one of the refrigerator-sized women she lived amongst. The footsteps continued all the way to the end of the hallway, then faded in the distance. Finally, she heard Jerry's rumbling voice once more. His face was bearded, and it seemed to emerge from within the bush forest of hair covering his cheeks.

"You told me they were following you. You told the police that. You pointed us this way. I know it's difficult, but, even if it didn't involve you and you didn't have so much at stake, this *is* a murder case."

"He proposed something to me once. I mean Tom."

"He had a suggestion?"

Vincenza hesitated once more. Then she thought again about what her lawyer had just told her, that Selva had been sleeping with a series of women, that she had been one among many. It was something she had sometimes felt. It was a bitter dish, and while the impulse for vengeance was not a strong impulse in her heart, it reminded her that she did not have any obligation to him. She had no reason to worry about his name or reputation. And as to the Church? It had always spoken of how essential truth was. Well, then…

There was something wrenching even so in talking about it. It did seem as though something was being pulled from her chest, like a hand was reaching down her throat and pulling out a lump of flesh. Yet, agonizing as it was, she revealed it, providing her lawyer with one of the last pieces to the puzzle.

CHAPTER 43

Todd Gelber awaited two police officers. It was two in the afternoon, and they were due at his office at four-thirty. Both his personal lawyer and a company attorney would be present. But, before they appeared, he had a vital task to perform. This wasn't to check his notes or look at old memos.

The film that everyone in the country was talking about he controlled. Yet there hadn't been time to watch it. Busy coordinating the service's hundreds of projects and dealing with his superiors in Silicon Valley, he had avoided viewing it as he believed that he could make his own schedule. This supposition had truth to it. After all, streaming services do not operate like television networks. They do not have to present their slate of upcoming shows to affiliate stations or the press at a set time: through what in the industry are known as upfronts. All the properties which the service has rights to it can roll out whenever it wishes. While a release can be coordinated with billboard ads and "screeners," copies mailed to critics, this can be done on short notice, and it is not obligatory. And talking about the film without bothering to see it had worked just fine in nearly every social situation presented to him: cocktail parties and dinner parties, conversations with agents and managers and directors. He had even performed adroitly when he had met with Vincenza and Sara. He had simply said what he did in making nearly every sales pitch: He loved their work, he would do right by them, and he would alert the world to their mighty achievements, artistry which was overdue for recognition.

In making these declarations, Gelber had parroted the details outlined to him in a report, "coverage" which told him what he should say about their performances and what he ought to think about the plot. He had followed this up by laying out a detailed, if wholly imaginary, vision of how and when the streaming service would promote it. The sale price had been $350,000, and, while he did not know what Vincenza and Sara's arrangement with their investors was, his guess was that they would pocket a third of the $275,000 in profit on its original $75,000 investment. Necessarily, as he spoke, he could see them eyeing the cake being constructed, piled layer upon layer. In their eyes, a mass of chocolate and butter cream and ganache and raspberry filling was heaping up. All their dreams were being realized, their hopes fulfilled. Obviously convinced as they were that the money meant that his company would give the movie a degree of prominence, their sense of assurance was further enhanced as in his conversation with them he had acted as if he were being wonderfully charitable, behaving as though he were the lord of the manor freeing a pair of serfs.

The purchase of the film had been completed in the week prior to Selva's death. What he had not told Sara and Vincenza was that on the same day that their contracts were returned to him, David Clarkson and Tom Selva's agent had stopped by his office, and he had reaffirmed his promise to them that he would never allow the movie to be shown. This pledge had been rendered meaningless by Selva's demise. That had turned this cheap "pickup" into an inspired acquisition, as the vow had cost him nothing. In return for his promise to Selva that the movie would not be released, Selva had agreed that he would play a supporting part in a planned action movie. That role needed to be recast. Yet Selva's timely end meant that millions of people now wanted to see Vincenza and Sara's movie, and he was being prodded with detailed questions from anyone and everyone about what he thought of it. He doubted, though, that he had enough time to see the whole picture now, as the detectives were on their way. Still, typing in a key code, he pulled up the video while an assistant brought in and set down a bowl of hot salted popcorn—no butter—on the glass coffee table in front of his office's expansive leather couch.

Starting to watch, Gelber nibbled on the popcorn. He had heard from friends that people in the publishing industry never had a chance to read, and, as a production chief, he was sometimes coming to feel that way about the movie business. When did he have a chance to see his films—or anyone else's?

Was the picture any good? That was one question to focus on, though his lack of sleep made watching movies an activity in which often he worked equally hard trying to stay awake. Pawing at the snack, he tried to absorb what he could of the story and the performances. Literally dark, it was full of meaningful glances and hushed voices, and the acting was of the school in which a person cannot say hello without pausing, aiming to convey the complexity of the moment. Even so, there was something quite real about parts of it. Selva was not bad, Lorelei was impressive, and Vincenza was sensational.

Yet, gazing at his watch, Gelber realized that he would not have time to watch the middle forty minutes. So, skipping ahead, he came to the final scene. This sequence did seem to jibe with what the coverage had said: The film might be well-received if they could add some music to the slower portions, while lopping out ten or twenty minutes from it. There was the hitch, though. The contracts that the women had signed gave them final say on changes. Yet the news reports said that the police had just raided Sara's place, and Vincenza was in jail. How was he to get their permission when they were facing murder charges and not available to come into an editing suite to go over the film, shot by shot?

This thought drew him back to the man who had spoken to him longest regarding the company's purchase of the movie, and, reaching for his phone, he instructed his secretary on a forthcoming call with David Clarkson. In the meantime, he worked feverishly. He had to review a summary budget for a conference call the following morning, and that was not something he could jibber-jabber his way through. He would be going over it with the company's CEO and CFO, and he needed to be sharp on every aspect. As this required utmost concentration, the time passed quickly, and he was slightly startled when his secretary informed him that the detectives and the lawyers were outside his office.

He looked about. His only food since an eleven a.m. meeting had been the popcorn, and the bowl was empty. Instructing his secretary to escort them in, he asked himself how his life had reached a point at which he was considered omnipotent, but he had no time for lunch.

In moments, he would call David Clarkson with recording equipment attached to his phone. Prior to that, the detectives wanted an account of their first meeting.

WHILE CLARKSON EXCHANGED PLEASANTRIES with Gelber's secretary, anticipating the sound of the production chief's voice on the line, he was also thinking back to their introduction, and he ran through the sequence of events that had set him in his present delicate position.

The movie was the spur. Or perhaps it was more accurate to say that it had been impelled by Armstrong's response to seeing it.

Holding the phone to his ear, Clarkson found himself placed somewhere he rarely bothered to go: the main cafeteria of the Church's headquarters. This was a mess hall on the far side of the building's fifth floor. A huge mural of the group's founder rose up on one of its walls, and an equally large picture of Armstrong faced it on the opposite side of the hall. Dressed in blue work smocks, the diners mostly ignored the renderings of the church leaders, intently gabbing with their friends. But he felt the two men's eyes. It was as though they were watching him. The combined height of the two figures in real life was not even eleven feet, yet each was twelve feet high as painted onto the walls.

Clarkson had come to the chow hall with the desire to break his routine of eating in his seventeenth-floor office. Then the call had come, and, as such, he had snuck out into the adjoining corridor, abandoning his tray and his meal in order to get a clearer phone line.

Exiting, he thought once more about how he had become involved.

Fearing that the movie might present an unsavory image of Selva, he had asked Vincenza for a tape of it. What he saw when he did obtain an unfinished copy troubled him—so much that he had brought it to Armstrong, and, while the Supreme Pilot was gratified by his foresight, this had prompted a series of urgent meetings. It had taken time to persuade Selva that the movie would be harmful and that they would work with his agent and manager to find him the intricate roles that his talent required.

The next step had been easier. Vincenza had told them of Gelber's interest in the film on behalf of the streaming service. Clarkson knew that it would not be seemly to ask for a direct meeting with the executive, and with this in mind he had purchased two invitations to a political fundraiser taking place at the new, much larger home in Bel Air that Gelber and his wife were moving into.

Designed in the mid-century modernist style, it was composed of an elegant if austere set of stainless steel and bone-white marble planes into which floor-to-ceiling windows had been fitted. Behind that lay a large, floodlit pool occupying most of the backyard. The drive to it had required them to slow down on multiple occasions, both to take in the sights of the spectacular homes that ran up the hillside it was on and to deal with the narrow road and its steep turns.

Parking the car down the block, Clarkson entered to the sound of water splashing. The clamor of the people in the outdoor pool was a relief as it covered up the noise of the lawyer's own breathing. The half block walk to the house and along its driveway had been that much of a climb.

Led through the massive entrance foyer, he and an aide were brought by the servants out back. There, along the patio, they found that the servers had lined up the drink stations, and that this was where most of the guests were. It was also the spot, Clarkson saw, where he needed to make his approach.

That had come early on: before Gelber had introduced the woman running for reelection to the senate, which they were there to fete. Gelber's smile suggested that he understood immediately: They were there on business. Leading them to a drink station, he had instructed one of the uniformed illegals standing behind it to provide them with gin and tonics. Handing them the libations, Gelber had drawn them aside.

The message was clear. He was a busy man hosting an enormous event, and there was little need for small talk. They could get right to it with regard to the matter they had come for. He didn't have all that much time anyway.

"That movie with Selva that's just been made? I think I might be able to help you out with it," he said. The expression that Gelber put forth when he said this was knowing and conspiratorial. It was as though he were winking with both eyes. "Seems the producers want me to buy it. I take it you're concerned that it might not present Tom properly as a representative of the Church?"

"To an extent, yes."

"Well, sometimes a film needs extra footage. Reshoots are required. We could purchase the film and allow you to help us with working on that. Fixing what needs to be fixed. However long that takes."

252

Gelber's suave manner told him that they were speaking the same language, a dialect that can only be called Los Angelese. Yes, he would bury the film, Gelber was saying, if Selva would do something for him in return.

Now, remembering the conversation, he heard Gelber's voice coming onto the line. Just as there are great beauties who carry their grace lightly, Gelber carried his power lightly. His tone was intimate and non-threatening. It was a stark contrast with Armstrong's. Wherever Gelber actually was, his manner suggested that he wanted to be right alongside Clarkson, that he liked him, and there was no reason that they shouldn't be working together. Clarkson listened, gratified. Gelber's solicitude was welcome at a time when he was up every night thinking about what might happen if the police discovered that he had initially avoided calling them about the discovery of Selva's body in the beach cottage.

"So what you were saying to him was that you welcomed the Church's input, but you couldn't and wouldn't compromise the artistic vision of the filmmakers?"

"That's right, officer. That's not what we're about. Especially in a case like this. The first time I saw the picture I realized that it was the work of artists. First-time filmmakers, yes, but genuine artists."

Finishing up with the detective's questions, Gelber gestured to find out if he should go ahead and speak with Clarkson. He watched as they silently indicated to get him on the phone. Although all present understood that the call would be on speaker phone, the assembled group hunched forward, leaning forward towards him, in anticipation.

"I'm glad we're on the line again, David," Gelber began.

"It's good to hear your voice."

"Yes…the movie is so talked about. Everyone's looking forward to when we'll put it on."

"Right. Of course…though you agreed that we'll look it over?"

"Of course…our problem is that we need a few changes, but, as you know, Vincenza is in that Ventura jail. And we need approval for changes."

"Well, then, I think I can help you."

"Yes?"

"Sara has given me a copy of the film with her revisions, and our Supreme Pilot looked it over. And he approves, too. I assume you wanted cuts. And some more music. We've done that."

"Great…but, in terms of story and character and performances, what are the changes like? Obviously, we can't be overly concerned about Selva's image now."

"Well, you saw the send-off—the memorial service—we gave him. He's one of our great heroes. Our James Dean. Our Heath Ledger. The believer who died too young. We need to protect that. Though that's not really the biggest thing."

"No?"

"You'll see."

"You can't tell me?"

There was a pause as Clarkson could be heard asking himself how much he should reveal. Gelber knew that if he remained silent that Clarkson would reveal his secret. And then he did.

"Between us," he said, "Sara was concerned that Vincenza had upstaged her. This version evens it out. Balances things."

"And Armstrong approves of that?"

"He said. They seem to really get along."

With these words, Gelber looked up to the detectives and the attorneys. Their faces showed that he had gotten them what they wanted.

CHAPTER 44

Ray Chalmers was among a clump of figures behind the two-way mirrored window. It was a coup of sorts that he was being permitted to listen in on Sara Kertesz's interrogation. That he was there told him that he was going to get a measure of credit for his work on the case, no matter that he had participated in the arrest of the wrong suspect. Because of that, he was not coming out of the affair as a hero.

As half a dozen figures stood in front of him at the window, he could barely see her. What was mostly visible was the back of a senior officer's double-vented blazer. A curl of Kertesz's yellow hair flashed in and out. He heard what was happening.

Sara Kertesz was almost a case study in the dangers of pot smoking. That hadn't prompted her to kill Selva. But it had caused her to make an amazing number of mistakes in covering up her crime. That she had placed the murder weapon where Abril Fernandez saw it was the least of her errors. Her phone showed the messages that had passed back and forth with Selva on the night she had shot him, and the cell tower records placed her close by. That was more than an hour from her apartment. By far her worst mistake, however, was not burning down the house with the body in it or throwing the corpse out to sea when she had the chance. Why had she instead stolen Vincenza's car and planted the body and the gun within it?

Chalmers listened as the detective laid out the evidence that they had compiled against her. He had also pointed out that forensic investigators employing luminol—a chemical agent with an affinity for iron which allows it to find bleached-out blood stains—had revealed that Selva had been killed inside the beach cottage. Her fingerprints were in half a dozen spots near where his corpse had first lain. And they had found the quantities of bleach and trace amounts of Selva's blood in her trunk.

The room Chalmers was in—the one adjoining the interrogation room—smelled as such rooms do. Odors of coffee, cologne, and sweat mingled. The polished linoleum floor was hard on his feet, and the lights flickering above his head were inducing a headache. Still, it was a thrill to be there. It was an opportunity to learn, too. The detective in charge was a master. He was as good as anyone Chalmers had ever observed. Because he spoke with a noticeable Valley drawl, his final vowels were elongated, and he used this almost as a trick. The way he said the word "Hello," it had three syllables rather than two, and he knew how to twist each extra intonation towards a specific emotion: sympathy, earnestness, sarcasm, or menace. As he had worked through the first three, he was shifting to the last. She could save herself from a life sentence in one way and one way only, he explained: by telling them the truth, cooperating, and providing them with such evidence as there might be against James Armstrong.

The sound of her sobbing was painful. Though Chalmers knew she was a murderer, it affected him. Indeed, somehow, that she was partially concealed from view made it more unpleasant. It was reminiscent of a dog's wailing.

Chalmers watched as the detective sat down and folded his arms. He would say no more until she stopped crying and confessed. He had her. Beside her was her lawyer, and her profile came into view as she pivoted towards him, wiping away her tears as she whispered into his ear. This went on for some time. Then the lawyer turned back to the officer and an accompanying figure from the prosecutor's offer. Could they give them a proffer: a guarantee of reduced sentencing in return for her testimony? The attorney's tone indicated defeat, and Chalmers could almost make out a snicker from their side.

"Do-*oo* you-*ew* rilly think we-*ee* need to do-*oo* that?" the detective asked. It was apparent that he was half-smiling.

This commenced the confession. Chalmers knew from the case files that people often mentioned the suspect's exuberance and cheeriness. For that reason, her collapse as she told her story seemed to go further down, deeper inside. She could not just tell the story and be relieved. It was dire. Yet it also had a strange quality of performance, and the formal, almost stilted way she spoke told him that on some unconscious level she had been influenced by scenes she had watched—or rehearsed—in the past.

"Selva told me to come to the beach cottage that night," she began. "He and his agent and David Clarkson were going to get Todd Gelber to bury the film. I hadn't told Vincenza what was happening. Tom agreed to let me come by to talk about it. The only reason I had the gun was because it was in my glove compartment for protection. Because Tom had talked to me about how proud he was of his performance I thought I could convince him. Get him to agree to it. Releasing the movie, y'know."

She paused, letting out a sigh.

"Armstrong was there?"

She nodded. "When I got there, Selva told me that they had wanted to have sex with a woman together. That it was something they had talked about. Apparently, they had asked Vincenza to do it. She wouldn't. But Tom said if I did it with him and Armstrong that maybe Armstrong would consent and let the movie come out."

"And did you-*ew* have sex with them? Both?"

Several seconds passed before she responded. The sidewise motion of a lock of her hair showed that she had nodded again. "Afterwards... well...then they told me they couldn't help me on this picture. But maybe they could on something else. They were laughing at me."

"And...?"

"I walked out. I leaned against my car. I was seeing red. Literally. I was that angry. All my hopes were about to be destroyed. They thought I was just something amusing to fuck and fuck over. I sat down in the car. And then I realized that I had the gun, and I opened the glove compartment. I came back with it, and, yes, I shot Tom. Armstrong looked at me. He was scared. Terrified. He thought I was going to kill him, too. He said he could help me. You understand: He didn't want people to know he'd been there or what had happened. He knew what it would do to his reputation, to his claim of being a moral figure—'The Supreme Pilot' who would save us all. So I had him move the body into my car's trunk, and I told him that I would throw it into the ocean, close as we were. And he said that he would see to it that the movie did come out and that my performance in the movie stood out. He promised. At that point he left."

"Why didn't you throw it in the ocean?"

"I got to thinking. The movie was my only chance. But Vincenza had stolen it. Her performance. It was what people would be talking about. Armstrong said he would get it so the finished film made me look good. But how could he do that? It struck me there was one way. If she was in jail, I could supervise the editing. Hey, I had already killed someone...I know: It was not only wrong. It was stupid."

"How did you get the body into Vincenza's trunk by yourself?"

"I had a copy of her car keys. I picked it up and slanted it on a hillside directly below mine with the cars set rear end to rear end. Then I opened the trunks and used gravity to get it from one to the other. Smart, huh?" She paused. "You know what I'm thinking, officer?"

"Tell me."

"The producers force women to bend over. I got to be a producer, and I still had to bend over. For both of them."

CHAPTER 45

The letters arrived in huge bags. They were outnumbered three hundred to one by the emails. There were so many that Sara Kertesz's website crashed hour after hour. It was impossible to say how many messages might have reached her otherwise, and she could only imagine the number of folks who were contacting the prosecutors, the state attorney general, and the governor on her behalf. There were editorials in the newspapers, and once more there were trucks with camera crews parked outside the jail. Inside, they had given her the same cell that Vincenza had been in. Now everyone waited. The world was like an expectant mother approaching her due date.

The halt was prompted by the desire for answers to two questions. The first was when there would be an agreement between her defense lawyers and the Ventura County prosecutor. Each day her lead attorney spoke off the record with a handful of reporters, providing "background" in which he indicated an urgent wish to take the case to trial. He was desperate, he said, fervently intent on arguing before a jury that she had acted out of momentary passion and that hers was an act of justifiable homicide. He was going to prove that. He wanted to show it, irrefutably, definitively, and incontestably. He couldn't wait. The prosecutor's fear was less that he could persuade twelve of her peers among the citizenry of this, than that he could find just one juror who would refuse to convict and that a hung jury and mistrial would result.

There was enormous and growing sympathy among the public. Polls showed that vast numbers of men and even more women thought that she should not be prosecuted for the murder, that she was the victim. As such, Disney, Netflix, and Amazon had all been compelled to remove Tom Selva's movies from their streaming sites, and he was now universally spoken of with the degree of hatred accorded to mankind's greatest foes: Adolf Hitler, Joseph Stalin, and shrink-wrapping.

The adoration existed inside the jailhouse. Her fellow inmates looked at her fondly and with an underfed guard dog's protective studiousness. Truck drivers accused of beating their wives lent her maternal expressions. Rapists nodded their heads when they saw her at the jailhouse commissary. Butch toughs gave her stolid and respectful looks of affirmation. And it wasn't only the other prisoners. The guards showed grudging appreciation. She had displayed guts. She had stood up for herself by killing the bastard. It seemed that everyone had some measure of affection for her and appreciation for what she had done. It was as though she had acquired the immeasurable appeal of bug spray along the Amazon but in a formulation that smelled like calla lilies.

Nonetheless, the lawyers had informed her that California law said that she could not profit by writing a memoir or a script about the case for a full ten years after she was released from prison, and in theory Selva's widow could sue her in civil court for damages. So she could not make any money directly from the shooting, and it was even conceivable that she was liable. She would not be anything but broke when she got out.

The second question revolved around when that would be, and if she could resolve her deal with Todd Gelber and the streaming service.

How much could she compel them to show of her best scenes and how much would they insist on presenting Vincenza's finest work? That was what she pondered day and night. Would all her training and skill be brought to light and displayed to millions? Might she receive award nominations and appreciation for her work? Would casting directors see it? And would that reverence still be held for her talents when she was released?

She knew that her testimony would send James Armstrong to prison. He had been an accomplice after the fact, and, like her, he potentially faced a sentence of fifteen years to life. However, as state law notes that a defendant may show "circumstances of mitigation or that justify or excuse it," and this applied more to her than to him, his sentence might be greater, though he was not the perpetrator. There was the further matter that she could provide character witnesses who would testify on her behalf, but, removed from his position by the Church of Life, he could not. What complicated matters was her seeming attempt to shift blame onto her friend. How might prosecutors make use of that if her lawyers did not reach a deal with the state's attorneys?

Sara Kertesz was twenty-nine. What she wanted was a sentence that would permit her to leave prison—with time off for good behavior—while she was still young enough that she could marry, have a child and, most critically, be employable as an actress. Since parole was possible at two-thirds of the maximum sentence, that meant that she needed an agreement for her to receive a sentence of no more than twelve years. With parole, that would get her sprung, out of the hoosegow, when she was thirty-seven or thirty-eight.

Gazing at the women in jail, she saw the danger. So many grew corpulent. She would have to war against the carb-heavy prison diet. She had to stay thin. She couldn't become one of those doughy creatures. Yet she would not have ready access to that most vital instrument, a bathroom scale. And there would be no yoga classes, no Pilates. You couldn't even have clothes that were fitted to promptly warn you of weight gain. Imagine!

And, yes, she had to see to it that she wasn't completely overshadowed by Vincenza's performance. These were the two great battles. It was a ceaseless conflict. But she knew that she would get one more opportunity to perform before an even greater audience. That would come when she testified against Armstrong, telling the story of how he and Selva had successively made use of her body parts and of their callous expressions afterwards. She rehearsed this testimony in her mind many times each day, sharpening her performance so that tears were held back. On behalf of her reputation and the streaming service, they would stream down her face at just the right instant. Her voice would have the right sexy hoarseness to show that she would be a natural in parts that called for a fetching bad girl or a neglected housewife. It was all a matter of using her sense memory and proper breath control.

The library in the jail was small. But she had no difficulty finding copies of *Measure for Measure* and *Medea*, and she rehearsed their speeches, refreshing the lessons she had learned through the years. Each day she recited the orations, and when mealtimes came she offered the greater amount of what was on her tray to the other prisoners, winning her additional fondness.

A whole month went by in this fashion. Then her lawyers informed her that Gelber and Vincenza had consented to inclusion of a complete version of her favorite take of the early scene in the film in which she chastised Tom Hutchins. They had also negotiated an arrangement by which Vincenza's total screen time would be kept to nineteen minutes of the movie's ninety-four-minute length. She would have equal time: *literally*. The lawyers also said that "the people" would request that she receive a sentence of nine to twelve years in return for her testimony. With time off and parole, that meant she could be freed as one of America's most famous and admired fighters for women's rights when she was only thirty-five or, at worst, thirty-six. That was still young enough to get a starring role in a network series or a welcome cable gig. As much noise as there was in the jail, she slept better inside it than she had in years. Her future was set.

She had it in writing.

CHAPTER 46

The streaming service had a lot invested in Vincenza and her movie. They had signed her to write and star in a follow-up, and they were attaching her to various scripted dramas they were developing.

In consequence, they were employing every method possible to promote the film. She was to appear on seven talk shows in the week before it streamed: *Live with Kelly and Ryan*, *The Tonight Show Starring Jimmy Fallon*, *Jimmy Kimmel Live!*, *The Late Show with Stephen Colbert*, *Today*, *The Kelly Clarkson Show*, and *The View*. Later, she was to do a sit-down interview with *60 Minutes*, and she would be discussing #MeToo on *The Rachel Maddow Show*. She was to fly to Las Vegas where she would stay in a hotel room for three days of rapid-fire print interviews. She was to appear on three magazine covers. *Harper's Bazaar* was to require a full-day shoot with three stylists.

She was also authoring a short book—ghosted for her—on how to overcome personal betrayal. Its message was the importance of forgiveness. In that vein, she was making a point in her interviews of talking about Sara's testimony against James Armstrong. She was presenting Sara as a victim of him, rather than a victimizer of her.

Smaller lifestyle items and articles were constantly appearing about her as well. A *Los Angeles Times* style section article described her move from her one-bedroom in Hollywood to a split-level she was purchasing in Laurel Canyon. And the gossip columns were occasionally reporting on her love life, most often by displaying photos of her on the arm of the good-looking osteopath she had started dating.

She had felt both relief and sadness in saying good-bye to the dispensary and the people she had worked with there: the Israeli brothers, the gay store manager, her preternaturally gorgeous but wooden co-worker.

Although the book was largely the work of her ghostwriter, she had spent several days with him. This was to provide him the material: her experiences and reflections. In part this meant speaking about her days in the Church and their mistreatment of her. The greatest part of the time, though, was spent on Sara and on what she had learned from her. She tried not to speak much about what it felt to find out that her business partner and supposed friend had tried to edit her acting feats out of their movie and then had sought to make her look like a murderer.

Even so, in going over matters with the writer, she was compelled to think more broadly. The discussions made her aware of how hard it was to have a real friend in the business. And it made her contemplate someone else: the woman who gave her life.

In most respects her mother had failed as a parent. This had not ended when Vincenza left home. It was not easy to be indifferent to the fact that her mother had made snide remarks to the reporters who appeared at her Minnesota doorstep when she was universally presumed to be Tom Selva's killer. But, freed from the Church of Life, Vincenza found herself ruminating not only on her mother but on the prior religious training she had received. While she did not want to be a synod member again, she pondered their teachings. Two seemed relevant: Honor Thy Father and Thy Mother, and Judge Not That Thou Shall Not Be Judged.

In jail she had known piercing loneliness. Not as she had felt it as an adolescent but as a full-grown adult, and it gave her a better understanding of what her mother must have felt as a widow with a small child and little formal education. She had not really thought about this, and it made her conscious of the compassion underlying the synod's teaching.

She did not know how famous she would be. She was not sure if she could write another successful movie. She was unsure how great her range as an actress was. But, aware that the hour had come to heal the rift, she found herself in early June waiting outside the airline baggage claim at LAX. In moments, her mother was to appear. Although it had been months since she had felt heart palpitations, they were there. Her osteopath beau had offered to accompany her, but she sensed this was something she had to do herself. No reporter was alongside her, and she was wearing sunglasses in the hope she would not be recognized. She did not want to sign autographs. She was frightened that she would cry.

The weather was as beautiful as it is on any day in Los Angeles. The sky was cloudless and blue, and a coastal breeze was drawing in as the taxi cabs and rental car company vans zipped past.

It had been more than a decade since she had seen her mother, and, while she had no fear that she would fail to recognize her, she wondered how much her looks had changed and what her mother would think of her appearance.

There had been several steps to their meeting. There was the decision to call, the dialing of the number, and the call itself. Each was difficult. Indeed, she had only realized how profound marijuana's grip on her was when she contemplated them. She had continually *wanted* to toke in jail. But she felt that she *needed* a drag before she had picked up the phone. In many respects, it was the hardest thing she had ever done: harder than leaving home. Auditions were low stress by comparison. One act was as demanding as opening a parasol, the other like breaking boulders with a penknife.

Now she watched as the crowd of people coming off the flight stumbled ahead towards the baggage claim. She was reminded of how enormous Minnesotans could be, not only fat, but tall and strapping. Compared to the people of Los Angeles, they were mountainous. But where was her mother? Vincenza had sent her the money for the ticket, and she was supposed to be putting her mother up in her new home. Was paying for the ticket a mistake? Might she have skipped out on the flight? Was she ashamed of her daughter or afraid of the reunion?

Her palms were sweaty. She had scanned at least sixty faces without seeing the one she sought. And then: There it was. Her mother had aged. She had put on at least thirty pounds, and her face had grown lined. The creases were especially apparent around the throat, the forehead, and the eyes. Her hair was dyed now, colored an unreal black to hide obvious gray. But the eyes were vital, and she was smiling. Approaching, she signaled her desire to hug. The feeling that followed of her body pressed against Vincenza's own was satisfying, cleansing, welcome.

CHAPTER 47

Planning the honeymoon had proved almost as difficult as the wedding, and the nuptials had been delayed twice.

In fact, depending on how you counted, you could argue that Claire had put off the ceremony half a dozen times. She didn't like the ring. She wanted a smaller, more intimate occasion—but then she realized that there were relatives they had to invite, which meant they needed a larger venue. And although she was put off by the study of Hebrew required for a formal conversion, she was intrigued by the notion of a Jewish wedding. Wasn't that a storied tradition of the entertainment industry, one trod before her by Elizabeth Taylor and Marilyn Monroe?

The conversion idea was finally let go of. The big issue that remained was the prenuptial agreement Billy had to sign. While he was amenable to most any document, her lawyers couldn't agree among themselves what it should say. The result of all this was that she was more than just a little bit showing by the time that a Universal Life minister asked them to undertake their vows in the ballroom of a Seattle hotel her family owned. She was six months pregnant and, weighted by the train of her bridal gown while traipsing ahead in three-inch heels, she alternated between nearly falling backwards and tipping over forwards as her father escorted her to Billy and the minister.

The honeymoon was equally complicated. With pre-production work on her *Fatal Attraction* remake rapidly advancing, she didn't want to be overseas in a distant time zone when the movie required her to cooperate with two huge entertainment conglomerates: the streaming service *and* Viacom. Then there were all the troubles of dealing with the stars and the locations and the director. At the same time, she was with child—a daughter, as it turned out—and she was unsure about how their little one might respond to the suspect drinking water of Latin America. That meant they couldn't go south. Yet Sonoma, Napa, and the Willamette Valley were out because she couldn't consume alcohol. And, since it was the end of summer, there was no point in going to a ski resort. That eliminated Boulder, Banff, and Whistler.

Sitting on the beach in Honolulu, Billy was reminded that the one place he had told himself that he would never go for a honeymoon was where he was. Claire was in a one-piece bathing suit, and she was indeed glowing. If it was possible for immaculate skin to be more so, it was. Yet were it also possible for an evolutionary advance to take place by which a phone became a human body part, that might be so, too. Her drive was extraordinary, her attention to her spouse less so.

Everything was a discussion. Who was going to change the diapers was sure to be, and sex was already so much a negotiation that he asked himself if he should be undertaking his conjugal duties without his lawyer present.

In the morning, as they were sitting in the hotel lounge where he was devouring his regular omelet and she picked at her egg-white one, they eyed a television set broadcasting the latest news on the Selva murder trial. The reporter detailing events was a beautiful young woman with an enormous crest of bleached blonde hair. She was among a cluster of reporters who stood in front of a long, white, Georgian mansion fronted by palm trees. As it turned out, this was the

Ventura County courthouse. Her chirping voice seemed to declare her intent to giggle even when her face conveyed perfect seriousness and gravity. Only half-awake, it took Billy a moment to grasp what she was saying: As public reaction to the circumstances of the case grew, pressure was increasing on the prosecutors to cut a deal by which Sara Kertesz would receive a reduced sentence for second-degree murder. Some were saying the plea agreement might call for a sentence of ten years, or perhaps even less. The reporter announced this in her curious style that combined bounciness and solemnity.

Now, as he stretched out in a hammock, Billy noticed additional news related to the case was popping up on his phone's web browser. An Associated Press report said that the Pilot Crew—apparently some sort of board of directors of the Church of Life—had selected David Clarkson as the new Supreme Pilot, in place of James Armstrong. A spokesman for the Church, reading a formal statement, had explained the decision:

> Mr. Clarkson is only the third Supreme Pilot we have chosen in our storied history. We have selected him as he brings together the qualities of devotion and high ethical standards. These attributes make him uniquely prepared to serve in this august role.

The report went on to say that "insiders" said that Clarkson had "distinguished" himself in his work for the Church by his refusal to do anything improper. This, they explained, reflected his background as an attorney. "He always knew how to say no to James," the insider noted, adding, "That's a crucial part of the reason we picked him."

This account seemed not to be quite right to Billy. But the sun was making him sleepy, and he was content to drift off. When he awoke a few minutes later, he heard Claire barking out directions to an underling back in her Los Angeles production office. He could see already that while he was on the beach, the marriage was not always going to be a day at the beach. Still, he remained astonished, amazed, and mostly delighted that she had become his bride. She was lovely and smart, and she was going to be joyful when she first gazed at their daughter's face. He had always regarded Claire with some measure of wonderment, and she was even his type.

Claire did present him with many criticisms, though. He didn't stand up straight enough. He folded the bed sheets wrong. He packed the suitcases too tight. When he spoke to people in the industry he was too frank; he was inclined to forget that if you criticized a terrible movie which was a hit that you were pissing on someone's child's college fund. The list of his failings and the number of things he needed to work on was considerable, and there were times when it rankled.

He had mused on this in the days leading up to the wedding.

It particularly struck him on the day before they had gotten on the plane to fly to Seattle. Hanging out in in the *Fatal Attraction* production office, he had picked up a copy of one of the trade magazines. In it, he saw another of the innumerable mentions of Vincenza. Her sudden celebrity was not what sparked his thoughts. It was her gentleness. Hard as it was not to reflect upon this, he would occasionally find himself thinking about her. But he understood that he was lucky. Honolulu was warm, and the landscape was lush. It was not what Los Angeles was, though. Both cities offered delicious weather. But Los Angeles was filled with things to see and do—museums and orchestras and screenings and theaters and restaurants and public gardens and a thousand other activities and delights. More, he would be beside a woman for whom he felt awe, and, endowed with a heart rich in hope, he reminded himself that love at its best was something two people grew towards. Los Angeles was the citadel of dreams, and, whatever was to be, Billy Rosenberg wished then to lie upon the beach, half-awake, idly imagining welcome days to come.

ABOUT THE AUTHOR

Jonathan Leaf is a playwright and journalist. His drama *Pushkin* was selected as one of the four best plays of 2018 by the *Wall Street Journal*. He has been nominated in the Innovative Theater (IT) Awards for Best Play of the Year for *The Caterers* and has received rave reviews for his work in the *New Yorker*, the *Wall Street Journal*, the *New York Daily News*, the *New Criterion*, *BroadwayWorld*, *Show Business Weekly*, *National Review*, and many other publications. Since March 2017, he has premiered five new plays in New York, San Francisco, and Paris.

As a journalist and critic, his writing has been featured in *National Review*, the *Daily Beast*, *Spectator* (USA), *Tablet*, *Mosaic*, the *New York Post*, *New York Press*, *City Journal*, *Humanities*, the *Weekly Standard*, *Modern Age*, *First Things*, *The American*, *The American Conservative*, the *New York Sun*, and many other publications.